TROUBLE FOR DINNER

They came out on the street and they looked right over at the restaurant.

Just then Teresa came in with my coffee. She saw my expression and she stopped. "What is it? What's the matter, Kearney?"

"It's them. They're comin' across the street. If there's to be a fight I'll try to get them outside so's we won't tear things up."

"You'll do what you have to, Kearney, and leave the cleaning up to me. I've mopped up blood before this."

Here they come. Right at me.

THE PROVING TRAIL
LOUIS L'AMOUR

BANTAM BOOKS · TORONTO · LONDON · NEW YORK

THE PROVING TRAIL

A Bantam Book | January 1979

2nd printing ...... January 1979   4th printing .... May 1979
3rd printing .... February 1979   5th printing .. September 1979
6th printing .... June 1980

ISBN 0–553–14283–6

Published simultaneously in the United States and Canada

Bantam Books are published by Bantam Books, Inc. Its trademark, consisting of the words "Bantam Books" and the por-
trayal of a bantam, is Registered in U.S. Patent and Trademark
Office and in other countries. Marca Registrada. Bantam
Books, Inc., 666 Fifth Avenue, New York, New York 10019.

PRINTED IN THE UNITED STATES OF AMERICA

15 14 13 12 11 10 9 8 7 6

THE PROVING TRAIL

Chapter I

All winter long I held them cattle up on the plateau whilst pa collected my wages down to town. Come first grass I taken them cattle down to Dingleberry's and I told old Ding what he could do with them, that I had my fill of playin' nursemaid to a bunch of cows.

He made quite a fuss, sayin' as how pa had hired me out to him and I'd no choice, bein' a boy not yet eighteen.

So I told him if he figured I'd no choice, just to watch the tail end of my horse because I was fetchin' out of there. I knew pa was down to town gamblin', workin' with my money as his base, but pa was a no-account gambler, generally speakin', and couldn't seem to put a winnin' hand together.

Nonetheless he might have enough put by to give me a road stake, and I could make do with five dollars, if he had it.

Only when I rode into town pa was dead. He was not only dead, he was buried, and they'd put a marker on his grave.

It taken the wind out of me. I just sort of backed off an' set down. Pa, he was no more than forty, seemed like, and a man in fair health for somebody who spent most of his time over a card table.

There was a lot of strangers in town, but one man who knowed me and who'd knowed pa, too, he told me, "Was I you I'd git straddle of that bronc an' light

1

a shuck. Ain't nothin' around town for you no more, with your pa dead."

"How'd he die? It don't make no sense—him dyin' right off, like that."

"That's the way folks usually die, son. Everybody knows he's goin' to die sometime, but nobody really expects to. You light out, son. I hear tell they're hirin' men for work in the mines out in the western part of the Territory."

"How'd he die?" I persisted.

"Well, seems like he killed hisself. I never did see the body, mind. But Judge Blazer, he seen it. He shot hisself. Lost money, I reckon. You know he was always gamblin'."

"Hell," I said, disgusted, "he'd not kill himself for that! He'd done been losin' money all his life! That man could lose more money than you'd ever see."

"You take my advice, boy, an' you light out. There's some mighty rough folks in this town an' they won't take to no wet-eared boy nosin' around."

That couldn't make no sense to me, because I'd been around rough folks all my life. We never had nothin', our family didn't, scrabblin' around for whatever it was we could find after ma died an' Pistol—that's my brother—taken off. It just left me an' pa, an' we'd gone from one cow camp or minin' camp to another. Now pa was dead an' I was alone.

Pa wasn't much account, I guess, as men went, but he was pa, and a kindly man most of the time. We'd never had much to say to one another but hello or good-bye or how much money was I holdin'? Nonetheless, he was pa an' I loved him, although that was a word we'd have been shamed to use.

Pistol, he was my half brother, ten year older'n me, an' he'd taken off a long time back, six or seven years back. Pa kind of hinted that Pistol had taken off along the outlaw trail but I never did think so. Pistol always seemed the kind to ride them straight up the middle.

The Bon Ton was down the street, and I was surely hard up for grub. I'd been so long without eatin', my belly was beginning to think my throat was cut, so

I bellied up to a table in the Bon Ton and ordered, thankin' my stars a body could still get him a good meal for two bits.

Until I set down there, I'd had no chance to give much thought to pa. We'd sort of taken one another for granted, or so it had seemed to me. Now all of a sudden he was gone and there was a great big hole in my life and an emptiness inside me.

Nothing had ever seemed to go right for pa. A couple of times we had ourselves a little two-by-twice outfit, but the first time it was get run off or fight, an' ma didn't want us to fight so we pulled out. Then the Comanches run us off the next place, stealin' our horses and cows an' leavin' us with a burned-up wagon and no stock. Next time pa was about to make out, ma took sick, and it needed all pa had just for doctor's bills and such. After that pa took to gamblin' reg'lar and it was all bad cards and slow horses.

Man at the next table was talkin'. "Never seen such a thing," he was sayin', "not in all my born days. When they raised him that last time, he taken out a six-shooter an' there for a minute nobody knew what was going to happen. Then he put that gun down in the middle of the table. 'Ought to be worth twenty dollars,' he says, 'and I raise you twenty.'

"Two of them stayed, and when the showdown came he was holdin' a full house. Well, sir, that started it! You never seen the like! The cards began runnin' his way and it seemed he couldn't do anything wrong! If they could have gotten the governor into the game, he'd have owned the Territory! I tell you, he must have won eight, maybe ten thousand dollars!"

The waitress brought me beef and beans and filled my coffee cup. She was a pretty redhead with freckles, and when she leaned over to pour my coffee, I looked up at her and she whispered, "You be careful! You be real careful!"

"What's that mean?" I said. "I never said a word."

"I don't mean that. Was I you, I'd fork that roan of yours and ride right out of town and never even look back. If'n I was you, they'd never see me for the dust."

"Why? What have I done? I ain't been to town for months, and no sooner do I ride in than folks start tellin' me I should leave."

"You better," she warned, and walked away.

Well, I drank some coffee and it tasted mighty good. Then I went to work on the beef and beans, half-hearin' the talk at the next table about that card game. "It was that six-shooter did it. He'd been losin' steady until he staked that six-shooter with the pearl handle and the little red birds inlaid into the pearl. I declare, I—"

Well, I just stopped chewin'. I set there for a full minute before I leaned over to that man and said, "Sounds real pretty. Did you say red birds in a pearl handle?"

"That's right! Talk about lucky! That gun worked a charm! Soon's he put up that gun his luck changed an' there was no stoppin' him."

"Medium-sized man, with a mustache?"

"Had him a mustache, all right, but he was a tall, thin galoot. Wore one of those Prince Albert coats, a black frock coat, y'know." He peered at me. "D'you know him?"

"The gun sounds familiar. I got an eye for guns, and a man wouldn't be likely to forget anything like that."

"He sure was lucky! Won him maybe nine, ten thousand dollars! More'n that, he won the deed to some big cattle outfit up north. He seemed to make all the wrong moves, yet he kept pullin' down the high cards."

The other man at the table looked around. "Only reason he didn't win all the money in the world was because those other fellers didn't have it. He just won all they did have. I seen it."

They went back to talkin' amongst themselves, and I finished what was before me. Meanwhile I did some thinkin'. Now, I'm not quick to think. I act fast but I consider slow. I like to contemplate a subject, turnin' it on the spit of my mind until I have seen all sides of it. This here shaped up like plain, old-fashioned trouble.

I was right sorry for pa. I'd be sorrier later on, for

things never hit me all of a sudden. Yet maybe I shouldn't be sorry for him, because pa died right at the peak of the greatest run of luck he'd ever had.

He died winners, and not many gamblers could say that. Certainly nobody expected pa to beat the game, but he had. If he had come off that run of luck alive, he'd have lost it all had he continued to gamble. So he passed out a winner.

Shot through the skull, though. Now how come that?

Whose was the bullet? What finger squeezed off that shot?

Now I could see why folks were suggesting I get away while I could. They didn't want too many bodies clutterin' up the town, and me bein' his son and all ...

I walked across the street to Judge Blazer's. He was not only a judge but the coroner as well.

He was a-settin' up there on the porch of that ho-tel, tipped back in a chair smokin' a big seegar. He seen me comin' and squinted his eyes to make me out.

I promise you I didn't look like Sunday meetin' time. I'd been all winter up in the mountains, and it was almighty cold up there. I was wearin' all the clothes I owned, and I'd made a hole in a blanket for a poncho.

"Judge Blazer," I said, "you buried my pa. I've come for his belongin's."

He just set there. Then he taken the seegar from his lips. "Now, now, son, you know your pa never had nothing. He was never much account at anything at all, and all he done for the past year was gamble. We done buried him our own selves, and he had just three dollars and six bits on him when he passed on. He had him a gold watch and his six-shooters. One was in his hand, the other was on the bureau." He hitched himself around in his chair. "You're welcome to 'em."

He got up and went through the door ahead of me. He was a big man, and fat, but folks said he was almighty strong, that little of what looked like fat was really fat. I never cottoned to him much, but had he known he'd not have cared. Who was I but a youngster still wet behind the ears? *He* thought.

In his office he waved at a table. There was a roll-top desk, a big iron safe, a brass spittoon, and there was this table. There lay one of pa's guns in the holster with his gun belt. The other gun lay free on the table. Pa's old black hat was there, too.

Judge Blazer taken three dollars and six bits from a drawer and put it down along with a gold watch. "There you be, boy. You he'p yourself an' run along. I got business to attend to."

Well, I taken up that gun belt an' strapped her on. She settled down natural-like against my leg. Then I pocketed the watch and the money and swapped my beat-up old hat for pa's black one. Then I spun the cylinder on that second gun, and it was fully loaded. Pa was always careful with his guns. He kept them first-rate.

She was working and she was ready.

"Judge?" I was holdin' right to that six-shooter, kind of casual-like, but ready. "Seems to me you're bein' forgetful, I guess a man like you, with business and all, could forget."

He turned around slow and he stared hard at me. He looked from me to the gun, then back at me. Maybe I was only seventeen, but pa an' me had cut the mustard in a lot of mean places. He didn't look no different than a lot of others we'd met.

"Forget what?" he asked.

"All that money. Pa had him some winnin' hands that last night. He won a lot of cash money and he won property, and I don't see any of it on that table."

"Now, now, son! You've been misinformed. I think—"

"Mister Judge," I said, keeping my voice quiet-like, "this here gun don't have so much patience. Could get right hasty, in fact. Now, if you'd like, I can round up twenty, maybe thirty witnesses who saw that game. There's a lot of strangers in town, Judge, and they ain't afeered of you, an' many of them seen what happened last night. The whole town's talkin'. You hold out one penny on a poor orphant boy who's just lost his pa an' I think those boys would be huntin' theirselves a rope. Now I can guess why ol' Dingleberry was so upset about me pullin' my freight. You'd likely told him to keep me busy up yonder until all this sort of blowed over."

He didn't like it. No man likes to give up that kind of money to what he figures is a no-account boy. That was probably more money than the judge hisself had seen all to one time, and he was in no mood to let loose of it. On the other hand, there I stood with a six-shooter and maybe I was trigger-happy.

"You pull that trigger, boy, an' you'll hang for sure."

"I don't know anybody got hung for shootin' a thief," I said.

His face flushed up red and angry. His eyes got real mean. "Now, you look here!"

Me, I just tilted that gun a mite. "All you got to do to prove me wrong is hand over that money and those deeds. If you want to go to court about it, we can arrange to hold it yonder in the saloon where pa won the money."

He didn't like any part of it, but he didn't want to hear what a jury of rough-and-ready western men would say, either. They believed in fair play and most of them had seen the game.

Reluctantly he dropped to one knee in front of the safe, and I moved right behind him. Maybe I looked green, but not so green that I didn't know some folks kept a six-shooter in their safe to watch the money.

Sure enough, I seen one. As he reached his hand for it, I said, "Judge, when your hand comes out of that safe, it better have nothing in it but money. You lay hold of that gun and you still have to turn around to shoot. I don't."

He got up, very careful, holding the money in his two hands. He placed it on the table in front of me, and I told him to back off, easy-like.

"Son," he said, "I wasn't holdin' out on you. I meant to take care of this money for you until you come of age. Fact is," and I'd bet the idea just occurred to him, "I've been fixin' to get myself appointed your guardian by the court." He smiled like a cat lickin' cream. "A young boy with all that there money, he needs advice. I figure to send you off to school to get you some eddication."

"You ain't my guardian or likely to be," I said.

"On the contrary." He was pleased with himself now. "I'll draw up the papers. Appoint myself your guardian. I'll take that money an' invest it for you."

"Pull in your horns, Judge. You made your play an' you've come up empty. Just give me that deed."

"Ain't worth the paper it's writ on," Blazer protested.

"Just hand it over," I insisted, and he done so. He didn't like it, but he could see my thumb was holdin' back the hammer, and if I was so much as nudged that gun would tear a hole in him big enough to drive a Conestoga wagon through.

Backing to the door, I stepped into the street, pulled the slipknot on the tie rope, and stepped into the saddle. That roan was tired. He was plumb beat, but he sensed I was in trouble an' he taken out of there like a scared rabbit.

There was a road into town and there was a road out of town, and it stood to reason I had to take one or the other, so I took neither. I took the trail to my cow camp, which I figured would be the last place they'd look.

First place, nobody rightly knew where it was but me, and there was no need to pass Dingleberry's place in gettin' there, so there'd be nobody to report my passing. That cow camp had been home for the roan for some time, so he taken the trail at a good gait. Twice I glanced back. Nobody was in sight.

They'd study on it and Blazer would figure it out, but not until they had wasted time on other trails, and by that time I hoped it would be too late.

Only I'd better hurry. If it came on to snow before I got off the mountain—and there could be heavy snows up yonder—I'd be in trouble.

If a man got snowed in up there at this time of year, he might never get off. It was slide country and all the trails in or out were subject to snowslides.

The year had been an open one with little snow. Cold as it was, the grass was good, cured on the stem, and the cattle had done well. I'd kept alert, ready to move them fast if need be, and there were some valleys close by that offered shelter. In that country a man got out fast or he was stuck. That had been all right for me, as I'd had plenty of grub stashed up there and fuel close to hand. Trouble was that during the winter I'd used up most of the grub and the fuel as well.

The wind blew cold off the peaks and the trickles of melt had stopped flowing, which meant it was freezing on top. The roan, tired as he was, stepped faster. From where the trail topped out, four or five miles shy of the high grass, I turned in my saddle to look back.

Nothing in sight, nothing at all. But I knew they were back there, and I knew they were coming.

How much money I had I didn't know, but it was a-plenty and Blazer figured to have that money. He wouldn't be coming alone. He'd have however many he figured he needed, no matter what reason he gave them. He was a judge, probably no more than a justice of the peace, I thought. Still, he knew more about the law than me and he might be able to get himself appointed my guardian. He could even appoint himself and make a good story of how I was a wild kid who needed taking care of. Meanwhile he'd have his use of, and the spending of, my money.

When I saw, far ahead, the dark shadow of the cabin, it was already coming on to snow. I pulled up, although the roan wanted to go on in. I sat in my saddle taking a long look at my hole card, and it didn't shape up to very much.

How did I know nobody knew of that place but me? Wasn't I taking a lot for granted? That gold money rested heavy in my saddlebags and so did the paper. The gold might be just too much weight, going off the mountain in the deep snow. Besides, if they got me I didn't want them to profit by it.

It was then I thought of the cache.

Chapter II

It was a crack in the rock, that was all, hidden in a niche of the wall. It was a crack not over six inches wide and maybe two feet deep about ten feet off the ground. I'd found it a handy place to cache a bite of lunch, time to time, or some extra ammunition and coffee in case the cabin burned down whilst I was with the cattle.

The cabin was still a good two miles off, although I could see a kind of black blotch where it stood. Swinging the bronc over to the niche, I stood up in my stirrups and put the gold away back in that crack and then the bills and replaced the rock that closed the crack.

Three hundred dollars in paper money I kept. I hid five twenties under the sweatband of my hat, another five in a slit in my belt, and the last five I wadded into a tight ball in the bottom of my holster. That last made my gun ride a little high, but the thong would still slip over it, although a snug fit. I was figuring on using my waist gun if I had to use any.

Then I headed for the cabin, circling a little to come up on the back side through the aspen. Back there about fifty yards from the cabin and down over a little aspen and spruce-covered knoll there was another cabin. This one was built mighty strong of square-cut logs and was warmer than the stable near the cabin. I led the roan in-

to it and dished out some corn I kept there for cold
spells.

Then I started for the cabin. There was a side of
bacon there, some beans, flour, salt, sugar, and coffee.
There was also some dried apples and odds and ends
of grub. I had me a feeling I was going to need it.

This here was springtime, but in the high country it
wasn't a dependable thing. I'd seen the spring come with
flowers and all, and then off the mountains come a
storm and there'd be another ten to fifty days of winter.

The high mountain pasture which we called the plateau was actually no such thing, but rather a series of
high mountain valleys above timberline or right at it,
where grew the richest of grass. Most winters they were
free of snow, and warmer than some lower-down country due to what pa called a local weather pattern—
winds off the desert, I guess.

Pa had known about this place and he had gone to
Dingleberry with the suggestion that he'd graze a few
hundred head of Big D cattle in the high country and
I'd see to them, for so much a head and wages for me.

How pa found this place or heard of it I never did
know. He had never been given to talk. I was just beginning to realize how little pa had told me about himself, his early life, or his family. I'd not paid it much
mind because pa was always there to ask in case I
wanted to know, but now he was gone. His death not
only left me alone but it cut me off from whatever past
there was, and whatever family we might have had
somewhere.

When I got to the cabin, all was quiet and I went in.
It was ice-cold, so I taken the time to put a fire together. Then with the flames crackling, I went to putting
grub into a burlap sack. I worked fast, all the time
thinking maybe I should just spend the night where I
was instead of heading out across that mountain country in the cold and the dark.

I packed my sack of grub down and tied it behind
the saddle, still thinking I should unsaddle and give
us both a rest. The roan was tuckered and so was I,

but I recalled the mean look in Blazer's eye and I knowed he'd be comin' after me, cold or no. Be a long time before he had a chance at that much cash money again.

There was a small paper sack with some .44s in it lyin' on the floor in the cabin, and I decided I'd better take them with me, so I walked back to the cabin and pushed open the door.

Something loomed in front of me, big as a grizzly, it seemed, and my hand went for my gun, but then I remembered I'd hung the gun belt over the saddle horn and the spare gun with it whilst I was working around.

What hit me was a fist, but it felt like the butt end of an axe. I staggered, and something fetched me a clout from behind, knocking me through the door into the lighted cabin. I sprawled on the floor, my head buzzing, but I wasn't let lay. A big hand grabbed the scruff of my neck and flung me into a chair.

"Where is it, kid? Where's the money?"

Dazed, I looked up at Judge Blazer. There were three other men in the cabin. The only one I knew by sight was Tobin Wacker, a teamster who drove freight wagons and was said to be the meanest man anywhere around. He was a brawler and a bully, outweighed me by fifty pounds, and he was three, four inches taller. I don't know why they had the other two, because with Wacker they surely didn't need anybody else.

Blazer grabbed me by the shirtfront and half lifted me out of my chair. "Where is it? Where'd you hide that money you stole off me?"

"It was took," I lied. "I figured it was you."

"Took?" He stared at me.

"Two fellers with guns. They taken the money and told me to get gone. That if they ever seen me around town they'd blow my head off. One of them had a shotgun."

"You expect me to swallow that?" Blazer had a mighty unpleasant look to him, and I was scared. All the same I had sense enough to know that once they had that money, I was dead. They'd never leave me alive to protest or make trouble for them.

"I figured you sent 'em," I said. "They taken everything. My guns, my horse . . . they cleaned me out."

"Kid," and Blazer's voice got real quiet, "you're a liar, and I know you're a liar. You can tell us where it is or we'll beat it out of you."

"Look," I said, "I don't know—"

He hit me in the mouth. I tasted blood and came off that chair, and that Wacker, he just grabbed me, grabbed my arms while Blazer went to work on me. He slugged me in the belly, then kneed me in the face when I bent over. He straightened me up and slapped me back and forth across the face until my head rung like a bell. Then he stepped back and kicked me in the groin, and they dropped me on the floor.

They set down then, and one of them added fuel to the fire. "Gettin' cold," he commented.

Wacker, he kicked me in the ribs. "Better tell us, boy," he said. "We got all night."

"Maybe you got all spring," I said, spluttering it out between split lips.

Blazer stared at me. "We have. We got all spring. We can beat you until you tell us, so make it easier on yourself."

He surely didn't take my meaning, and it didn't look like he knew what could happen up this high. Down yonder at town it was warm in the daytime, the flowers were out, and the trees budded. I mean, it was sure enough springtime down yonder, but that didn't hold up here in these hills.

"Make some coffee," he said to one of the others. He looked down at me. "Where's the coffee?"

"I taken it all down when I quit," I said. "Wasn't much left, anyway."

"I got some," this gent said, and he opened the door to go out. A gust of wind and snow come in the door.

"Would you look at that," Blazer said. "Snow!"

I was beginning to really hurt. Felt like I'd got myself a busted rib. I tried to sit up, but it hurt so I lay back down. My head was beginning to clear up, but my face was sore and my head ached. And now I was gettin' mad. I was feelin' almighty mean toward those men. I tried again to sit up, and Wacker, he just reached out and kicked me in the face. Lucky I jerked back and he missed my chin, but the rough sole of his boot taken the hide off my cheek.

"You set still, boy. You tell us an' we'll leave you be. You don't tell us an' we just keep on beatin'. It's gonna be a long night for you."

"The longest," I muttered through split lips. "Maybe your longest."

The man at the fire turned halfway around and looked at me. "What's that mean?"

"Listen to the wind," I said.

Blazer glanced at me. "Wind? What about it?"

"Snow," I said, "lots of snow. I've seen it when these late snows come so's a man couldn't get out for six, eight weeks. I hope you boys brought plenty of grub or fat horses. You'll need it."

The man at the fire looked at Blazer. "Is that right?"

"He's lyin'. This is springtime." Nevertheless he looked uneasy. "This is April."

"I seen it so's you couldn't get in or out before June," I said. "You boys say good-bye to your women-folks?"

He backhanded me across the mouth. "Shut your trap!" he said.

After a minute I said, "Man a few year ago started across the mountains with some trappers. Come spring he showed up in mighty good shape. They backtracked him and found he'd killed an' eaten all the others. They call that place Cannibal Plateau now."

The coffee was ready. "Heard about that," Wacker said. "It sure enough happened."

"Lucky you boys have Blazer," I said. "He's good an' fat. He'll—"

He kicked me. Then he got up on his feet and stomped on my fingers. He kicked me again in the belly, and I felt a stab of pain. He jerked me up by the shirtfront and punched me in the wind again. "Where's that money?" he said.

"Stole," I muttered. "That money was stole. An' it must've been you who murdered pa."

He dropped me like I was too hot to hold. Then he stepped back and kicked me in the ribs. I was turned half over, and he kicked me in the kidneys three, four times. I didn't say anything.

My face was against the floor, and the cold was coming up through the cracks, but all I could feel was pain. I hurt like I'd never hurt before.

"I better put the horses up," one of those men said. "That's a cold-sounding wind."

"Get at it, then," Blazer said irritably. "Come morning we'll pull out."

I laughed. I didn't feel much like laughing, but I done it.

He went out and I lay there. They had two cups and they taken turns at the coffee. All of a sudden the door slammed open with a blast of cold air, and amid considerable cussing they got the door closed.

"I got the horses in," the man said. He was a sourfaced man with a scar on his jaw. "Judge? He may be tellin' the truth. He don't have no horse."

"They taken my horse, too," I said.

"Hell, he's a-lyin'," Wacker said irritably. "Come morning we'll find the horse and the money, too."

"By morning," I fumbled at the words with swollen, bloody lips, "you'll be snowed in, the pass closed for maybe six, eight weeks. An' don't think about game. There's none up this high, this time of year."

"And by morning," Judge Blazer added, "we will either have the money or you will be hammered to a pulp. We've only begun, you know. If you wish to survive at all, you will tell us."

I looked down at my hands. My eyes were swollen almost shut, my head was thick with pain, and the hands I saw through the slits left to me were mangled beyond belief. Yet I would not talk. If I told them, I would die. As long as I did not tell them, I had a chance.

Suddenly, without warning, Wacker kicked me in the

kidney. Agony shot through me and I gasped. Blazer struck me again across the face.

"And now you'll die." I formed the words, made the sounds, clumsy as they were. "The passes will be closed soon, and there will be no getting out."

"Suppose he's right?" one of the other men said suddenly. "I don't like it, Blazer. Those passes are almighty narrow, and the snow's a-fallin' fast out there."

Wacker walked to the window and peered out. For the first time he seemed uneasy. "Aw, that's a lot of crap!" he said irritably. He walked back to the bunk and sat down. The wind moaned around the eaves, and suddenly he got up and went again to the window. He could see nothing, I knew. It was all dark and still.

I had seen the flakes that had blown into the room. They were thick and white now, and that kind of snow would pile up fast. They wouldn't get out, but neither would I. Except . . . except that I had an idea of another way out.

Maybe. I'd never tried it. An old Indian had come up that way and told me about it over the meal I'd fixed for him.

Could I find it in the dark and the snow? Could I find it even without them? He had not been very explicit, but Indians rarely were.

Blazer got up and went to the door. He peered out, then shouldered into his coat and went outside. When he came back, his manner had changed. "Dick," he said, glancing over at the man who'd made the coffee, "go saddle up. We're riding out."

"What about him?" Wacker asked.

"He'll tell us before we go. We're through fooling around."

Dick went out the door. Three of them left. I tried to grin with my bloody, broken lips. "He'll lose them horses in the snow. You'll die here."

He picked me up and I struck at him. My fist caught his cheekbone and it must have hurt because he kneed me in the groin, then began that ponderous slapping of my face, each blow jarring my skull. The man was strong. Very strong.

He began hitting me, slowly, methodically, steadily. I made no effort to fight back. I had strength. I had some reserve, and I'd been waiting. My time would come.

I took the blows. He smashed a fist into my belly, struck me on the ear, slapped me until my head rang.

"Let me have him," Wacker said. "I can make him talk." Across the room my eyes caught a bloody image in the cracked mirror over the washbasin, a bloody caricature of something that had been human. That was me.

"Do what you're of a mind to," Blazer said, arm-weary from beating on me. "Just keep him alive until he talks. He's got that money."

"Suppose his story is straight?" the other man said. "He just might have been robbed. Somebody might have known where that money was. Sure it is that nigh ever'body knew his old man won it."

Blazer wouldn't buy that. Without his belief that I had the money, he had nothing. He was wasting his time and he did not want that at all.

I heard a crunch from the doorway. Dick was coming back. Blazer had dropped into a chair near the fire. Wacker pushed me off at arm's length. He was a cruel man and much stronger than Blazer. He'd kill me. Dick fumbled with the latch, and suddenly I lunged.

Only a quick step forward, my left palm came up under Wacker's elbow, my right came down hard on his wrist. There was a snap of bone, and Wacker screamed. I shoved him hard into Blazer, and both of them tumbled toward the fire. Then I threw myself at the door.

Dick was coming in, had just opened the door when my shoulder hit it, knocking him sprawling in the snow with me almost astride of him. I scrambled to get up, smashing my knee under his chin in the process, and then I was rolling over and over in the snow.

I fought myself to my feet. Instinctively I went for the woods. Behind me I heard a shout, cries of pain, and cursing. I stumbled and fell, crawled madly toward the trees, sprawled again, and got hold of a tree and pushed myself and pulled myself up.

For a moment, groggy and hurt, I leaned against the tree, my breath coming in rasping gasps, each one like a knife grinding against bone.

I tried to look around, but my eyes were swollen almost shut. I made it to another tree, then another. I fell, sliding down the tree into the snow. Yet I knew from a lessening of the wind that I was in the aspens. I struggled on.

My horse! They had not found my horse. If I could only . . .

I fell again and again. Now the snow was blowing in a howling blizzard. I did not think. I fell, striking my side and sending a spasm of pain through me. I had a broken rib, maybe more than one. From the feel of my nose, that was broken, too.

Scooping up a handful of snow, I wiped it across my battered features. Then grasping the slim trunk of a tree, I pulled myself erect again.

Somehow my sense of direction remained with me. The cabin was on my right rear now. The small shelter where I'd left the roan was ahead of me, lower down . . . twenty yards?

Fighting to keep my feet, I worked my way across the slope from tree to tree. Suddenly it was there. Then I was inside, and the roan nickered a welcome.

I fell flat, but managed to push the door shut. The room was cold, but secure . . . secure.

For how long? They would search. They would find me. I had to get away. Could I find my way across the valley? Down its long length? How far? Two miles? Less.

Once in the broken country beyond, there would be some shelter from the wind.

I leaned against the horse and tightened the cinch. Then I opened the door and crawled into the saddle. Ducking my head low, I urged the roan out into the storm.

He must have known I was in a bad way, for surprisingly he did not resist.

Out into the storm, up into the aspens, out between the grove and the house. I could vaguely hear them shouting inside. I walked the horse past and pointed him down the valley, and the poor beast trusted me.

Here where the wind blew, the snow could not drift. Here we could canter, and we did. Out across the empty land, toward a crack in the rock that I only hoped I could find, or he could.

Behind us, death. Before us, freezing cold, miles of hard riding . . . possibly a chance.

Turning briefly, I looked back. I could see a faint glow in the darkness through the snow. The window.

From my scabbard I fumbled my Winchester. With frozen, numbed fingers I steadied the rifle, and then I fired three fast shots through that window.

Shoving the rifle down into the scabbard, I rode on into the night and the snow. At least I had left them a defiance. I had thrown them a gesture. Whatever else they knew, they knew I was not defeated.

And now, the storm . . .

Chapter III

It was cold, bitter, bitter cold. I had to find the opening of that Indian trail, and it was narrow, scarcely to be seen even in the best of weather, but the roan and I had been down that trail several times for short distances. Would he know now where I was going?

The wind was directly in my face, and to catch a breath I had to hold my head down, try to get my mouth and chin behind the edge of my coat. The snow was growing deep, even out here on the flat. Several times the roan stumbled. He was dog-tired, I knew, and in no shape for such a trip as this.

The wind was like a wall of iron, cold, cold iron against which we pushed and pushed. Suddenly the roan slipped and almost fell. He scrambled, regained his feet, and stood trembling. Then I remembered. Just to the right of that opening there was a sort of gentle slope where the ground fell off several feet in a gradual slant. Was it there? Was that why the roan had slipped?

Taking a chance, I pulled his head over and urged him forward. He took a tentative step, then another. Liking the level ground, he went on, and suddenly something black loomed beside us and I knew it was the big spruce. I urged him in close to it and swung down.

Every bone in my body ached, every muscle was bruised and sore. I was in no shape to walk, yet I must save the roan. We needed each other, that horse and me, if we were to survive at all. From here I thought I could follow the trail, for it wound down along through the trees and rocks, narrow, tricky, but possible.

Leading the roan, I walked on, stamping my feet from time to time to shake off the numbness from the cold. We could not go on like this. Somewhere, somehow, we had to find shelter. An overhanging cliff, a wind-hollowed cave, some fallen trees—anything. We had to find shelter and we had to have a fire.

Pausing, I peered into the storm, turning my head slowly, trying to find something, anything. And there was only the snow, the staggered ranks of the spruce, and the howling wind that lashed the trees like a gigantic whip. We pushed on and on.

Again I paused, trying to judge the distance we had come since finding the trail—if this was it. A quarter of a mile? A half mile? More . . . probably a little more. My brain seemed dull. It worked slowly, but I fought desperately to remember. Had there been a place in the part of the trail I knew, any place that offered shelter? A riding man in wild country naturally looks for such things, but I could remember nothing.

We started on. I walked and walked. Then suddenly I slipped. My feet shot from under me, and I fell heavily. For a moment I lay there, ready to quit. The roan nudged me with his nose, urging me to get up. I put my hands down to push myself up.

Ice. My hands were on ice. That was why I had slipped . . . ice under the snow. I struggled erect and stood there, my shoulders humped against the wind. Ice meant water. This must be the stream the old Indian had mentioned. The stream that flowed from a cave.

A cave?

I turned left up the mountain and walked gingerly on the ice, holding to the bed of the small stream. We walked on, the roan following meekly enough. The wind seemed to ease . . . or was that my imagination? We plodded on, one step at a time. The wind was easing off . . . or else we were in the lee of a cliff . . . something.

No longer was I a thinking, reasoning being. The cold was numbing my brain as well as my feet and legs. Enough of intelligence left to tell me that either we found shelter quickly or we would both die.

I slipped, almost fell. This time I gathered myself together more slowly. I took a step on. The ice was tilting ahead of me . . . or was tilted. It was a slope, a steep place in the drop of the stream. Working myself to the right, I tried to find an opening in the thick brush along the bank. It was a wall, stiff, frozen branches, closely intertwined. We climbed, and this time the roan slipped and fell.

It was all both of us could do to get him back on his feet. I stood gasping with effort, pain stabbing my side. Something was black before me. There seemed a break in the wall of brush. I went into the narrow opening, pulling the horse after me. Suddenly we were out of the wind. I put my gloved hand to my face. It was stiff and cold.

There was a path or opening. I followed along, and suddenly the cave was there, a black opening. I went in, leading the roan.

It was dark and still. I peered around, seeing nothing. My hands were numb, feeling like thick clubs. I beat them against each other, against my legs, then tucked them into my armpits. Numb with cold, I began to move, stiffly, slowly, sweeping the snow from the saddle, from the roan's back.

I must move and keep moving. My eyes slowly were adjusting to the darkness, and I could see I was in a room no more than twenty feet in diameter, off which seemed to run at least two dark passages. There was scattered wood on the floor, left from campfires of the past. Overhead there was an opening, a sort of crack through which smoke could find a way out.

When I stamped my feet, it was like they were made of wood, yet stamp them I did. Working very slowly, I got a few sticks together, but my hands were too clumsy to hold a match. What I needed was simply to keep moving, and here, out of the chilling wind, I might slowly recover the warmth my body needed.

Fumbling with the cinch, I succeeded in loosening it and swinging the saddle off the roan. With a quick smash of the saddle blanket against the rock wall, I cleared it of most of the accumulated snow and ice, and began to wipe the roan, rubbing warmth back into it, and at the same time into myself.

It was a long time, for my movements were clumsy from the cold, but slowly my own blood began to flow more freely. Kneeling down, I gathered some slivers together, a few pine cones and some sticks from a pack rat's nest. With infinite care I put together some dried leaves and part of the stuff of the nest itself. Then I struck a match. It had long been a matter of boyish pride that I could start a fire with but one match. Fortunately, it worked for me now.

The flame caught, blazed up, licked hungrily at the long dry sticks. I added fuel, extending my still-cold hands to the warmth.

As the light grew, I peered around to see what kind of place I had come to. There was a considerable pile of fuel stacked against the walls, and an old tin bucket, several Indian pots, a gourd dipper, and some odds and ends of rope harness. Somebody, Indians no doubt, had been using this cave.

At the door I scooped up a bucket of snow and put it near the fire to melt and warm up. When the water was warm, I took it to the roan, who drank long and gratefully. With my coffeepot, which I had in my gear, I made coffee.

While the water was coming to a boil, I wiped my Winchester dry, and my pistols also.

Thoughtfully I looked at the twin six-shooters. They were expensive, but hard up as he had often been, pa had never parted with them. For the first time I found myself curious about that.

Why? Why would pa, the least violent of men, have carried two guns? He never wore them both in public, and I had never seen him draw a gun except to clean it.

It dawned on me then that I actually knew very little about my father. Little? Did I actually know anything?

In the dark and lonely cave, with the storm howling outside and the bitter cold, I crouched by my fire with its light flickering on the walls and thought of my father, that strange and lonely man.

For I knew now that he had been lonely. Only now did little things come back to be remembered—the clumsy ways he had tried to show affection, and the lost man he had become when ma died.

We never talked of her. Whenever I mentioned her, he got up, left the room, or turned from me. I know now it was because he liked to think she was not dead, that she was just out somewhere and would soon be back.

I remembered him as he was, in his threadbare frock coat with its worn velvet collar. Even when shabby, he had something of elegance about him. Yet why did I know so little? Was there some reason for being secretive? Or was he just not given to talk of his family? If there was a family.

Where he was born, why he had come west, or where he met ma, I never knew, nor had I given thought to it until now.

Once, sitting in our room at the hotel, he had read something in the paper that irritated him. He slammed it down and with a sudden anger that was so unlike him he said, "Son, get an education! Whatever you do, get an education!"

It was cold. I went to the door of the cave, into which the wind whipped from time to time, and peered out. I could see nothing. That we were back from the faint trail we had followed, I knew, but how far back? And when the storm ended, would we be visible?

Again I checked the guns.

From the pile of wood I took a fair-sized log and added it to the fire. It was almost warm in the cave now. At least we would not freeze.

What would happen back there? Would they try to get out? Or would they be trapped in the old cabin? There was a little food left, how much I did not know, but a little. There was not enough to last one man even a week, let alone several men, and some of them would die.

Between the cave wall and the fire, I made my bed and lay down upon it, my guns beside me. Hands clasped behind my head, I returned again to the thoughts of my father. I hadn't spent much time with him, not as much as I could have. There'd been a couple of times when he seemed to want to talk, but I was in no mood for listening. I'd been rude at times, and it shamed me to recall it. He had wanted to tell me something, I think, but I'd been only a youngster and full of myself and not anxious to hear a lot of talk about the past or his boyhood. Because of that I'd missed learning what he might have told me.

Dozing on the bed, I suddenly recalled ma's voice saying, "Why don't you go back? Or is there some reason why you cannot?"

If he made a reply to that, I did not hear it. Only her words, "I am not thinking of us, only of you."

"It is too late," he said then. "It would not be the same." And then, after a mintue or two, "I dare not . . . I must not start that all over again. It is better that they never know."

I was very young then, and the words meant noth-

ing. Just grown-up talk. But why did I not forget the
words? Why did I remember them now?

Pa was gone now. He was dead.

Yet he had not killed himself. For one thing I knew
about pa—he wasn't a quitter. Until the end, fail as he
might, he would be in there trying.

That started me thinking about his gambling. When
ma was alive, he had never gambled. Come to think
of it, he had not gambled until just the last two or three
years.

One night I'd seen him throw down a deck of cards
in disgust. "I'd just as soon never see a card again!"
he said suddenly.

"Why don't you quit playing if you don't like it?" I
asked him.

He stood there for a minute looking at nothing and
then he said, "It's the only way. It's the only chance
now. Just one good winning! That's all I ask!"

At the time I did not believe him. Now I began to
wonder. Little bits and pieces of things began to come
back to me as I lay there in the half-warmth of the
cave.

Ma was gone. Pa never seemed to want anything. I
mean he was not much for spending money, even when
we had it. All of a sudden the answer was there. He
wanted it for me.

I sat up on my bed and put a stick into the fire, and
then another. Of course! Why else did he want it? I
remembered a couple of times when he looked at me
wearing that old blanket-poncho of mine, and my boots
with the heels almost wore off, and my beat-up old hat.

"Damn it," he said once, "I wish—"

He never finished what he was going to say. He just
taken his hat and left, and that night he lost the thirty-
odd dollars we had between us.

Next morning I made six dollars breaking horses at
fifty cents a head. I got tossed a couple of times, but I
rode them. When you don't eat unless you ride, you
ride. It's simple as that.

One time when I was sick, he stayed up night after

night caring for me. I was eleven then, or twelve. I just
taken it for granted, and never really thought of his
health. Only time I thought much of that was when I
come in the room one time and pa was washing. It
was the first time in all the years I saw him with his
shirt off, and I saw those two bullet wounds low down
on his left side.

I made some comment, but he brushed it off and
changed the subject. I kept after him, so he finally said,
"I got shot one time. It doesn't matter."

Lying there, I tried to piece it all together but I
came up with nothing, and it began to irk me. Who
was pa, anyway? Why couldn't he go back? And if he
could have, where would he have gone to?

By that time I'd warmed up some, and I went to the
cave opening and stepped outside into the shelter of a
corner of the cliff. The snow was swirling out there,
falling fast and blowing just as much. If they were in
trouble back at the cabin, I was in trouble out here.
Any time you get caught ten thousand feet up in a
heavy snow, you're in trouble, and I was. Outside
there was a deadfall, a tree that had toppled over close
to the cave, and I tried to drag it inside, but it was
frozen to the ground. I broke off a big branch, though,
and it cracked like a pistol shot.

I got that branch inside, then some slabs of bark
and other fuel lyin' about. It would help a little, when
the ice melted off it.

It was a long, long night. Every few minutes I'd
have to wake up and add fuel to the fire, and on a
cold, windy night a fire can eat up a lot of wood. Fortunately, there was a good bit stored inside.

Come dawn I awakened stiff with cold and my fire
down to gray ashes. After a bit I got it going again and
built it up good and warm.

I went to the cave mouth to size up the situation.
Everything was white and still. The wind had died
down, but it was cold, real cold. It must've been thirty
below or better, and it didn't look like it was going
to get better fast. Furthermore, if they came looking,
they would find me. I had to have the fire to keep from

freezing, and they'd smell the smoke if they got anywhere close.

For a long time I stood shivering, studying the layout before me. There was an Indian village down off the mountain somewhere, and the trail should take me there, but an Indian trail in the mountains can take a body into some almighty scary places, and somewhere there might be a lot of ice. Yet when I thought of what food I had, the fuel that was left, I decided I had to chance it.

The snow crunched underfoot when I went back inside. I added a couple of sticks to the fire and then I saddled up. The roan didn't offer any arguments, so I guess he didn't take to that dark old cave no more than I did. About an hour after daybreak we rode out of the cave and taken the trail to wherever we were going.

We walked a spell, then trotted to warm up a mite, and then I got off and walked to keep warm. I had pa's watch and I figured to keep going at least four hours, and then see where we were. Meanwhile, I'd keep an eye out for another camp, as I had no idea how long the roan could take it . . . or me.

We dipped down into the spruce, ragged, windblown trees that grew shaggier and shaggier. The snow was knee-deep, and in some of the canyons off the trail it looked to be twenty, maybe thirty feet deep. But the trail led down, circling among the trees, rounding boulders dropped off the ridge.

When I'd been riding or walking for four hours, we just weren't anywhere. I saw no tracks of man or beast, and my feet were like clumps of ice again.

Once again the trail led upward, and I found myself riding across a great tilted slab of rock covered with snow. From where I came upon it to as far as I could see in the low clouds that shrouded the peaks, there was at least three miles of unbroken expanse. Nowhere was there a track of man or animal.

A lonely wind prowled above the snow with eerie, threatening whispers. In the vast silence even the roan seemed uneasy, and I was glad when I glimpsed a way off into the forested valley below, yet I held back, looking doubtfully at the steep slide that would take us down the first fifty feet or so. But the roan tugged at the bit, so I let him have his head and he went right into the notch and down the slide without hesitation.

Now we were in a thick, dark stand of spruce, a place of absolute silence. We crunched along, but here, too, I saw no tracks. Animals were simply not stirring, and of course the bear and the marmot were both hibernating, although there was no telling about a bear. He might wake up, be hungry, and go on the prowl even in the deepest winter.

At nightfall I found a corner of a cliff that gave us a break from the wind. I found a slab of rock that I could tilt up to serve as a reflector for my fire, and I got the roan in close to the wall, then built a fire.

There was wood aplenty as there is apt to be in high mountain country where wind and frost wreak havoc with trees. It was a cold night, but come daylight we were on our way again, and then all of a sudden the trees petered out and there we were, facing a trail one horse wide, covered with snow and probably ice under it. Down below, in a deep, wide valley, I could see a thin trail of smoke. So there were folks down there, of some kind, there was warmth, probably food. And we had to use that trail to get there.

It was unbroken snow. What lay under it a body could not guess, but we were going to have to go that way, and one stirrup would be hanging out in space with maybe two thousand feet of open air under it.

I tell you I swallowed a couple of times. I looked at the trail and felt the cold sweat start. The roan seemed edgy but willing. He started for the trail, tossed his head a couple of times, then with ears pricked he started forward.

"Boy," I said, "if you slip—!"

He taken a step, then another. My boot scraped the side of the cliff, the other hung out in space. The roan walked on and headed for a bend around which we could not see. One thing I knew, that horse had to keep going. He couldn't back very well on that narrow path, and it was a cinch I couldn't get off unless over his hindquarters, which I wasn't aiming to do.

He walked forward, stepping like he was on eggs. He'd been a wild mustang in his time and no telling where he'd gone then, but I hoped it was nothing like this. We edged around the corner of the cliff, and the trail sloped steeply away ahead of us. I kept my eyes on the trail, trying to think that horse for every step, trying to hold him on there by sheer willpower. Only once did I glance aside, when some movement in the valley drew my eye.

Maybe a dozen to twenty Indians had come out on the snow and were looking up at me. If I'd thought that trail was hairy before, I had no doubt of it now. Those redskins were out there to watch, and if it was that bad, it must be as mean as it could get. Indians take most any kind of a trail, but it looked like nobody took this one come snow-time.

But that roan was steppin' easy and light. Once in a while he'd blow through his nostrils, scared as I was, but he knew the only way was down and he went right along.

All of a sudden the narrow part played out and the trail widened. I taken a long breath and I felt the roan do the same thing, then we trotted along the rest of the trail, took two or three switchbacks, and then we were cantering up to that Indian village.

It wasn't much, just three tepees up against some aspen, but smoke lifted from those tepees and I was glad to see them.

For ten days I stayed with those Indians. Old Tom Beaver was one of them, and I'd fed him many a time up on that plateau. When I saddled up to leave, they were pulling down their tepees, too. "If anybody comes looking," I said, "you don't know anything."

Lying there in that Indian village, I had time to think back to pa and to wonder who had killed him.

Blazer? Maybe . . . but why had pa always carried a gun?

Of course, most men did. Certainly all of them did

when traveling, because there could be a lot of occasions when a six-shooter was essential. Occasions that had nothing to do with outlaws, Indians, horse thieves, or whatever.

And pa could shoot. I'd seen him shoot, and he was good, better than many a man who carried a reputation as a gunfighter.

When I came down off the mountain, it was to a strange town. There was a church there, because I seen its steeple from afar, and there was a double row of storefronts and a scattering of houses.

There were three two-story buildings, a store, the bank, and one with a sign that said Hotel.

There was a plump, white-haired woman dusting when I came in. She went behind the counter and looked at me with a wary eye. I had on pa's black hat, which fitted, my blanket poncho, and those run-down boots. I hadn't shaved in several days and must have looked like the wrath of God.

"Room will be two bits," she said, "two bits each night, payable in advance. Four bits if you want a bath."

I grinned at her, and her face lit up. She smiled back, friendly-like. "I'll want a room for two nights at least," I said, "and definitely a bath. I been riding some rough country."

"You look it," she said cheerfully.

So I dug down and come up with a dollar, which I gave her. "Hungry?" she asked.

"I could eat a wolf," I said.

"We're fresh out of wolves," she said, "but we got us a cougar."

"All right," I said, "I never et cougar but I'm up to it." I thought she was funnin' me, but she wasn't. Not a-tall.

"My pappy was a mountain man," she said, "and he had the pick of the finest meat in the West, just for the shooting. He always rated cougar meat the best there was. After that come beaver tail and buffalo tongue."

"Bring on your cougar," I said. "Just be sure he's declawed and defanged, 'cause I'm a mite tuckered."

"Bath first?"

I just looked at her. "All right, all right, you can eat first." She indicated a door. "Right through that door, and don't go to makin' sheep's eyes at the waitress. She's my niece and she's seen a sheep."

Chapter IV

A man should always bathe before he eats. I didn't, and that choice got me into more trouble than you could shake a stick at.

I mean had I gone upstairs and had a hot bath, that man wouldn't have been in the restaurant when I went in there. He'd have been off down the country, gone clean out of there, and I'd never have met up with him.

Sure, I was hungry, but it wasn't the first time and I could have waited. They'd already shot their cougar and he wasn't going anyplace. I mean the meat would have been there, and that pretty waitress would have been there, too. Only difference would have been in that man.

I'd just left trouble behind, and I walked right through that door into twicet as much. It wasn't only that the man was there, it was what I said and what he saw.

I went through the door and he set there with his back to me. There was nobody else in the room but that girl, who was just coming through the door with a coffeepot in her hand. Had I seen her first, it might have changed everything, too, because she was right

pert and pretty, but what I saw was that man's back,
a man in a black frock coat, and before I could think
I said, "Pa?"

He looked so much like pa that it just come out of
me, without me thinking, but it turned that man sharp
around, and sure enough, he had a cast of feature
much like pa's only he was younger by ten years, and
there was something else about him. Pa had a touch
of gentleness in his face, where this man had none.
His features were cold, handsome, clean-cut, but you
needed only to look at him once to know there was no
mercy in him, none at all.

"Pa?" he said. "I'm not your pa." And then his
eyes dropped to my gun.

The blanket-coat was off and slung over my arm,
and he could see that gun with its pearl handle and its
red birds. I seen his face change. The expression, I mean.
His scalp kind of drawed back, and when he looked
up at me it was like a wolf ready to jump a rabbit.

"What made you think I was your pa?"

I laughed, kind of embarrassed. "I didn't, really.
Only when I come through the door, your back looked
like—I mean, he's got him a coat like that. I'm sorry, I
just made a mistake."

I started across the room toward another table, but
he spoke and his tone was quiet. "No need to eat alone,
boy. Sit here with me."

If that wolf I mentioned could have talked, he
would have said something just like that, but what was
I to do? If I could have thought faster, I might have
excused myself. Instead I turned around, pulled back
a chair, and sat down, and if there'd ever been a chance
to avoid trouble, I missed it right then.

The girl brought me a cup and a plate with grub
on it. There was meat, cougar meat from what they
said, and there was some rice and beans. It looked
good to me, and I set to, all the while wondering about
that man at the table with me.

"Travel far?" he asked.

"Come down the mountain," I said. "Been ridin'
herd on some cows up yonder."

"Looks like you quit at the right time." He sipped his coffee. "This pa of yours . . . with the coat like mine? He herdin' cattle, too?"

"Not right now. Ain't seen him in a while."

He kind of prodded at me with questions, but I wasn't telling him anything. Least of all where I'd come from. By this time Judge Blazer may have had the word out to pick me up.

As we sat there eating and sort of talking along, I began to get real bothered. This man had a gesture or two just like pa and a way of lifting an eyebrow like him when he was skeptical of something. Many a time I'd known kinfolk to have the same mannerisms and gestures—whether they inherited them or picked them up from seeing them used, I don't know—and it began to come over me that this man did not only look like pa but that he might even be related to him.

What I wanted to know was who he was and where he hailed from, and in western country you never just up and asked a man his business or where he come from. You just waited until he told you, if he was of a mind to. Yet I could try.

"How's things back east?" I asked.

"Times are hard," he said. He studied me coolly, and I felt the thin edge of fear, and it angered me. I told myself I was foolish, that I was afraid of nothing. Besides, why should I fear him? Or anybody? Yet something about him haunted me, and it may have been his resemblance to pa.

"You and your father," he asked, "have you been here long?"

"We move around," I replied. "A man takes work where he can find it."

"Your pa now? He was from back east?"

I chuckled. "Ain't ever'body? Nobody come from this country but Indians, and from what they tell me they came from somewhere else, too."

He threw me a hard glance. He didn't like me any better than I liked him, and as we talked back and forth he would come out with a question or, more often, just some leading comment. He was fishing for information, and I wasn't giving him any. Truth to tell, I knew mighty little about pa. I'd never guessed how little until he was gone, and with him the chance of learning more.

Now, maybe I'm only seventeen, but most of my years been spent working around over the mountains or desert and plains country, and I'd learned a thing or two. This man carried a six-shooter, that was plain to see, but he carried a sleeve gun, too, one of them gambler's hideout guns, derringer type that fires two shots. Mighty good for close action across a card table. I noticed it because of the way he favored his right wrist when he put it down on the table and the way he held his arm. Only a mite different, but to somebody who knows it was plain enough.

"Staying in town?" he asked, finally.

"For a while. I been up in the hills so long I'm growin' grass in my ears. I want to just set and look at the street for a while."

He didn't like that, and I had an idea—I don't really know why—that he wanted me away from there.

"Too bad," he said, casually, "I thought we might ride down the country together."

"Ain't good weather for travelin'," I said. "It's too durned cold to suit me."

I was itching to get away from him, but I had an idea he might just pick up and follow me. Yet I was curious, too, and wanted to know more about him. If he was some kin of pa's, I might learn something about pa from him, or about pa's family.

Yet every instinct I had told me this man was dangerous, and more than that, he was evil. He had the look about his eyes and mouth of a man who was short-tempered and cruel. And I trust my instincts.

His manners were those of a gentleman, but fine manners do not make a fine man, and I was alert for any clue as to what he planned, where he was from, or where he planned to go. He was no miner—that much I could see—nor was he a cowhand. A gambler? Well . . . maybe.

The girl with the freckles was watching me, and she seemed bothered by something. After a bit I finished my coffee and pushed back my chair.

"I'm almighty tired," I said. "Good night."

I arose abruptly and, without so much as a glance back, I left the room. I had moved quickly, hoping to catch him kind of off balance, and that was just what I done. It hadn't seemed like I was fixing to move, but looked like I was going to set for a spell, which was how I'd wanted it to look. I wasted no time in the lobby but went right upstairs to my room. Once inside, I shut the door and put a chair under the knob so's it couldn't be opened.

It was in my mind to open the window, get out, and leave, taking out of there just as fast as I could travel, but it was a miserable night and I was bone-tired.

The thought that come to me was almost as good. He didn't know what horse I'd been riding, because he'd been in town for some time before I arrived and had no reason to be curious about me until I walked into that eating room and spoke to him.

I'd been cold before and could be again, so I opened my window wide and then got into bed.

The wind blew through that window, icy cold, and I done some shivering. Must have been an hour later somebody tried the door, turning the knob real slow and careful. The door didn't give because I had that chair under the knob, and after a minute or two the knob was released and all was quiet. About that time he seemed to get the message of that cold wind comin' from under the door, because of a sudden I heard a kind of an exclamation and then quickly retreating footsteps. After a minute I heard the sound of a horse ridden rapidly down the street. Cheerfully, I closed the window and got back into bed.

There were two ways I could have gone if I'd left town by the trail, and he'd have to check them both out. Meanwhile I'd get some sleep.

Lying there in bed, I studied about it. This man, whoever he was, had tried my door—leastwise, I could

think of nobody else who might try it. He had seemed
suspicious of me, and he resembled pa. Now, what did
all that amount to?

Exactly nothing, except that man had apparently
ridden out of town trying to overtake me, thinking I'd
flown the coop.

Why?

Pa was dead, murdered by somebody. Somebody
who was either Judge Blazer or one of his friends, or
who was somebody else. If it was somebody else, he
hadn't murdered pa to rob him, because Blazer did that,
or tried to.

Suppose Blazer hadn't murdered pa, but just found
him murdered and took advantage of the chance? That
sounded more like Blazer.

Then that implied somebody else had done it, somebody who didn't even know pa had all that money, and
from his looks and the state of his clothes, figured he
hadn't anything worth taking.

If that was the case, it had to be somebody who had
known pa before, somebody from out of his past.

"That's storybook stuff," I said aloud. "You got no
reason to think anything of the kind."

Why would anybody from pa's past want him dead?
Pa hadn't been east in years (if that was where he come
from), and so far as I knew, he'd had no letters from
yonder.

All of which left me nowhere but asleep. When I
opened my eyes with daybreak, the thought was still in
my mind but had gotten nowhere.

After washing up a mite and brushing my clothes as
much as I could, I combed my hair slick and went
down to the lobby. All was quiet and there was nobody around, so I stepped over to the desk and turned
that register around and looked at it.

There was my name, and above it—the only one who
had checked in during the last three days—was the
name Felix Yant. It was a name that meant nothing
to me, and I had an idea it was a name the man had
assumed. Yet what was his purpose?

The restaurant was empty, but there was a rustle of

sound from the kitchen and an occasional rattle of dishes. I pulled back a chair, rather noisily, and sat down. I wanted to eat and get out.

The girl with the freckles looked in and then came quickly over. "You're early. Not much is ready, but we can make you some flapjacks."

"Fine. How about some eggs?"

"I'll see." She hesitated. "Did you know that man who sat with you?"

"Never saw him before." I looked up at her. "Do you know him?"

"No, but he told my aunt he was looking for mining properties. He rides out a good deal."

"In this weather? Seems a bad time to look for a mine, when the ground's covered with snow and you can't even see how it lays or what the formations are."

"We thought so, too."

She brought coffee and, after a little while, a stack of hotcakes and maple syrup. "We've got some eggs. My aunt says you can have them." She hesitated again. "She likes you."

"Well, that's a help. Maybe I should stick around."

"There isn't much work." She lingered. "This is mostly mining around here, and some lumbering. Over the mountain and to the south there's cattle. Are you a cowboy?"

"I'm whatever I need to be to get a job," I said, "but I've put by a little."

She looked at me thoughtfully, for it was a rare man in those days who thought of tomorrow while punching cows. I didn't feel it necessary to explain that it wasn't my saving that had provided the money. Still, come to think of it, it had been my capital. Thinking of that made me feel better, and for the first time it seemed maybe I was entitled to that money.

"I'm Teresa," she said. "Sometimes they call me Terry."

"My name's McRaven. Kearney McRaven. And sometimes they call me just anything they can think of." I grinned at her. "I ain't seen such a pretty girl in a long time."

She flushed up a mite but she liked it, too. I was no hand at making talk with womenfolks, but pa, he'd always had a friendly way about him. "Say something nice to them," he told me once, "and particularly waitresses and such people. You've got to remember they put in a long, hard day, and many people grumble a lot. It does no harm to speak a friendly word."

Well, I was willing. Fact is, I could have been more than friendly with that there Teresa if I knowed how to go about it.

"He ever talk much?"

She knew who I meant, all right. "No . . . scarcely at all. But he watches. Nothing that happens around him happens without his seeing it." And just at that minute he came in.

"Good morning," he said cheerfully enough. "You rise early."

"On a cow ranch you're up before the sun," I said. "I was never no hand to lie abed, anyway."

Felix Yant was what his name was? Should that mean anything to me? I hadn't heard the name before, so far as I could recall, and my recall was pretty good, yet the man worried me. I felt he knew more about me than he had any use for, and I didn't like it. Gave me a feeling of being watched.

He seemed friendly enough, and began to talk of the mountains, the trees, then got to comparing these mountains with those back east. I listened mighty sharp, wanting to pick up a clue.

He had hands like a gambler. They were slender and white, beautiful hands, actually. I suspect he was what is called a gentleman, but I had a feeling if he was, it was more by birth than by instinct. Yet he was an interesting talker, and once started he could hold a body spellbound.

"This is all very well," he said, waving a hand at the surroundings, "but one needs to travel. You need perspective, some basis for comparison."

Seemed to me he was talking as much for Teresa as for me, and there's nothing like a smooth-talking

man to have a way with womenfolks. This here little
one-horse town seemed mighty empty when he began
talking of San Francisco, New York, London, Paris,
and suchlike. Seemed to me he'd been everywhere and
seen everything and remembered most of it. Teresa
was looking at him all starry-eyed, and that didn't set
well with me. I began to feel sore. I wished I had a
story to match him, but when all you've done is play
nursemaid to a few cows, it doesn't leave you much to
spend on conversation.

"Me an' pa traveled some," I said defensively. "We
covered most of the West, time to time. I been to
Dodge, and down there in El Paso . . . that's right
acrosst the river from Mexico!"

"So it is." Yant was amused and showed it. Then
he slipped it in so casually I almost spoke up. He said,
"Your father ever talk of taking you home? To his
home, I mean?"

That was one thing pa never mentioned, but I felt no
need to say so. "Time to time," I lied. But I wondered
why he had never mentioned it. Why had he not talked
of home? Told me of his family, the place where he
was born? The memories of his childhood?

And then suddenly something did come back. I'd
been very young then, a mere child, and there'd been a
woman in the room. I remember she was slender and
dark-haired with large, lovely black eyes . . . or almost
black. I do not know where she came from, how she
came to be there, or where "there" was, except that
she was wearing a cloak and she had come in out of
the night.

Did I remember anything? Or was it all my imagination? "I've only a few minutes. I'm afraid . . . deathly
afraid! He's coming back, Charles, and you know how
he is! I'm afraid! If he ever finds out that I've even
talked to you, he'd kill me. I mean it. Literally."

"You mustn't be here. Leave . . . get away while
you can. I only wish I—"

"There's nothing you can do, Charles. There's nothing anybody can do! And if you come back, that would

be the end of everything. They believe you did it,
Charles. They all believe it . . . except grandfather. I
don't believe he does."

"Well, I didn't do it. We had trouble, I'll admit that,
but it was nothing, and I'm not a vengeful person."

Did I remember all that? Why had I remembered it
at all, when I had forgotten so much? Maybe it was
her beauty, her sudden arrival out of the night, and the
intensity with which she spoke.

How long had it been? Thirteen years? Closer to
fourteen, I thought.

It was the only time I remembered a woman coming
to our rooms, wherever we lived . . . that is, the only
time when pa was home.

There was that other time, the time I never liked
to remember, the time I never told pa about, when the
witch-woman came.

I'd been alone in the room, but that was years later,
and I was eight years old. I remember that because it
was my birthday and pa had promised me something
special, a real treat for my birthday.

I never got my treat, and that I remembered most
of all because pa always did what he promised, except
that time. That was the time he got sick, he almost
died . . . and for months after that he was sick.

Was it because of the witch-woman?

Chapter V

Settin' there over breakfast he riled me. Talkin' smooth was one thing, but he looked so *elegant*, always lookin' like he'd stepped out of a bandbox, as they used to say. Made me look shabby.

Well, I had me a little money, so I made up my mind right then I'd get fixed up. Finally, he got up and left, but he'd been talkin' smooth and easy-like and it got to me, him making himself big in front of Teresa. So I said, "I'm tired this morning. Some damn fool was ridin' his horse up an' down last night, away after midnight. You'd think folks would have the sense to stay inside when it's that cold."

It stopped him, and he turned his head to look at me just like a rattler does when he fixes to strike. There was no laughter in his eyes, nor no smoothness in his tongue. "Sometimes, they tell me, when you hear a rider in the night, it's a sign of death."

"I never heard that," Teresa said. "That's a new one."

"I heard it," I lied, "it's somebody ridin' a dark horse to his death."

He looked at me with those flat, cold eyes, and I looked right back, and then I grinned. I don't know how I done it, but suddenly everything seemed funny. I'm like that. Solemn occasions seem to arouse the humor in me. It wasn't that way with him, for when I grinned, he got up. I could see the temper in his eyes

41

and knew right then his weakness was his impatience.
He was a man who hated to wait, hated to be thwarted
or put off, hated anybody that didn't sidestep for him.

"We'll meet another time," he said, and turned sharp
around on his heel and went out, leaving the money
to pay for his breakfast.

"He doesn't like me," I said dryly.

"He doesn't like anybody," Teresa commented.

"He likes you," I said.

She shrugged. "Not really. And I'm afraid of him,
really afraid."

After I finished my coffee, I went out. Being cold
winter like it was, not many folks were moving about.
We hadn't had much snow, but it was surely cold. I
went down to the general store and looked over what
he had. It wasn't much.

I bought myself a couple of pairs of black Frisco
jeans for rough work and a sheepskin coat. Then I
bought some shirts, a pair of gray striped pants, and a
black suit. They were hand-me-downs, of course, and
would have the sharp creases that come from the shelf,
but would no doubt lose them in time. I bought some
socks, some underwear, and a few odds and ends, and
then went to my room to bathe and change.

When I opened my pack, I seen right away somebody had been through my gear. After living out of a
pack for years, a man gets so he packs for easy handling, and somebody had been through my things, then
had neatly repacked them, but not as I'd had them.

Now who would do— It was him! It had to be him
. . . but why? What was there about me that would
interest him that much? What was there to bring him
to this country at all?

Suppose . . . just suppose he tied into all this
mystery about pa and his past? Suppose we were related? Why would what we did matter to him?

A man like him, he would be apt to do something
only for money or hate. This might be one or the
other, and it might be both.

But what would he be looking for? Fortunately,
what money I had was on me, but I didn't think it

would be money. I'd never had anything else worth taking, and no personal papers of no kind, and as for pa, he never carried his papers—

I just sort of backed up and set down. Pa's papers—those two big brown envelopes he had for so long . . . where were they? And what were they?

Pa an' me, we'd knocked about the country a good bit, hunting work here and there, and pa had always carried those two brown envelopes in a sort of buck-skin case he had with a belt run through it. Yet it had not been on him when he was killed, and in fact, I hadn't seen it for some time.

Kidlike, I was mostly concerned with my own affairs, and somewhere along the line pa had left those envelopes with somebody or hid them somewhere, and I'd no idea where they were.

There was a lot I had never known and had never thought to ask about that was suddenly important to me. If there were any answers, they would be in our past. Somewhere down the drifting path we had taken over the years, pa had left a clue.

Those papers now, in those brown envelopes in the leather case . . . pa hadn't lost them. He'd just plain left them somewhere, and if he left them he left them a-purpose, someplace where they would be safe until needed. He had carried those guns, but he was never a quarrelsome man, although I'd seen him shoot and knew he feared no man. Yet death finally caught up with him.

Murder . . . and if I was not careful, I would be next.

Somehow I never doubted that. It was just the way things shaped. I could see it coming, and had I been out on the trail in the snow, I would now be dead. Or if I hadn't locked my door. What I should do was run . . . yet I knew I'd never get away. This man would be a bloodhound on a trail. Hadn't he found pa and me after all those years?

First, I'd better not let him think I was smart . . . if I was. He had to believe it wasn't going to be all that hard to win or he would suddenly try much harder, and to kill a man in our day wasn't all that hard. He could start a quarrel, then shoot me down . . . if he was fast enough.

That, of course, was the question. I'd never had a gunfight, nor wanted one. No man in his right mind does. I heard tell of a kid or two running around trying to get a reputation, but it was a rare thing, and only some half-baked youngster whose cards were badly mixed would be that crazy. I knew I was fast, and pa had taught me to shoot.

Running went against the grain, even if I could get away. On the other hand, I might be better out in the hills than he was, and it might make all the difference. Yet with him around and knowing what it was about, I'd be better off to try to blunder into some hint of why he was here, and why it was important that pa be dead.

He either hated pa something fierce or there was money involved. Or maybe some family feud.

Just thinking about it would help me none at all, and if I was going to survive, I was going to have to do some thinking.

When I got all dressed, I looked at myself in the mirror and looked just what I was, a country boy all dressed up to go to town. I didn't look right to myself, and wouldn't to those folks out there, including Teresa. I had nothing of that casual elegance Felix Yant had. He was the kind of a man who would have looked well-dressed in his long johns. He had manner and style. Well, pa had it, too. Why not me?

I taken off that new suit and hung it up. I just put on a pair of Frisco jeans, a gray flannel shirt, a black handkerchief at my neck, and my new sheepskin coat. But I did not forget my guns. Nor my knife . . . which I'd carried all my life. Never can tell when you might come on somebody needs skinning.

Next I taken that coat off again and set down at the bureau, which would do for a table. On the edge of an old newspaper I started to write down the towns we'd been in. I never realized there was so many.

When I got to counting towns, I found that in the past four years we'd stopped or worked in twenty-two different places. Part of it was that pa had an itchy foot or some other reason for moving on, and the rest of it was that work was scarce and few jobs lasted long.

For two months pa worked for the stage line. He was an agent and bookkeeper in Eureka, Nevada. I'd had a job herding cows right near town, a herd that had been driven in to supply beef to the miners. We went over to Pioche from there, and it was a rough town, a boom mining town with a man named Morgan Courtney walking the streets, a hard, irritable man always on edge for trouble. Pa took the place of a teller in a bank there, for the regular man had to go to a funeral in Salt Lake or somewheres. I taken a job washing dishes in a restaurant.

One way and another we moved across the country, from Placerville in California to Kansas City in Missouri, with stops at Fort Worth, Fort Griffin, Santa Fe, and Silver City, and then back to Dodge and up to Yankton.

Where had I last seen those brown envelopes? He'd had them in Eureka, because he kept them in the company safe whilst there. I recall stopping for them before we rode out. And he'd had them when he was teller, that time. I had seen him roll the buckskin wallet up in his bedroll when we left Dodge, and I thought I recalled pa having them in Kit Carson.

Georgetown! Try as I might, I could not remember them after we stopped at the Hotel de Paris in Georgetown. Pa was friendly with the owner, a Frenchman, and they often talked French together. I recall pa telling me Louis Dupuy was a man he could trust. "He's a hard, opinionated man, but nobody can push him, buy him, or sway him. I'd trust him with my life."

So there it was . . . maybe.

Which didn't help me one bit, for that was clear across the country from where I was. There were a lot of passes choked with snow between here and yonder, and I had a bloodhound on my tail.

About then I began to get an idea. It was a crazy sort of thought that came into my mind and stayed there. Part of it was because I thought I might be better off in the wild country than he would be. Nobody tried to cross those mountains in the winter. Up high there, the passes were often packed with twenty to thirty feet of snow, and it was cold, really cold.

But west and south of here was some desert like you've never seen, and it come to me that maybe I should head off west right into the midst of that desert. I'd pick a stretch where I knew the water holes and I'd lose him out there. It sounded simple, but I wasn't at all sure. Felix Yant was not a simple man.

Getting into my coat, I went off down to the restaurant again. Seemed like the only place I was going these days, but where could a body go, it being so cold and all?

Teresa looked at me and smiled. "You look very nice, Kearney," she said. I felt like I was blushing, and maybe I was.

"We've got some hot soup," she suggested. "Lots of beef and vegetables."

"Sounds good," I said, and I meant it, but at the same time an idea hit me. What I should do was take out of here at midday or later. A traveling man starts early to get the light for traveling, but if I were to take out suddenly, I might just get a lead on Yant before he knew I was gone.

Chances were I wouldn't, but it was a thought. I'd been stopping by the livery barn to see if my horse was all right, and I'd continue to do that, stopping by in the afternoon so there'd be a pattern.

The soup was good. Only trouble was, in the midst of it I looked up and I seen Tobin Wacker and Dick riding into town. There was no sign of Judge Blazer or the others.

I started to get up, then sat back down. That was mighty good soup, and it might be before I had more. My eyes followed Wacker and Dick as they rode up to the saloon and got stiffly down. They looked to be wore out. Even Wacker, big and burly as he was, staggered a mite when he stood. Might be because they'd been in the saddle for some time.

They went into the saloon, and I finished my soup.

It was time I did some thinking. Had they come down here hunting me or were they just getting out of the mountains? It looked to me like they'd had a rough, rough time.

Teresa came in and sat down across the table from me. "You're in some kind of trouble, aren't you?"

"You could say that," I agreed, "but it's none of my seeking."

"Is it him? Mr. Yant, I mean?"

I shrugged. "I don't know," I said. "I don't know what he wants or where he comes from, but he worries me."

Suddenly it all began to come out. Maybe I was lonely, maybe I just needed to get it all straight in my mind. Anyway, I told her about me an' pa, our drifting and the like, and I told her about pa's big winning and what followed after. I didn't know what was to happen, and maybe I just wanted something to be on record, with somebody, and she was a good listener. Anyway, what man doesn't like having all the attention of a pretty girl?

The more I talked, the more it began to shape up like this Felix Yant was kin to me. At least, I had something he wanted, or didn't want, to find.

"You scared of him?" She looked at me with those blue eyes, and I looked into myself for the answer. Was I scared of him?

"No," I said, after a bit. "I ain't . . . I'm not scared of him, but he worries me, because I don't know what he's after. You know and I know that nobody but a crazy man would be out here inspecting mining properties with all this snow on the ground. You can't see the formations, how the land lays, or anything. I don't know why he's here, but it ain't that."

"What are you going to do?" she asked.

"I got to do some detective work," I said, and I'll not deny using that word made me kind of swell up a little. "I've got to go back along the country aways and maybe find out where pa came from and where Yant comes from."

"You be careful," Teresa warned.

"You can do something for me," I said, "if you're of a mind to."

"What is it?"

"Those two men I spoke of? The ones who just came into town? If they should come in here, try to hear what they say if you can do it without seeming to. I'd like to have an idea what they have on their minds."

"I'll do it." She got up. "I'll get you some hot coffee."

From where I sat, I could see up and down the street while sitting back from the window. Those two had gone into the saloon and they were having a few. Tobin Wacker was a right quarrelsome man when drinking. I knew nothing about Dick except the company he kept and the fact he'd been one of those who attacked me on the mountain.

What had become of Judge Blazer? There was just no way he was going to get back to where he came from after that snow, and he wasn't the kind of a man to stay in any cold mountain cabin when he could get off the mountain. It began to look to me like Judge Blazer was dead.

They came out on the street and they looked right over at the restaurant. They looked up and down the street and then they started over. Dick, who was about average size for our time, was maybe five foot eight. I guess he'd weigh maybe one fifty. Tobin Wacker was something else. He was maybe six inches taller than my five foot nine, and he was a good seventy pounds heavier than my one sixty. If I was going to tangle with them, it wouldn't be for fun. I'd have to take Dick out with one punch so's I could devote my time to Wacker.

Just then Teresa came in with my coffee. She seen my expression and she stopped. "What is it? What's the matter, Kearney?"

"It's them. They're comin' across the street. If there's to be a fight, I'll try to get them outside so's we won't tear things up."

"You'll do what you have to, Kearney," she said coolly. "My pa was a fighting man, and I've heard him say it a thousand times, 'Land the first punch. The first punch wins nine out of ten fights.' You land the first punch, Kearney, and leave the cleaning up to me. I've mopped up blood before this."

Here they come. Right at me. I pushed a chair to one side so's my feet wouldn't get tangled.

Chapter VI

When he came through the door, the first thing Tobin Wacker laid eyes on was me.

He stopped right in the door, looking like he'd seen death. If ever I saw a man scared, it was him. Whatever he expected when he came in, I wasn't any part of it. Maybe he figured me for dead. I don't know what was in his mind, but whatever it was, he had no idea of fighting.

"Howdy, Wacker," I said. "You had enough or are you huntin' some more?"

Rightly, I should have been over there where I could nail him before he got out of that doorway, and before his partner could make it through.

They came on into the room, and when Dick seen who was there, his face turned white. Puzzled me, what they were so scared about. From behind me, from the entrance to the hotel lobby came a low, quiet voice. "Need some help, McRaven?"

It was Yant.

"Thanks." I was irritated. Was it him they was . . . were scared of? How long had he been there, anyway? "I can skin anything I can catch."

"We ain't huntin' trouble," Wacker said, rubbing his big meat-hooks on his pants. "We just come for some grub."

Recalling my talk about cannibalism, I said kind of wryly, "What's the matter? Didn't Blazer last you?"

You'd of thought I lashed them with a whip. They just turned and busted out of that door and went a-flyin'.

Yant walked up beside me, still watching the door. "Now what was *that* all about?"

"Nothing," I said, "we had trouble awhile back. I thought they'd come for more."

"So did I," he said.

"Thanks," I said.

"Thanks? For what?"

"Offering to help," I said.

He pulled back a chair and sat down opposite me, and for once that poker face showed something. He was puzzled and angry, but with himself, I thought. "Think nothing of it," he muttered, and I began to wonder if that offer to help hadn't come naturally, without him thinking of it at all. If that was true, I felt better about him, but still, why should he help me? This was a country where a man was supposed to saddle his own broncs and fight his own battles. Yet he had offered to help.

"Have something," I said. "I was fixing to eat."

He didn't say anything, but he did order when Teresa came in. He was in what some folks call a brown study, I mean he was figuring something out and he didn't like it. If it was true that he figured on killing me, and I surely believed it, he had missed a good chance of having it done for him. He had offered to step in when all he needed to do was stand aside and let it happen, whatever it was. I was going to barrel right into them, but I'd no idea I could whip them both, the shape I was in. My ribs still hurt me once in a while, and my nose was swole. That old Indian woman had set it best she could, and strapped up my ribs.

"They were afraid of you, McRaven," Yant said. "Why were they afraid? Who are you? What are you?"

"I'm an orphan," I said, "who herds cows when he can find the work. That's all I am."

"And all you want to be?" he asked sharply.

"Now, I never said that. Ever'body has some notion of being more than he is, I expect."

He stared at me out of those level, cold eyes. "Did you ever go to school?"

"Not so's it would count. Time or two I went for a spell. Never liked it much, though. I liked pa teaching me."

"He taught you?"

"Surely did. From the time I can first recall. He'd read aloud and then we'd talk about it. I guess come graduation time in a proper school it wouldn't count for much, but he surely taught me a lot. He taught me to shoot, to throw a knife, and how to hunt and to live off the country. Then he taken me to the cotton markets in New Orleans and Mobile and showed me how business was done there, and how it was done in stores, and where the money went that they took in.

"We talked to cattle and wool buyers, to horse traders and steamboat men. We worked in mines, and he showed me how they operated. He used to read to me from the classics, and after he read we'd talk about them, and about people he met. He was a quiet man, but uncommon shrewd."

"You knew those men?" he asked. "I mean the ones you had trouble with?"

"We went round and about awhile back. Maybe they didn't like what they got."

You didn't like it, either, I told myself. *You taken a beating up yonder.* But even as I thought that, I remembered they'd been up on the plateau quite awhile. There was no more grub than for a day . . . two at most. Yet it had been more than two weeks and they looked to be in good shape. Maybe that was why they were scared. Maybe what I'd said about Blazer hit them right where it hurt. I'd spent about ten days with those Indians, and I'd been a few days getting to where they were . . . that was all hazy now. Had it been two or three days? I couldn't recall.

"Your English is very bad," he said to me then.

I just looked at him. "That just ain't none of your business," I told him. "Besides, I can talk better if need be. Sometimes folks think you're puttin' on airs if you talk so hifalutin."

"They'll not think that of you."

"Didn't aim for them to." I pushed back my chair and got up. I was tired of this talk, and I had some thinking to do.

"Can you use that gun?"

"I can."

"We'll have to take a ride out of town, and you can show me."

Well, I just looked at him. "Like hell we will, mister. My pa taught me never to draw a gun unless I meant to use it. Showin' off with guns is for tinhorns. If you ever see me with a gun in my hand, mister, it'll be because I got good reason. A handgun isn't a toy to pleasure yourself with. I carry it because I live in a rough country. I herd stock where there's wolves and cougars, and some of the stock is mighty mean itself. I need a gun, mister."

With that I walked out and left him sittin' there, and I went for my horse, mounted, and rode out of town.

He was standin' on the walk in front of the restaurant when I rode out, and a moment later, watching from behind some trees on the slope of a hill, I seen him cantering out the way I'd gone. When he was gone by, I rode down to the stable and put up my horse. Then I went up to my room and stretched out on my bed.

Hour or so later I heard him ride back, and I grinned at the ceiling. He'd had him a ride and he'd missed finishing his dinner. If he was going to keep track of me, he had his work cut out for him.

Chapter VII

Curiously, I began to look forward to those meetings with Felix Yant. He irritated me, and I was wary of him. I was sure he meant to kill me, but there was a quiet elegance about him that I envied, and his obvious assurance, which I lacked . . . except maybe when I was out in the wild country.

Oddly enough, I think in his own way he liked me. Not that it would have stopped him from killing me if the chance offered, but there was something in each of us to which the other responded. He was like pa, which may have been part of it, but in some ways I was freer with him than I ever had been with pa.

Yet I doubt if he had an ounce of human sympathy for anyone or anything. Whatever he was, he was complete in himself. He asked for nothing but to remain as he was, and if there was money involved, I believe he wanted it to give him isolation. Solitude is a hard thing to buy if one expects bodily comfort, too, and he was a man who liked to take his ease. He reminded me of a rattlesnake on a warm rock, just content to be there.

To have the solitude he wanted demanded money, and he was not the kind of man to turn outlaw. No matter what anybody says, an outlaw's life is a hard one. He spends most of his time dodging the law, hiding out in the hills or in shacks away from town. If he's half-smart, he won't flash money around to make people curious as to how he got it, and in most ways it is a rougher life than making an honest living.

Felix Yant would have none of that. He had a distaste for the crude, the uncomfortable, and the ignorant. He had nothing but contempt for most people, and it showed.

"What are you going to do with yourself?" he demanded suddenly of me. "Do you expect to spend the rest of your life just looking between a horse's ears? Haven't you discovered that the world belongs to those who can use it?"

"What's wrong with me? I'm gettin' along all right."

"Are you?" He eyed me coolly. "You're just like a million others, just walking blindly through life. Why don't you get out of the rut you're in and get an education?"

"You mean go back to school?"

"Of course not. All any school can give you is the barest outline of an education. You have to fill it in yourself. Read . . . listen . . . taste. An ignorant man has such limits on his possibilities of enjoyment. He is denying himself all the richness in life. Just as with food, your taste in all things needs experience of flavor. Education is in part just learning to discriminate between ideas, tastes, flavors, sounds, colors, or whatever you wish to mention. The wider your range of taste experience, the greater your possibilities of pleasure, of enjoyment.

"If evil and hardship come upon you at least you will be aware of what is happening, and you will have some understanding of why. It is better than falling under the axe like some dumb brute in a slaughterhouse who has no awareness of what is happening to him. A wise man can even experience the approach of death with some awareness. It may be the final experience, but it is experience."

There was nothing much I could say to that. Yet it ired me to be taken with such contempt. Pa had read a lot to me, and I'd read a good bit myself, when we could find the books. And there was more to be learned than just from books. There was music in the mountains, and lessons wherever grass grew, and a body who kept his eyes open could learn anywhere.

"Why did you come west?" I asked him straight out. "You could live the way you want to back wherever you came from."

"That I could," he said dryly, "and I shall soon be back there again, living as I wish. Often to attain one's goals one has to take a few extra steps." He looked straight at me with a kind of amused contempt. "I have one minor chore. When that is done I shall return, live the life of a country gentleman and leave the pushing and shoving to the rest of these pigs."

I had an idea what that minor chore was, and it made me sore to have him speak of it thataway.

"I ain't been east since I was a youngster," I commented, "although pa used to talk about times when the azaleas were in bloom. He was always a man who loved fine horses, too."

"He sounds like a most interesting man. Did he give you that gun?"

"He was murdered," I said, "by some coward who was afraid to face him. Shot in the back of the head. Had he seen his murderer he would have killed him first."

Yant shrugged. "Then the murderer, as you call him, was wise not to be seen, was he not? Yet it sounds more like an execution than a murder."

"Does it? I wonder what gave you that idea? Executions are carried out by what pa used to call 'duly constituted authority' and in a legal manner. Anyway, pa never did anything to be executed for."

"Did he not? I doubt if you were with him all his life, and most men have done something for which they should be hanged."

"Do you speak for yourself?"

He turned those hard, straight eyes on me. They stared unblinking, and I met his gaze. After a moment he shrugged. "You must learn to guard your tongue, boy. A man must answer for his words when he talks with men."

"I've talked with men since I was six," I said coolly,

"and am prepared to answer for anything I say or have said. Anyway, you spoke of men generally, and I merely wondered if you spoke for yourself too."

He did not like me and he did not like the way I replied to him, so he got up and walked away without speaking or looking back. I watched him go, suddenly conscious that Teresa was at my side. "Be careful of him," she said. "I'm afraid of him."

She sat down across from me, and for a moment we looked at one another. I'd never known many girls, or how to deal with them, but with Teresa it seemed no problem. "What are you going to do?" she asked suddenly. "Are you going to stay here? There isn't much to do, you know."

"I'd be gone," I said "if it weren't for you . . . and him."

A few people came and went, and after waiting on them she came back to sit with me. Betweentimes I thought about my father and Felix Yant. Somehow there was a connection, and I meant to know what it was.

"If I leave suddenly," I said, "just remember I'll come back."

"Maybe," she said. "Men always say they will come back, but they rarely do."

"I will."

She was silent a minute, and then she said, "He was talking to them, to those men who came in here that day."

To Wacker and Dick? Now what did that mean? What could he get from them that he did not know already? Or was he going to let them do the job for him?

"Tomorrow," I said, "watch for me. But don't expect me."

"Watch for you?"

"So he will think I am coming."

I rode out quickly at sundown, back a half hour later. He watched me from behind his curtain but did not follow. Was he so sure I'd be back?

Immediately I went to bed. I had eaten earlier, now I wanted rest, but I put my few things together first, and at four in the morning, with a cold wind blowing along the streets, I slipped out and went to the stables. Swiftly I saddled, keeping my face toward the door. Then I walked out and took a trail out of town, around the corrals and away from the street. When I passed from sight of any window in town, I started to canter.

It was still dark, and what warned me was a sudden catch of wood smoke on the air. Just a breath of it, then it was gone, yet instantly I was alert. The wind was wrong for the town, and there were no shacks out here that I knew of.

Instantly, I turned the roan into the deeper shadows along the edge of the forest and drew up, touching his shoulder gently with a gloved hand. Again I caught the smoke. A camp or a cabin of which I knew nothing . . . somebody was there . . . close by.

The roan walked at my signal, hoofs crunching a bit on the hard snow. Suddenly a man loomed up before me, rising out of a creek bed, but his rifle was not up, and I had the impression he had not meant to be seen, for when we glimpsed each other he shied as if he would try to hide, but there was no place, so he stood still. It was Wacker.

"So that's it? He set you to spy on me?"

He stood silent, watching me warily. "I think," I said, "I would be very slow about going to him with news of my ride. He won't like it when I come back into town."

"If you do."

"If I do. But wouldn't you like it better if I did not? Where is your bread buttered, Wacker? Would you rather have me gone where I cannot get people to asking questions, or in town where you have to worry?"

"I think he means to kill you."

"I have no doubt of it, Wacker, but you found that I do not die easily, and I'm tougher now. Go if you like, but if I were you, I'd let well enough alone. Go in an hour from now and tell him you saw me leave . . . choose whatever time you like." I grinned at him. "By that time I may be coming back."

He stood there looking at me, and I was wasting time. "What is it between you? He wants you bad, I think."

"Ask him."

"I'd ask him nothing. Not that one."

He stepped aside and I rode on, watching back, however, and trusting him not one whit. When there was a good two hundred yards and a bend in the road between us, I spoked the roan and we took the next mile at a good run, then slowed, steam rising from us in a cloud.

Felix Yant would be after me now. This would be his chance to kill. I had no doubt that he was a dead shot. His kind would be. An excellent horseman, also, but his horse was a finely bred eastern gelding, not a mountain horse. I felt very sorry for that horse.

My destination was Georgetown, but I headed west, away from it. I headed away from the high, snow-covered peaks with their passes choked with snow. I headed for the desert.

He had told me nothing of the years he had left behind, but I doubted they were akin to mine. He had lived well, I thought, or almost well, and he wanted more of that life. Now he would find how others lived, for I knew where he was to be taken. Mine were but seventeen, almost eighteen years, but they had been lean and hungry years, with long, lonely rides. Since I was old enough to recall, I had ridden the wild country, and I knew how to live there even like the coyotes who haunt the empty desert spaces.

Did he know the high desert in winter? Did he know those vast and empty spaces, sometimes spotted with patches of thin snow, always swept by cold and bitter winds? If he did not know, he would learn, for that was where I now went.

The roan knew. The roan was bred in those spaces, in the wild, remote canyon country and in the high deserts to the south of there. If Felix Yant wanted my hide, he would have to buy it with suffering, cold, and every bit of toughness there was in him.

Wild and broken was the land to the west, a land

of little water and less rain, a land where the rivers ran in canyons a thousand feet deep and where the springs were hidden in hollows of rock. Where a few Indians lived and no white man except a chance prospector or a trapper whom no one had told that the great days of fur were gone.

I rode down with the wind, down off a lofty plateau and into a canyon, then out to the lonely outpost store, where I led my horse to the stable. I had an hour, perhaps two. I went inside after watering my horse and giving him a bait of corn. Inside the store was warm, and an old man, very tall and thin with steel-rimmed spectacles, read a book by the potbellied stove. He looked over his glasses at me. "Not many ride in this weather," he commented.

"There's a man behind me," I explained.

"The law?"

"No . . . an enemy. I don't know how much of an enemy, but if he follows where I am going, he'll be wanting me bad."

I walked to the counter and ordered what I would need, a side of bacon, some dried fruit, flour, salt, beans, a few odds and ends, and some hard candy. It would help me through the times when I could not stop. I also bought one hundred rounds of .44s.

"You been out there before?"

"I have."

"Has he?"

"I don't believe so."

"West, south, and north," he said, "there isn't another white man for a hundred miles . . . more likely two hundred miles."

"Nobody at Lee's Ferry?"

"They come and got him. Or took him somehow. I don't think there's anybody there now."

He looked at me. "You're almighty young. Have you killed somebody?"

"Not yet," I said. "I'm hoping not to."

"If he ain't use to it, an' he follers you," the old man said, "you won't need to kill him. That country will do it."

He looked at me again. "You been there, you say?"

"I come across with my pa. I was a youngster the first time, standing about as high as the sight on a Winchester."

He nodded slowly. "With a tall man? A gentleman?"

"He was my father," I said gently, "and he was always a gentleman, and always a man."

"Ride well, son," the old man said, "an' make your grub last. I seen you come in. That's a good horse."

"This was his country," I said. "Pa taken him from the wild bunch over there back of the Sweet Alice Hills."

The land fell away in a vast sweep like a great, empty sea where no billows rolled, nor even waves. Stiff grass stood in the wind, scarcely bending, and the cedar played low, humming songs with the wind.

I rode away into the empty land, and there was no sound but the drum of hoofs upon the hard ground, and there was no dust, and scarcely a track to mark my passing.

Chapter VIII

What is it makes a man do the things he does? Time to time I've wondered about that, and it was pa who set me to thinking. I never realized that pa was running until it was too late. Sure, it occurred to me now and again that we moved a lot, sometimes leaving good jobs and places we liked. It was only now that I wondered if pa was running away from something, or simply avoiding an issue, a settlement he did not wish to face.

Pa wasn't scared. I'll give him that. Several times I'd seen him face up to mighty dangerous situations, always calm, easy, and in command. And he was a good man with a gun.

Something happened back yonder in his younger years that had brought him to grief. That something was tied in with the reason Felix Yant would come riding after me. Oh, I never doubted he'd come! And deep inside me I was sure it was he, and nobody else, who killed pa.

What bothered me was I felt an uneasy kinship with the man. Maybe we were related, but it was more than that. Sometimes when he spoke, I knew what he would say before he said it, and that was strange, too, for he was a different kind of man than I'd ever known.

Some things about me bothered him, too. He didn't like the language I used most of the time. What he hadn't yet realized was that it was a sort of a vernacular most western men slipped into, no matter how well they could talk or how much they knew of the language. Part of it was that the educated ones didn't want to seem to be putting on airs, as the saying was, but it was more than that. It was almost as if it was a dialect. We used a lot of contractions and Indian or Spanish words that came into our speaking natural-like.

Sometimes Yant, who was obviously new to the West, would stop and look at me to guess the meaning of what I'd said. I had an idea the words we used would in a short time become so much a part of the language nobody would even hesitate over them.

We used *lariat,* which was short for the Spanish *la reata,* and *hombre* was used almost as much as *man.* There were dozens of other words and expressions that sort of filtered into the everyday talk from the Indians, the Spanish, and the country itself.

Me an' that roan, we just taken off into the desert-like country toward the west. Not that it was desert, but it was dry—least you knew where the water lay. And all the advantage lays with a man who is making the trail. He can go where he wishes, stop when he likes, and I was of no mind to make it easy.

At first I didn't attempt to make myself hard to find. What I wanted most was distance, and I hit a fair pace and held to it. That roan could go all day at a kind of shambling trot.

I had no illusions about what I was getting into. Yant, if he had killed pa, was as cold-blooded as they come. He'd shot pa at point-blank range and in the back of the head, and he'd do the same for me if the chance allowed. Maybe I was better in wild country and maybe I wasn't. In any event, the man was a good rider and a tough, dangerous man, not to be held lightly.

If I could shake him loose, I'd strike out for Georgetown and hope that pa had left something there. If not, I'd have to rethink the situation and go over pa's back trail.

Wacker and the judge and them seemed far away and in another world. I was staking my life on outguessing Felix Yant.

There was nobody I could go to for help. Anyway, it wasn't the way things were done in the West. A man saddled his own broncs and he fought his own battles. He stood alone, on his own two feet. A gang was a place for cowards to hide, because they were afraid to stand out in the open. They wanted others to fight their battles for them and to shield them from attack.

The wind was cold, right off the snow-covered flanks of the mountains, which lay behind me now. How far I was going west I had no idea, only that somehow I had to shake Yant from my trail and then turn east once more.

There was ice on the edges of Cherry Creek when I crossed it. Then, deciding here was where I should start, I turned downstream, keeping my horse in the water for a couple of miles, then out on the east bank again, and by high noon I was skirting the La Plata on the west side, hunting for an arroyo I dimly remembered that ran off to the northwest. Sometime about an hour later, I saw it off to the west and cut across-country. There was a trail but I chose to avoid it, crossing to the arroyo itself. There had been recent rains, but cattle had gone up and down the canyon leaving a maze of tracks that in the soft sand had no distinction, one from the other. Keeping to the arroyo for another hour, I reached the old Ute Trail, which would take me west to the Mancos River.

Leaving the roan to graze on whatever he could find, I climbed a high shoulder near the trail and sat there for a good half hour, watching my back trail. I saw nothing, not even dust. Instead of making me feel good, it left me worried.

Suppose I was all wrong and he had not followed me? Suppose he had outsmarted me and guessed my intention and was waiting until I started east again? He was a shrewd man, and I returned to my horse feeling none too good.

The land through which I rode was lonely, desolate, offering nothing. Here and there great mesas thrust up from the land about, towering like islands from a vanished sea. Off to the south was the tableland of Mesa Verde, its great promontory like the bow of a ship outlined sharply against the sky.

Everywhere there was a thick stand of cedar, and wherever there was an open space, it was grown up to sagebrush. From time to time up some branch canyon, there was a glimpse of spruce trees along the flanks or in the ends of the canyons. It was rough, broken country with many fallen slabs of rock and talus slopes. I needed a place to hole up. If Yant lost my trail, he might give up on me.

At the head of a canyon a trail branched off to the northwest. No Indian tracks, although this was Ute country, only a scattering of deer and other animal tracks. I was catching a sense of the country now, remembering it from a time long since, when pa and me had holed up here for a spell.

Red Horse Gulch was somewhere off to the south, and if I wasn't guessing wrong, this trail led to a spring.

I turned the roan along that trail, and from the way he quickened his step I had an idea there was water ahead.

Believe me, I was mighty uneasy. Felix Yant might be green to this country, but he'd ridden and hunted a lot and it would take some doing to fool him. I was banking that he'd sight-hunted mostly, or trailed game with dogs, and that he wasn't much of a tracker. Yet to underestimate an enemy is always dangerous.

About a half mile or so from where I left the Ute Trail, I found the spring. First off I let my horse have what he wanted, drank myself, and filled my canteen. Plenty of game tracks but no horse tracks.

Squatting beside the spring, I considered what lay before me and behind me. Odd part of it was, I was kind of enjoying this cat-and-mouse game. The trouble was —and this I had to keep in mind—that it was no game. It was being played for keeps, and all a man needed was one mistake.

Right now a man was on my back trail who was deadly as a rattler. He'd shot pa in the back, so it showed he didn't have any mercy in him. It may have shown something else . . . that when it came right down to it, he was scared of pa.

Seemed strange that anybody could be afraid of pa, who had always seemed the gentlest of men, yet Yant had taken no chances with him.

The spring was in a small branch canyon, and I didn't much like staying there for fear Yant would come down the draw and catch me there, so I straddled the roan and started down canyon. Here and yonder the trail went up the flank of the canyon to get away from great blocks of rock that had broken off the wall and tumbled to the bottom, blocking any trail there might have been.

Here and there I saw broken pieces of pottery, so Indians had lived here before. Pa had told me of some cliff dwellings along this canyon and another branch that ran back toward the east and north.

Where the canyon forked, I turned right and found myself looking up into the high arch of one of those shallow, wind-hollowed caves where the old cliff dwellers liked to build. There was a cliff dwelling there, too, but it was different.

There was a ledge crossed that cave some sixty feet from the bottom of the arch, and on that ledge was built a house. Only ruins were left, yet pretty substantial ruins. How a body could get up there was more than I could figure, but a man sitting up there with a rifle could cover anybody coming down that canyon where I was.

The cave was right at the junction of those two canyons, and the more I looked at that cliff house, the more I wanted to see what was inside. Certainly once a man got in there, a body would surely be in a fix trying to get at him. If I could get in.

Riding up the canyon was no easy matter. There was a sandy strip in the bottom where water had run during rains, but great boulders and slabs of rock had fallen across the way in several places. There was more pottery down here, or bits and pieces of it, and there were several ruins tucked back under the brows of the cliff. Back at the junction those canyon walls were maybe five hundred feet high, but a little less toward the canyon's head. Near the far end I glimpsed what seemed to be some ruins in behind some spruce trees. Leaving my horse cropping at some brush, I scrambled up there and found the ruins of a house and the edge of what might have been a kiva, one of their round ceremonial centers. It was mostly filled with rock that had sloughed off the roof of the cave. The place was cool, still, and almost entirely hidden from below. In a couple of pools water stood, runoff from recent rains that had not evaporated in this shaded place.

Returning to my roan, I found a place where it could be hidden behind a thick stand of spruce, a fairly level area, although small. Here, too, there were broken fragments of pottery and some ears of corn that were only three or four inches long and no larger around than my finger. Stripping the gear from the roan, I hid it as well as I could with some fallen branches and the like. Then, taking my rifle and canteen, I went back down the canyon, working my way along the steep

side, following what must at one time have been a foot
trail, that took me higher and higher along the canyon
wall.

Several hundred feet above the canyon floor I found
a crack in the canyon wall where stood the notched
trunk of a cedar. Rigging a crude sling for my rifle, I
hung it over my back to have both hands free for
climbing. Slowly and carefully, aiding myself with
handholds or fingergrips on the rocks, I mounted to an
excessively narrow ledge, then by another notched pole
to a still higher one.

Working my way along and up, I reached a ledge
that led to the cliff house. Once settled inside, I un-
slung my rifle and peered out through a crack in the
crumbling wall. From here I could look down to the
junction of the two canyons. It was an easy rifle shot,
but did I wish to kill?

Settling back, I studied my surroundings. On my
right, almost under my elbow, was the edge of the
kiva, a round ceremonial room with some of the ancient
timbers still in place although the roof had long since
fallen in.

There was a door, broader at the top than at the
bottom, for is not a man wider at the top? And often
carrying a burden on his back or shoulders? And another opening that gave access to an area beyond.

There were bits of broken pottery lying about and
a number of small corncobs, less than a third the size
of those with which I was familiar. Corn had been
domesticated, apparently, but not developed to our
present standard. I took a short drink from my canteen
and settled back to rest.

All was quiet in the canyon. Occasionally a rock,
loosened by some animal or by the workings of nature,
would tumble off into the canyon below. Once I heard
some small animal scurrying.

My horse was reasonably safe. Shielded by trees as
he was, and somewhat above the canyon floor in the
old ruin, there was small chance he would be discovered. It would need someone totally lacking in
caution to go up the canyon to its end, completely

exposed to rifle fire from a dozen possible places of hiding. Felix Yant was not, I was sure, such a man.

What I needed was a little rest, time to think and to plan, and a chance to observe my enemy, if such he was, and to learn what manner of man he was.

Slowly the afternoon passed. I dozed, awakened, dozed again.

At last, peering through some broken brick atop the wall, I saw a bird fly up.

Somebody coming? Suddenly I began to sweat. Suppose they had seen me climb up here? If such was the case I could well be trapped, for impossible as the place was to attack, it was almost equally impossible to leave without exposing myself.

At night? The thought of attempting that cliff in the darkness gave me no pleasure. I was agile enough, and had climbed a lot among rocks, but at night? Not if I could help it.

Nothing happened. All was still. Watching, I thought of Yant, of those cold, measuring eyes that seemed to possess no more human feeling than those of a rattler.

That he was a relative I accepted. His resemblance to pa was too uncanny for it to be otherwise. Yet how related? And if related, why would he wish to kill *me?*

An estate of some kind? Money motivated more things than hatred, yet there could be both.

The two mysterious women who had come to visit us returned to mind. One had been friendly, yet I had been so frightened of the other I had never even told pa . . . and she had tried to kill him. To poison him, somehow. I knew that now. Pa had been deathly ill after her visit.

Who could she be? And why did they wish us dead?

I was alone. I knew nothing. And they were seeking me out. Suddenly, I was uneasy. I felt cramped, closed in, eager to be out and away. Yet to move now would be fatal. I must remain where I was, let them search, let them seek me.

Georgetown. I was sure now that was where pa had left his papers. He and Louis Dupuy had struck up a friendship, and the man Dupuy was a strange, bitter, self-isolated man, influenced by no one, beholden to no one. If pa wished to leave those papers with someone, he could have chosen no better man.

A stone fell from the canyon wall opposite, a pebble that bounded from rock to rock. My eyes searched the rock wall opposite. Much broken rock, clumps of cedar, and some lower brush. The rock atop the cliff was largely water-worn and smooth, but here and there were hollows that held water. It was from these natural reservoirs, most of them small, that the cliff dwellers had obtained some of their water.

A faint flicker of light on metal, seen and gone. A rifle barrel?

There was silence in the canyon. Easing my rifle forward, I waited. The last thing I wished was to give away my position, and to move might be fatal. I had water enough for another day and night if I was careful. I had a little food. It was unlikely they would find the way up that I had used, impossible for them to use it by night, so for the moment I seemed secure.

Peering through a crack in the rocks, I saw a man suddenly appear opposite me on the rim of the canyon. He moved out in plain sight and just stood there.

Puzzled, I watched him for several minutes before it dawned on me that he was there to draw my fire, or to somehow make me give away my position. I remained very still. The man disappeared, and a moment later there was a shot. The bullet struck the rock outer wall of the cliff house.

Careful to make no sound, I crawled through the T-shaped door into the inner room, which was completely enclosed. There I would be safe from ricochets.

Apparently they had no idea where I was or if I was even in the canyon, and if my horse made no sound we might well deceive them into moving on.

Another shot, and this time the bullet struck the back wall of the cave, and the ricochet smashed into the rock wall. For a long time then, there was no sound. I took a swallow of water and waited. There were no more shots. After a while I moved out of the inner room and peered through the rocks. Nobody was in sight . . . nothing moved.

Somewhere thunder rolled and a wind stirred the cedars across the canyon. Leaning my head back against the rock pile where I sat, most of it debris or slabs fallen from the wall of the cave, I dozed.

I awakened to the patter of rain and a crash of thunder followed a flash of lightning. That one was close. Sitting up, I looked out. Here I was sheltered, but the canyon was veiled by a curtain of rain.

Chuckling, I clasped my hands behind my head. They would have to find shelter, and I just hoped they did not also find my horse. But they had seemed unaware of any caves or cliff houses further up the canyon and had evidently missed them.

For a long time I slept, and when I awakened it was cold and dark. It was raining softly now, and thunder was a muted sound, far off. Listening, I heard nothing but the rain. I thought of my horse and of the trail I must follow to reach it. To wait until daylight would mean I would be exposed and helpless on the canyon wall, yet if I could make it by night I might successfully slip away.

I lay still for a while, reluctant to break my comfort, for despite the hard rocks upon which I lay, I had rested well. Yet the longer I lay still, the more urgent became the need to move. Carefully, I reviewed the steps I had taken in mounting the cliff. Dare I attempt it by night? In the rain and the dark?

Finally I sat up and looked around. It was very dark, for the sky was still heavy with rainclouds and no star could be seen. My father had told me the spirits of the dead were believed by the Indians to still linger in these cliff dwellings, and I did not doubt it. Lying alone in one of a night, where nothing else lived, subtle stirrings could be heard, and sometimes mumbling and distant chanting or the sound of flutes. So it was said and so it was believed. I heard stirrings enough, but the earth itself makes sounds and the wind finds holes to whistle through.

Maybe . . . who was I to argue the point? In any event, if the spirits lingered here, they were no enemies of mine, or should not be, for I wished them no harm, nor their dwelling. This had been a shrewd place in which to build, where attack by night was virtually impossible.

Gathering my few things about me, I slung my rifle over my shoulders to have my hands free. Then I crept back over the narrow ledge, bending far over because of the low-hanging rock above me. At one point I knew to step carefully, for a deep crack cut through the ledge to the back wall, a drop of several hundred feet if one made a false step.

Inching along in the darkness, I found that despite the darkness my eyes could pick out places for my feet, and eventually I found the two notched poles down which I must descend.

For a few moments I crouched there at the top of the first. Below me gapped the blackness of the canyon depths, above me loomed the cliff. I listened, but heard nothing. That pole worried me. It simply stood there, unfastened to anything. The slightest overbalance and it would fall, and I would go with it.

However, it did stand in a sort of notch that concealed it from observation and helped to hold it in place. At last I got a good grip on a corner of rock and turned slowly around and felt with my toe for the first notch.

My toe missed it, and desperately I felt it sliding down the pole. Then it caught on another step. Gingerly I lifted the other foot and took a long step downward. The pole wavered under me, and I leaned toward the rock to hold it still. Then I took another careful step downward . . . how many steps had there been?

It started to rain again, a hard, pelting rain. Step by step I worked my way down to the rock ledge on which the pole stood. Now a little to one side, and the other pole. It was the longer of the two . . . I thought.

Working my way along the ledge, I found the second pole and descended it warily. When my feet were once more on solid ground, I breathed a sigh of relief.

Now to my horse . . . if he was still there . . . and someone was not waiting there, lying in wait for me.

Now the heavy rain was in my favor. Not only did it mask the sounds of my movements, but nobody would be abroad in such a rain.

I hoped.

Chapter IX

There was no sound in the canyon, no sound but the rain on the rocks, on the brim of my hat and my shoulders. The ruin cloaked by trees where I had left my horse lay hidden in the deepest shadow. Warily, I paused before descending over the mound of fallen rock and earth.

Here the rain was muted by the cavern and the trees. I listened, holding my Winchester ready in my two hands to use as a club or to fire.

Nothing stirred. I took a tentative step forward, waited a bit, then another step. All was still. Another step, moving a little to the right, closer to the edge where the walking was better. My boot toe kicked a rock and it fell, bounding off a rock, then falling into the kiva.

Instantly I dropped to a crouch, rifle ready to fire. Had there been anyone waiting, the sound of the pebble falling should have drawn a gunshot.

Waiting . . . listening . . . how much time did I have? I must be out of the branch canyon and well down the main canyon before first light.

Suddenly something stirred. A footfall? I straightened up and took a step forward. Then my horse nickered softly. Moving closer, I felt his nose at my shoulder. "Hello, boy." I spoke quietly. "Have you missed me?"

Feeling about in the darkness, I found my saddle, blanket, and bridle where they had been left. The roan welcomed the bit, and smoothing the hair on his back, I shook out the blanket to free it of any grains of sand. Then I saddled up. Taking each step with care, I led the horse to the edge of the trail. Once there I waited, listening. Then I removed my slicker from the blanket roll back of the saddle and donned it.

The rain fell steadily. There would be a danger of flash floods once I got out of this branch canyon. Around me the rocks glistened with wet. Leading the roan, I felt my way cautiously down the slope to the canyon floor. Here there was a strip of sand, already running with water.

With a palm I swept the saddle free of water and mounted. Warily, rifle in hand, I walked him down the canyon, keeping him to the sand, where his hoofs made almost no sound.

This must be the one they had called Lion Canyon . . . probably with reason, and probably why the roan was eager to leave.

At the mouth of the canyon I hesitated. If I remembered correctly, this larger canyon was about five miles longer. At the end it joined the still larger canyon of the Mancos River. The trail, if I recalled correctly, held to the east side of the river and back from the bank, which was where I wished it to be.

Once well past the entrance to Lion Canyon, I moved the roan into a canter. Five miles in the darkness and rain? Perhaps a half hour if lucky, three-quarters of an hour if I was not. I doubted if there was danger of a flood here, but once in Mancos Canyon the chances were increased tenfold, for there were many canyons that fed into it, particularly those from the high mesa north of the river.

By daybreak they would find no tracks. All would be washed away by the rain. The Mancos might be too

deep for them to ford, and that might hold them up . . .
if I could get across it myself.

It was somewhat lighter in Mancos Canyon, because it was wider. I rode to the edge of the river and
drew up. The dark waters rushed by, at least three times
as wide and probably three times as deep as normally.
An instant I hesitated, then I urged the roan forward.
Snorting a little, wary of the water, he walked, hesitated, then plunged in. A moment of deep wading and
then he was swimming. The current was strong. We
swept downstream, struggling toward the far bank.

Then suddenly he was scrambling for a footing, and
then we were out of the water and weaving a way
through the rain-heavy willows. Turning, I glanced
back.

There was only the dark, rushing water, still rising,
and the wide jaws of the canyon, black against the
night. The trail was further east and north. Emerging
from the willows, the roan found his way to the trail,
and I turned him northwest. Above us to the northwest
and mostly north was the vast bulk of Mesa Verde,
split with a myriad of canyons. When my father had
brought me through here long ago, he told me of
whispers from among the Indians of strange castles
built in the cliff walls, ruined castles or dwellings of a
people who vanished long before.

Riding along through the rain, I kept thinking of
Teresa. Do no harm to stop by and make a little talk
on the way east. Seemed to me they'd waste time hunting me back there in the canyons. Me leaving no tracks
in the rain, they'd study on it no doubt and search
careful before they pulled out.

So far I'd seen nobody, which probably meant nobody had seen me, not in the dark and the rain. I'd
have to hole up and rest some, come morning, for the
roan was a good horse and needed to be treated kindly.
It was nigh to breaking day when the canyon forked.
One line went due north and the other took off toward
the east, which was my direction.

When we reached the main trail east, I just taken
off to the north of it, rode up the slope for a ways, and

found myself a place among the aspen. There was a hollow screened by aspen from the main trail. There I picketed the roan, and taking my gear back under the trees, I made a hurried shelter from some fallen aspen and brush in a space well covered by the aspen branches. Wet though the ground was, I put down my slicker and rolled up in my blanket to hope for the best.

It was nigh on to noon when I opened my eyes. For a moment I just lay still to listen, but heard nothing. After a bit I rolled my gear, saddled up, and lit out.

At Starvation Creek I drank, watered the roan, then cut down for the main trail. I taken a look back to the west, but nobody was in sight, although I couldn't see far. There were no tracks on the trail since the rain, so I taken out down the road.

Maybe I was a fool to go back, yet I wished to see Teresa. Why, I did not know. No doubt it was loneliness, for now I had begun to feel my father's absence more than I could tell. We had been much together, often not talking, yet together nonetheless, and he was all I had as I was all he had. At least, at the end.

Always the nagging thought . . . who had he been? Who was I? Kearney McRaven? The name did not sound right, although how a name should sound I did not know.

But who had my father *been?* And who was Felix Yant? Why had he killed my father, for I was now sure it had been him, and why did he seek to kill me?

Who were the women who came to visit when I was young? And where were they now? What part had they in all this?

The questions nagged at me, irritated me. Why had I been such a fool not to listen when I had the chance?

Nobody paid much mind when I rode into town. It was a late hour and, it being largely a mining town, folks had gone to sleep. Folks who handle drill steel and a single or double jack all day, or swing a muck stick, they don't have much use for late hours. This time of year things were slow, waiting for the grass to show and the warm weather to come.

I stabled my horse and fetched my gear over to the

ho-tel, and I just dumped her there at the foot of the stairs and went into the restaurant.

First thing I saw was her. She was across the room taking an order from a customer and she just stared at me, then went to the kitchen. Me, I dropped into a chair.

She brought food to those men at the other table and then crossed to me with the coffeepot and a cup. She filled the cup, her hand shaking so she spilled some in the saucer.

"You . . . you're back!"

She seemed surprised, and I couldn't make out whether she was pleased or not, but I guessed she was. "Seems as though," I said. "That's my horse yonder in the stable, and these are my pants, so this must be me."

"I thought . . . I mean I was afraid you were . . . dead."

"Time or two," I said, "I was cold enough to be. You got a nice slice of cow meat? Or cougar, for that matter."

Holding up the coffee, I said, "Been drinkin' my own make. Doesn't taste near as good as this."

"You'd better leave," she warned. "He's . . . he's here."

He. That would be Yant. *"Here?"* I couldn't believe it.

"He's been here. He said you'd be back . . . if you lived."

She looked up and I saw her face turn kind of pale and there he was, tall, neat, and well set out like a gentleman should be. He looked at me for a moment from those cold, cruel eyes, and I had no idea what he was thinking. Nor could I guess whether he was glad to see me or sorry. No doubt he expected me to be dead.

Teresa, she hurried off and he set down. Didn't even wait to ask my leave. He turned a chair around and set straddle of it. "You had a long ride for nothing," he commented.

"Maybe. I figure a man learns by travel, and I seen some country."

He looked at me sharply, irritated. "You *saw* some country. If your father was your teacher, he did a damned poor—"

"Mr. Yant," I interrupted him, "you leave my pa out of this. You say one more bad thing about him an' I'll blow your guts out."

He just stared at me. *"You?"* he said contemptuously. "Don't talk like a fool, boy. I was using guns before you were born."

"Maybe," I replied coolly, "but I'll be using them after you're dead."

We just looked at each other, and I was almighty glad my coat was open and I had one gun shoved out in my waistband. He saw that, too. If there was an edge, I had it.

"Don't be a fool, boy. You aren't dry behind the ears yet."

"That may be true," I said, "but this gun's full-growed . . . grown."

He stared at me, but I stared right back. Boylike, I hadn't no intention of being stared down by him. After a moment he shrugged. "You'll never live to be old enough. You're too cocky. You're too sure of yourself."

"Maybe I've got reason. Did you ever think of that? My pa was good with a gun, almighty good. The man who murdered him knew that, I think, and was too yellow to stand up to him so he shot him in the back. If the man who did that should come around, he ought to know that pa always said I could draw faster and shoot straighter than ary body he ever saw."

Teresa returned with another cup and coffee for Yant. She put both of them down and a moment later was back with food.

"Would you like—?" She was looking at Yant. "I mean, do you want to eat?"

"Yes, my dear," he said. "I believe I will join our young friend here."

Whatever was on Yant's mind was not shooting. Not at the moment, at least. In fact, I got the idea he was even relieved to see me. As he had no liking for me, I got to wondering why that was.

"Your father must have been quite a man," he commented. "You two traveled a lot, I take it?"

"We did.

"Were you always alone? No friends along the way?"

"Here and there," I said, "here and there."

"You should have gone to school," he commented. "Surely you stayed some places long enough?"

He sipped his coffee and seemed irritated when I made no reply. He was a most impatient man. "I mean, he could have left you with friends if he just had to move on. That way you could have gone to school."

"He liked having me with him." As I spoke, the idea came to me that he was fishing. He wanted to find out if we had good friends. He had the same idea I had, that pa might have left something somewhere.

Maybe, just maybe I could give him a false lead. "Oh, we had friends here and there," I said casually, "but pa didn't get close to many people. Of course, there was Jim Gillette. He and pa were close. There was some sort of a fandango down in Mexico . . . getting somebody out of jail down there and back across the border. Pa had some good friends in Mexico, and he helped somehow."

"Gillette? Wasn't he an officer?"

"Texas Ranger. He had some position in El Paso, too, I think. We stayed in El Paso some little time. Pa was working there, for the stage company, I think it was."

We ate in silence, and then I added the kicker. "Wasn't many people pa trusted, but Gillette was one of them."

Not to belabor the point, I moved on. "Pa met him on the buffalo plains first, I think. Or in Amarillo. Pa said when he first saw that town, it was built of buffalo hides. You know, they get stiff as iron, and folks had built houses and even stores from them."

Teresa kept watching us, but now I was wary of her, too. After all, she had been here and Felix Yant had also, and he was a smooth-talking man. Certainly he had more to offer than a no-account drifter like me. Or so it might seem to both her ma and her. And no doubt they'd begun to wonder why he was hanging about, this time of year. They would surely think it was Teresa rather than anything to do with me.

She'd been my reason for coming back here, but all of a sudden I felt uneasy about her. And right then I begun to be a mighty lonesome boy. It just seemed there was nobody in the world I could get close to. She'd been in my thinking ever since we met, but now I wasn't so sure. Since pa had been killed, I'd been alone, and I didn't favor it much.

She came over to see if our coffee was hot and she taken up the pot to go for more. "You're not too busy," Yant said. "Why don't you sit down for a minute or two? I am sure Kearney would appreciate your company as much as I would."

"Well, I—" She hesitated, sort of, looking at me.

"Sure," I said, "sit down."

Maybe I didn't sound too happy, because she looked at me funny-like, but she said, "I'll get some fresh coffee."

When she was gone, Yant looked at me, smiling a little. "A pretty one," he said. "I hope you do not mind her joining us?"

"Not at all," I said.

I was restless to get away. I wanted to be alone, to clean up, and to think of what I must do. To find him here was the last thing I expected. Who then had pursued me westward? Who had fired those inquiring shots into the cliff dwelling? Had he simply sat here while men he hired followed me? I had been a fool, and he had outwitted me at every turn.

What would happen when I started for Georgetown?

He would follow, of course. Somehow he had deduced that if my father had left me anything of his past, it must be at some place further east. Did he believe my hints about Jim Gillette? The man was no made-up figure but one well known there, and even he had recognized the name.

Teresa returned with a fresh pot of coffee, yet she

had no sooner seated herself than Yant arose, surprising me, and her, too, I believe.

"There," he said, "I shall leave you two together. No doubt you will have much to talk about. Your trip west, I imagine, was quite fascinating . . . and so sudden. You must tell Teresa about your experiences."

With that he was gone, and we sat there staring at each other. She was displeased, I thought, by his sudden leave-taking, but she tried to continue.

"What did happen out west?" she asked.

I shrugged. "Nothing much. Rain, cold, and a long ride. Somebody followed me from here, I think, and shot at me."

She stared at me. *"Shot* at you? Why?"

"I think it was those same two men, the two who came in here that day, just before I left."

"Who are you, Kearney?" she asked suddenly. "I mean *really*. You're never told me anything about yourself."

"I didn't figure you were interested."

"Oh, but I am! You told me about your father being killed. I'm sorry. That must have been awful for you. Did you send his body back home?"

Well, I just looked at her. "We hadn't a home," I said. "Home was wherever we hung our hats. He was buried in the town where he fell . . . like I'll be, no doubt."

"Fe—I mean Mr. Yant, he has a plantation back in Carolina. A beautiful place, he said, with a lovely old house and acres and acres of trees and planted land, right along a river."

"Good for him."

"He said he thought your father must have come from a good home, too. Before the trouble."

"What trouble?"

"Why . . . I don't know. I just thought . . . I mean he said that most men who came west like that had come because they were in some kind of trouble."

"Is that why you folks came west?" I asked bluntly.

She flushed. "It is not! And you've no right to suggest—"

"You just did it to me," I said.

She stared at me, half-angry. "Well, you told me yourself you and your pa wandered all over, never stopping anyplace at all. And then he did get shot. Somebody killed him, and they must have had a reason."

"What do you mean by that?"

We were alone in the room now, as the others had gone. I was angry and defensive.

"Well, he had done something to someone. Isn't that why people are usually killed? In revenge? Or in punishment?"

"Or because they have something," I said.

"You told me he wasn't robbed."

For a moment I did not reply, for what had been lingering in the back of my mind all the time suddenly was there, right before me. Of course that was why he was killed. Revenge or hatred might have had a part in it, but there was more than that. He had been killed because of something somebody wanted. As nothing had been taken that I knew of, it must have been something he did not have with him but something that belonged to him, and that meant property.

Property? Land? But if Felix Yant had a plantation in Carolina, why would he be worried about what pa might have?

I knew very little about such things. Only supposing they were kin. Suppose that plantation belonged to them both, and the only way Yant could have it all was to kill pa? And then he discovered me, of whom he had not known?

That was a lot of surmising, yet pa and Yant did favor each other. I'd mistaken Yant for pa, and they had mannerisms alike, and what was Yant doing out here, anyway?

"He wasn't robbed of anything he had on him," I said. "Maybe somebody was trying to rob him of something he owned. If that was true, then I own it now ... whatever it is."

"If your pa owned something that valuable, he'd be tending to it, not running around over the country letting his boy grow up every which way."

She was quiet for a few minutes and so was I. She seemed like a totally different girl, somehow. Had she always been that way, or was this something Yant had done to her?

"If I were you," she said, "and I thought I owned anything, I would find out what it was and claim it. Your pa, now, if he owned anything he would have some record of it, or he would have told you."

"He may have planned on telling me. Then he was killed."

"He must have told you *something*. If you tried, you could remember."

My coffee was cold. So was the night. I got up suddenly. "See you tomorrow," I said.

She started to turn away, then she looked back. "Kearney? I think you're angry with me."

"No, I ain't. Why should I be? You've done nothing."

"Mr. Yant likes you. He really does. He says you deserve a better future than this, and I think he would help you if you could just remember."

"Remember *what*?"

"Well, he said he thought maybe your pa had come from a good family, and that somewhere he'd had some records or something. If you could find those, you could be somebody yourself. He said he was sure you knew, although you might not think you did."

That, at least, was probably the truth. He wanted me to find those records. Maybe he was afraid that if something happened to me, those records would show up. It was then I thought back to Pistol. We'd always called ourselves brothers, but actually we weren't blood kin. Somewhere along the line Pistol just took on with us, and pa raised him along with me, only Pistol was older than me and before long he took off on his own.

Pistol, being older than me, might know something, but the last I heard Pistol was out California way. He taken his name from his skill, for he was a natural with any kind of shooting iron. He was almighty quick and he was steady, and that was how come he left us.

We'd been in Missouri at the time, and pa was down sick ... pneumonia, I think it was. Pneumonia was a real killer them days, and pa was in bad shape. A woman there was caring for him ... name of Kate Donelson.

Pistol an' me, we were just sort of waitin' around. My age was about ten, if I recall, an' Pistol was closing in on sixteen. Then these two men came to town.

I recall them clear. They were tall, straight men who never smiled ... not at least when I seen them. They wore black coats like the one pa had when he was shot, and like the one Felix Yant wore. I guess they were the style down south or back east or wherever. Mostly out west it was gamblers or lawyers who wore them, and often doctors.

These two men came to town, and I heard them inquiring for pa. The man at the livery stable, he told them he didn't know such a man, and he lied because he was friendly with pa. I started to tell them, but something in that livery man's face made me shut up.

I walked away and seen Pistol and told him. He asked me where they were an' I told him. Well, he taken a look and said we should get on home. When we got there, he went inside and buckled on his six-shooter. Now like I say, Pistol was almighty handy with one of them short guns but he never wore one in town ... only on the trail. Pa had asked him not to.

Me, I said as much this time, an' Pistol said, "Pa won't mind this time, Kearney. He surely won't. You see those men coming, you tell me and then you get inside, and do it quick."

Small town like that, there's always somebody who talks too much, an' somebody did. We was settin' on the porch ... I'd just brought Pistol a cup of coffee as he wouldn't leave those steps, not no way.

We seen ... saw ... them coming down the pike an' I says, "It's them!" He puts down his coffee and says, "You get inside and stay away back. This here's trouble."

"Trouble? Why?"

"Those men are huntin' your pa to kill him. I got to stop them."

Well, I'd been taught long ago not to argue when told to move and I done it. I moved inside and I went back to pa's bed and lifted one of his pistols from the holster. He opened his eyes and looked at me.

"What's the trouble, boy?" he asked, his voice weak and sick-sounding.

"Nothing we can't handle," I said, and went back to the door, then to the window. That window was open, and from beside it I could see those men. They looked at the house, at Pistol, and then they started for the steps, and Pistol says, "You lookin' for somebody?"

"It's nothing to you, boy. Get out of the way."

He stood up. "You just back off there," he says, quiet-like. "We ain't havin' visitors today. There's a sick man in there."

"Don't worry about that," the biggest one said. "He won't be sick much longer. We're doctors, boy, an' we got the cure."

"He's got him a doctor," Pistol said, and then he added, very quiet, "I ain't never killed a man yet, so don't you boys insist."

Well, they taken a look at him then. They'd been figuring him for some wet-nosed kid, and he stood there looking back at them and all of a sudden their manner changed.

"You never killed a man, boy? Well, we have. We've both killed our man, an' more than one. We'd as soon make it another if you don't move, and now."

Suddenly he laughed. He laughed right out loud and that surprised them. It was a real surprise because his laugh threw them off just enough and he went for his gun. It was only an edge and a mighty slight one, but Pistol was fast and he was sure.

He put two bullets into that big man faster'n you could wink, and then he shot the other one just as his gun came into action. Pistol taken a bullet through the side of his shirt, but that second man was already down.

I ran out on the porch, and Pistol turned on me. "You're hurt!" I said.

"No, I ain't, but the law here don't like me much and I'm leaving. You tell pa to get well. He's the best man ever!"

He turned and started up the street, and just as he turned his back, that big man who was lying there raised up on one elbow and pointed a six-shooter at his back. I was to one side of him and seen it, and next thing I knew, I'd fired, my shot being just a mite faster than the big man's.

Pistol turned and taken one quick look. "Thanks, Kearney . . . thanks."

And then he was gone, and people came crowding up. We'd been on a sort of back street where there weren't many folks, but they came back from the main street as soon as the shooting stopped. And right behind the first of them was that two-bit town marshal.

Nobody liked him much, because he was mean. He pushed through the crowd soon as he saw the shooting was over. I'd stuck my six-shooter back under the window-curtain so's it was lying on the sill, out of sight.

"Here! What's going on here?" he demanded.

"Those men threatened to kill pa," I said, "an' pa's sick in bed." That was something most of the town knew, as there were mighty few people in town and news got around, such as sickness, weddings, and such. "They tried to push in here and my brother, he stopped them."

Somebody in the crowd said, "Serves 'em right! Comin' after a sick man!"

From the way folks reacted, that seemed to be the general opinion, and nobody was quicker to sense that than the marshal. "Anybody know these men?" he asked.

Nobody did.

"What about you, boy? Did you know them? Why did they want to kill your pa?"

"I never saw them before. I don't know why they wanted to kill him. They must have hated him, to want to shoot a sick man who's on his back in bed with pneumonia. And they must have come a long way looking for him."

"Got what they deserved," one man muttered.

The marshal, he looked at me. "You sure your pa is down sick?"

"You can ask Doc Cory," I said. "He's treating him."

He looked at the bodies. One of the men had a white vest, and there was a bullet hole where the heart was. The other had two bullets in the body and a third in the head. That one was mine, but I didn't lay claim to it.

"Didn't figure that brother of yours was that fast," the marshal said.

"He's mighty good," I said, "maybe as good as pa."

They carried the bodies away, and that was the end of it. Pa got well and we dragged our freight out of there, but we surely missed Pistol.

Standing there in that restaurant, empty but for Teresa and me, I thought back to Pistol. I also thought of those two dead men and of Kate Donelson.

Pistol might know something, and so might Kate, if she was alive.

And those two dead men . . . maybe the folks in the town where they were killed had some record, from the stuff in their pockets or what gear they had.

It was something to go on, and it was time I got started.

Teresa, she looked at me. "What are you going to do? Are you going off again?"

"Might as well. Looks like you found yourself a man."

She flushed. "He's not my man. At least he knows how to treat a lady and he's not running off around the country all the time."

"You just see how long he stays once I'm gone," I said.

"Oh, my!" She stared at me. "You really think yourself important, don't you? He did not leave before, after you left!"

"Some others did," I said, "and he didn't figure he'd need to. This time I'm going east."

"He won't leave," she insisted. "When the snow is off, he plans to start mining."

"Good for him," I said, "and good-bye!"

I taken out of there, and picking up my gear, I went to the stable. They could keep their old hotel. I'd sleep in the hay. The good Lord knows I'd slept in worse places.

Chapter X

Daylight was an hour away when I fetched out of there, and I'd be lying if I said I'd slept well. Tired as I was, I surely didn't sleep. I'd been building ideas in my mind about Teresa. Except for that other freckle-faced girl I'd seen when I first come off the mountain, I'd had no girl in my thoughts.

If a boy is going to think about girls and such, he has to have some particular girl in mind, and I hadn't even *seen* one in eight or nine months. Teresa had seemed right friendly and I'd kind of warmed up to her in my mind, but Yant was a talker and I'd been gone awhile.

Me and that roan, we just taken out of there. The snow was off the passes now, and the trees were budding out in fine shape.

When I left town I was riding south, but I knew where I was going and a few miles out I took a dim mountain trail up Scotch Creek. That was high country

and rough, but I held to the old Indian trail and went
around a ridge and cut over to Hotel Draw.

If I was heading east I might need a sight of money,
and although I'd spent mighty little going west, a body
never knew when he might fetch up to needing. So I was
heading back to my cache on the plateau, or what I
called the place.

Sure enough, when I topped out, the snow was gone
except on the peaks around. The wind was chill but the
grass and flowers were coming up. On the sunny, south-
facing slope the tree-cover was higher, mostly spruce
so far as I could see, and the wild flowers would be
blooming in no time. Up that high a flower can't afford to waste time. They have to grow, blossom, and
put out seed before the next frost comes, and it's a
hurry-up job for them.

The sun was warm and friendly, and when I looked
across at the old cabin, it wasn't there. Standing in my
stirrups, when I topped a little rise I could see charred
timbers.

Burned. I felt a twinge then, for I'd spent some good
nights in that place. Burned by the judge and them, no
doubt.

I stayed shy of it, heading for my cache. There was
no time to waste around if I figured to get anywhere,
and already I was thinking of that town where pa
had been killed. It was fairly enough on my route,
and even if it meant taking a chance, I was going on
in.

A whiskey-jack made noises at me from a rock, hoping I'd go into camp. He followed along, keeping track
of me. Jacob's ladder was blooming, and I saw some
wand lily and alumroot here and there.

When I found my cache, I taken a long look around
and then reached up and fetched out my money. I'd
never yet counted it and wasn't about to do so now. I
stashed it away in my saddlebags and taken out of
there, heading out along a narrow trail through boulder
piles and uplifted slabs. Frost, wind, and sun had worn
the sharp edges off the rocks over the years, but here
and there among the piles of boulders there was some

dwarf columbine with a flower no bigger than my thumbnail.

Marmots whistled signals to each other as I wove a way through the rocks, but they didn't pay me much mind. Usually they whistle and disappear in the rocks, but they must have remembered me putting crusts of bread out for them now and again, because they just whistled and sat there, watching me pass. Maybe it was their way of saying good-bye, because I never figured to see that place again.

Old Dingleberry was nowhere around when I passed the trail leading to his place, and it was after sundown when I rode into the town where pa had been killed. There were lights at the portals of some of the mines, and there were lights along the street, mostly in saloons or eating places.

The roan was tired and so was I, so I fetched around to the livery stable. Old Chalk was there, and he seen me ride up. He knew that horse as well as me or better, and he said, "Howdy, son. It's been awhile."

"Anybody around town lookin' for me, Chalk?"

"Not so's I heard, son. The judge, he cut up somethin' fierce for a while, then he an' some others taken out. I reckoned they was huntin' you."

He didn't ask no questions and I didn't offer any answers. A man learns to keep his own affairs to himself. "Give old roan here a bait of oats. He's earned it."

"All right, son." Chalk watched me take my gear off the saddle, and if he noted those saddlebags were heavy, he didn't speak of it.

"Chalk," I said, "you knew my pa."

"I did so. A finer man never walked, although he was no gambler. Not until that last night."

"He was gamblin' for me, Chalk. I never guessed until it was too late. He was trying to get me a stake so's I could go to school and such. It was the only way he knew how."

"He might have gone to minin'," Chalk commented.

"Now, the way I see it," I replied, "pa didn't figure he had long, and there was a man on his trail . . . more than one of them." That reminded me. "Chalk, did you ever see a man around here, tall man, black coat like pa's, a man who favored pa some?"

"I seen him."

"Can you tell me when?"

"He come in the day your pa was killed and he rode out that same night. Had him a mighty fine horse."

"Thanks, Chalk."

"He the one who did it?"

"Seems like. I think he was family. I met him over yonder," I said, gesturing south. "He'll likely be along again, might even inquire after me."

"What should I tell him?"

"You haven't seen me. We'll meet up someday, and I figure on it, but there's some things I got to get straight first."

"Be careful, boy. He may be a pilgrim but he's a hard, hard man. I seen it in him."

"Chalk? Did pa ever talk to you? I mean, you know more about folks than anybody around, and I've got to find out where he came from." I kicked a toe into the dirt. "Chalk, I don't rightly know who I am. I don't know why that man killed pa, or why he's wishful to kill me."

"Your pa was not a talking man, son, but he was a good man and he was a gentleman. Good family. I could tell that. He come from the South, too. I'd guess Caroliny, maybe Georgia. I could get it by his accent, although most of it was lost. He had the pride, too. Southern pride. I fit again them in the War, but they was good folks, mostly, wrong to want to split the Union, but good folks. Your pa was such a one."

"Thanks, Chalk. I'll have a bite and go to sleep."

"Better get yourself a place first, because there's a lot of strangers in town. Been some good ore showin' up, and the boomers can smell it from a thousand miles off, the way they start comin' in."

"Chalk? Better have that horse ready. You hear any shootin', you saddle him, you hear?"

"Will do." Chalk hitched his belt and looked at me, then spat. "You take care of yourself, boy, and steer clear of grief."

When I had booked a room and left my gear in it, I went to the restaurant, but that freckle-faced girl wasn't there and the fat-bellied man with the rolled-up sleeves and hairy arms did nothing to brighten my evening but bring me grub. That was good, however, and a body can't expect too much of life.

When I'd had something to eat, I walked out on Blair Street. In just two blocks of that street there were thirty-two places where a man might get what he wished in food, drink, or women. There was Big Mollie's place, Diamond-Tooth Lil's, the Sage Hen, the Mikado, the Bon Ton, and Lola's. There was any kind of game you wanted, if it was gamblin' you were hunting for.

Here I was, weighted down with money, more than anybody on the street, I guess, but I'd learned not to flash it about, and looking at me nobody would guess that I had anything, especially as I was just rubbernecking around.

Truth was I was lonely, just wishful of setting down with somebody to hear them talk. I was turning back toward the ho-tel when I saw that girl with the freckles. She was hurrying across the street with a couple of packages, and I spoke to her, but she hurried on, paying me no mind.

"Ma'am?" I said. "I'll pack your groceries for you. We talked some awhile back in the restaurant."

"Oh?" She hesitated, looking at me, and I taken off my hat. She recognized me then. "You're the boy whose father was killed!"

"Yes, ma'am. You were the one warned me to be careful."

"Yes, I did. I was afraid for you." She stood looking at me. "Whatever happened to Judge Blazer?"

"Last I seen of him he was with Tobin Wacker and a man they called Dick."

"I was afraid they had found you."

"Here." I took the packages from her arms and walked beside her. "You lead the way and I'll pack these for you."

"I liked your father," she said. "He was a nice man."

"He was. A better father than I knew I had." I hesitated a mite. "Do you know where they buried him? I taken out so fast—"

"I'll show you, if you are going to be around."

"Well . . . I can't. There's things I have to do back east aways, but I'll come back. I want to put some flowers on his grave. Maybe a marker."

"There's a wooden cross with his name on it. We thought you knew."

"Knew? Why? Knew what?"

"That there was to be a cross. That note you left."

"I left no note."

"There was one. It was in the post office, addressed *To Whom It May Concern,* and it left some money for a decent coffin, burial, and a marker. We thought you left it."

Felix Yant. It had to be him. Shoot a man and then . . . he had to be kin, to do a thing like that.

"I reckon I know who done . . . did it. Anyway, I want some flowers on his grave. He'd have liked that. He was forever talking about the dogwood and laurel back home . . . wherever that was."

"It sounds like the South."

We had fetched up to a cabin with a little picket fence around it and a light in the window. She hesitated. "I'd like you to meet my mother, but not right now. I don't think—"

"Let me just set these things down inside," I said, "and I'll be on my way."

She opened the door and I stepped in behind her. There was a fire burning in a coal stove and there was a coal-oil lamp sitting on a table. Near it a woman was sewing. She was a thin, attractive woman, but she was some surprised when she saw me.

She put her sewing down quick and said, "I—"

"Now, ma'am, I just carried the groceries in for your daughter. I'll be leaving now."

Something got knocked over in the next room, and then a big man, unshaven and not too clean, showed in the door. He had no shirt on, just his suspenders over his undershirt, and he looked bleary, whether from being waked up or booze I couldn't tell.

"Who the hell are you?" he demanded, mighty rough.

"Kearney McRaven," I said. "I just showed your daughter home with—"

"Get out!" he said. "By the Lord, I'll not have any drunken saddle tramp coming around here! Get out!"

Putting the groceries down on the table, I said, very quiet, "Mister, I'm not drunk and I'm not a saddle tramp."

"I don't give a damn who you are! I said get out, and I mean out!"

Her mother stood up then. She stood up quickly and she did it with grace and dignity. "Henry, the young man is a guest. He just carried Laurie's groceries in."

He paid her no mind but walked into the room. "You get out," he said, "or I'll throw you out!"

"I am leaving," I repeated, "but, mister, don't you ever try throwing me out. I don't want to make any trouble for this young lady, but you've no call to talk like you've been. Now you just back up an' back off."

He stopped, glaring at me. He'd expected me to get when he yelled, but there I stood. Laurie's mother turned around quietly and said, "Mr. McRaven? Would you sit down? I was just about to make some coffee."

"Now, see here!" he blustered. "I'll be damned if—"

"Henry," she said, turning on him, "you've said quite enough. We would like to have you join us. If you do not wish to, I am sure your friends down at the National will be waiting for you."

He was angry enough to have hit her, but I was standing there and I guess he didn't like my manner.

"McRaven, is it? You're likely the son of that gambler who got himself killed."

"I am," I said, "and he was shot in the back, so I do not believe 'he got himself killed,' as you put it. He was never afraid to face a man with a gun or any other kind of weapon. And," I added, "neither am I."

He stared at me, a mean, ugly look. "There's them as are lookin' for you," he said, "an' I hope they find you!"

I smiled at him. "Just be sure you are not with them when they do."

He stomped back in the other room, and Laurie's mother gestured to a chair. "Please? I cannot let you go now."

"I don't want to cause any trouble," I suggested.

"You are not causing trouble," she insisted. "You are perhaps bringing to a head a difficult situation. Please sit down."

Well, I did so. First I took off my coat and put it over the back of the chair. My hat was on the table beside me, but when I sat down they could see my cartridge belt and pistols. She noticed them, as did Laurie.

"I just came in off the trail," I said. "I've been traveling some rough country."

"That is perfectly all right, Mr. McRaven. My husband fought in the War between the States and often against Indians."

The man loomed in the door again and was about to say something else. Then he saw the gun I carried in my waistband, and whatever he was about to say died on his lips. He disappeared.

"We do not often have visitors, Mr. McRaven, and Laurie works all day so we do not often go out. It is good to have company."

"Since pa died, I've been lonesome myself, ma'am. I haven't talked to a woman ... excepting one ... in quite some time."

"It is cold for traveling," she said. "Many of the high passes won't be open for another month. That poor Mister Nilson, you know? The man who carried the mail? Some believe he took what money was in the mail and skipped out, but I think he was trapped in a slide. He's been missing for months."

"It was a mean winter," I said.

"Your father was a southern man, Mr. McRaven? I did not know him, but he often talked to Laurie. She liked him very much. Said he was such a gentleman."

"He was from the South, but I never knew exactly where. He ... he never talked about it much. Only some days he would get to remembering and he'd mention places ... rivers and plantations and such. But I never did hear him mention a state or a town ... only big towns like New Orleans or Charleston, but he spoke of Boston, too, and Philadelphia."

"Mr. McRaven, I'd like you to know that man is not my husband nor is he Laurie's father. He is my brother-in-law, married to my sister until her death. He had no place to go and we took him in, and for a few weeks he worked and occasionally contributed to the expenses of living. For some time now he has done neither, but he considers himself the man of the house. You are not the first man he has ordered out."

"Why don't you tell him to leave?"

She smiled. "And if he refuses? What am I to do?"

"Ma'am, you tell him to leave and I'll see that he does, but if I'm not here, you or Laurie just go down to the marshal or some businessman you know and tell them. If that fails, you go to any saloon on Blair Street and tell them your troubles."

"They might hang him."

"Yes, ma'am, they might ... and good riddance. Even the roughest of those men down along the street won't see a decent woman abused."

The floor creaked faintly from the other room. The door was closed, but I had a feeling he had been listening. I put up a hand for quiet and drew my belt gun.

Laurie's mouth opened and I said, "There will not be any shooting."

The door opened suddenly, and he stood there with a rifle in his hands. "Now you git!" He raised the rifle threateningly, but it was not aimed, which was his mistake.

He started into the room and then he saw that six-shooter in my hand and he stopped so fast he almost fell.

"Put the rifle down," I told him, "and take whatever belongs to you and get out. Get out and stay out. If you ever come back here again or if you so much as speak to one of these women, I'll see you hang. I may not be around too long, but I shall talk to the marshal before I leave, and I'll also talk to some of the boys down along Blair Street."

He dearly wanted to shoot. He wanted to lift that rifle and turn it on me, but he knew he didn't have a chance. "Who the hell do you think you are?" he blustered.

"I'm a friend of the family," I said.

He blustered and he grumbled but he went. He was a loafer and a bully but a man of no courage, yet I recalled my father warning me against taking such men too lightly.

When he was gone, I moved my chair so that I couldn't be seen from outside and holstered my pistol. "Sorry, ma'am. The only other thing was to throw him out bodily, and that might have torn up the room somewhat."

"Thank you, Kearney, thank you very much. He has been. . . oh, obnoxious! And getting worse every day."

She refilled my cup, and I sat back and enjoyed it, my eyes straying to the books on the shelf. There were a couple of novels by Sir Walter Scott, *Little Dorrit* by Charles Dickens, and *Vivian Grey* by Benjamin Disraeli.

She saw me looking at the books. "They are presentation copies," she explained. "My husband knew them all, and his father went to school with Sir Walter. They were pupils of Mr. Luke Fraser, in his second-year class. He lived off Canongate Street, and they often walked home together. Later he moved to a house near that where John Knox died."

"What did your husband do?"

She smiled. "Nothing very well, I am afraid, but he was a fine man for all of that and I loved him dearly. He wished most of all to paint, but his paintings did not sell. Then we were married and he had a small inheritance, so we came to America. He had known Sir Walter from childhood, but he met Mr. Dickens only when he came to London, and he knew Mr. Disraeli, then, too. In New York he taught painting and the piano, but the life was confining, so he joined the army at last. He became a sergeant major, and when the Indian wars needed men, they made an officer of him."

"I don't even know your name," I said.

"Oh! I'm sorry!" She put her hand to her mouth. "I am Anne McCrae and my daughter is Laurie."

We talked long, and when I left it was to walk back to the hotel and to bed. First I stopped by the livery stable to see old Chalk. "Well, you don't look in no hurry, so I guess you'll be stayin' over."

Taking a few minutes, I told him about Mrs. McCrae and Henry.

"Know him," Chalk said. "He's no-account. He's lazy and he's a boozer. They're well rid of him. An' don't you worry none. They're fine folks an' we'll take care of them."

He looked at me thoughtfully. "You figure on coming back here, son?"

"I do."

"That there's a fine girl. We here in Silverton think a lot of her and her ma. They're good folks, gentle folks."

"I know." After a moment I said, "Chalk, there's a man hunting me . . . maybe more than one. I think one of them is the man who killed my father. The others are men he has hired."

"We talked of that. I'll keep my eyes open."

In the hotel I put a chair under the knob again and lay down to sleep with my six-shooter on a chair alongside the bed where I could lay a hand on it.

Yet I didn't go to sleep right away. There were movements in the hallways and horses passing in the street. Lying on my back, hands clasped behind my head, I thought back to my earliest memories.

Finally I got up and went to the small desk in one corner of the room. I found a tablet in the drawer, and taking a pencil, I started to note down all I could recall.

Lying on a boat dock or some such place with the sun on my back . . . the long-legged birds in the swamp . . . that time down on the sand by the sea, a lonely place . . . an old hulk half buried in the mud that pa wouldn't let me go near, and the big, empty old house with the shutter banging . . . the gnarled old man in the faded green cloak who came to our house one night when pa was away, a man all crippled and twisted . . . or so he seemed.

Pa talking. "No, I will not have her in the house! I will have nothing to do with them!"

Somebody said something about a curse. "Curse? I know nothing about that, only they contaminate everything they touch! There's evil in them . . . evil!"

A door had closed and I had heard no more.

Just odds and ends of memories, although I remembered my father had reacted strangely when I told him of the old man in the green cloak.

And then there was the night that ended something and began something else, the night my father came home, bundled me up, and took me away, and we never went back.

Names . . . there had been names—Old Tolbert . . . Faustina . . . Weber . . . Naomi . . . There were many, but none of them seemed connected with anything. At last I returned to my bed and slept.

When morning came, I went to breakfast and it was Laurie who served me. She came quickly to my table with coffee. "There are eggs," she whispered. "If you want them, you'd better order, because there are not many and they do not last long."

"I'll have two, scrambled."

Suddenly the door opened and two men came in. Both men wore badges on their vests and they looked quickly around the room. When they saw me, they turned and walked to my table.

"McRaven? My name is Burns. I am making inquiries about a man named Blazer. Judge Blazer."

Chapter XI

A moment only, I held myself very still inside. This could be trouble, serious trouble.

"I met him," I replied.

"So we understand. Would you explain what happened?"

Laurie came over, looking frightened. "Laurie, would you bring some cups for these gentlemen? And some hot coffee?"

Briefly, I explained about herding Dingleberry's cattle in the high country, coming down to find my father murdered and then to hear of his heavy winning the night before. Then I told them about my showdown with Blazer.

"I went to his office and he held back the money my father had won, evidently imagining I had not heard of it. So I told him I knew of it and impressed him with the necessity of turning it over to me."

"And he did?"

"Well, I had to nudge him a mite. He didn't take kindly to the notion of giving up all that money."

"And then?"

"Mister, I hadn't any friends around that I knew of, so I taken out. I figured they'd look up and down the trail for me, so I went back to the hills."

" 'They'?"

"Yes, sir. He brought some men with him. Tobin Wacker for one. They followed me."

Choosing my words with care, I explained about the fight in the cabin, how I was badly beaten and escaped into the storm.

"Indian woman fixed my nose. They broke it. She put the bone in place and put some kind of wax or something over it that stiffened up tight. They took good care of me."

"You never saw Blazer again?"

"No, but I saw Tobin Wacker and that man called Dick. I saw them in Rico."

They asked me a sight of questions, and I was itching to get away. It was time I started for Georgetown, but there was no way I could leave them.

"Do you believe Blazer killed your father for his winnings?"

"No, sir. I don't believe he killed my father. I think he just saw all that money and got greedy."

"The last you saw of him was in the cabin? But you saw Wacker and Dick in Rico? And the cabin had been burned?"

"Blazer's missing," the other officer said, "and we have to find him . . . or his body."

"My guess would be in the ruins of that burned-out cabin. When Wacker and Dick saw me in Rico, they were scared. That doesn't make sense. Why should they be scared of me? And that Wacker, he wasn't afraid of anything. Only I had seen them with Blazer on the mountain before that last snow."

"We will look around." They got up. "Are you going to be around town?"

"Not for a while. I am going east . . . Cherry Creek, and around that part of the country."

They exchanged a glance. "It would be better if you stayed here until this Blazer affair is straightened out."

For a moment I said nothing and then I replied. "I cannot. For business and personal reasons I have to go east, but I will come back here when I have done what needs to be done."

They just looked at me, and finally I said, "There's a man hunting me, and Wacker and Dick have been helping him. I don't know why he wants me killed, but if I go east I can find out. I figure if a man is gunning for me, I should know why."

Burns laughed. "Seems reasonable. All right, you go. Think you can be back here in thirty days?"

"I'll try."

Burns pushed back his chair. "That's good enough for me. Meanwhile we'll have a look at that cabin."

"Mr. Burns, you'd better pull back. Unless you know the country, that cabin isn't easy to find."

With salt and pepper shakers and the cups, I showed him where the peaks and passes were. He needed no diagram. There'd been two thousand head of cattle driven over trails of as many miles with no more direction than I was giving these men.

When they had gone, Laurie came over. "Kearney, what is it? Are you in trouble?"

"No, ma'am. They're just investigating. Judge Blazer hasn't been seen and they're looking into it. Why, I don't know, but I suspect Blazer was up to something himself. When he wasn't with Wacker and them over at Rico, I knew something was wrong. He would have come with them or back here. The way I see it, he never got off that mountain."

"When are you going?"

It came to me of a sudden. I'd been thinking about daybreak, but the words were saying themselves before I had a chance to think. I said, "I'm going now. This minute." I got up. "Laurie, I told them I'd try to be back in thirty days. That's what I'm aiming for, but if something happens, I may have to go further east. If I do, and if I can, I'll write."

The roan was ready. I mean that was a trail horse, never so contented as when going somewhere, and when I'd saddled up and strapped on my gear, I taken out of there. It was too late in the day and it was a lot else, but I taken out, and the next good stopping place was more than twenty-five miles away.

The trail I followed around those mountains to Ouray would have scared a gopher to death.

The trail was clear if narrow, and I was moving along at a good clip, yet I didn't like it. The further I went the more uneasy I became, for the country was confining. Most of the time I was riding along trails cut into the walls of a canyon, and if a man should be trapped in such a place, he was a goner. There was simply no place to hide for long stretches.

Then it started to rain. When thunder rumbles in those narrow, rocky gorges, you just naturally curl up. It pulls in all the edges, if you get what I mean. By the time I got to where I could see the lights of Ouray nestled in the valley below, it was pouring down rain, and every once in a while the sky would split wide open with a crash of thunder and a flash of lightning. They were all close by, hitting those 13,000-foot mountains all around the town.

There was a dim light over the door of the livery stable, and when I rode in, an old man with handlebar mustaches stuck his head out of the office door. "Put up your hoss, boy! An' come in for a cup of java!"

First time I'd heard it called that since Texas, where they had names for everything.

Stripping off my gear, I rubbed the roan dry and put a bait of oats in the bin. Then I went up the ladder to the loft and forked down some hay. By that time I was ready for coffee.

Walking down the middle of the barn, I peered into all the stalls. No familiar horses, which did not necessarily mean anything. I'd learn more from the hostler.

He was setting back in a swivel chair in front of a rolltop desk and he had him a dime novel he was reading. It was about some daredevil who kept rescuing fair maidens from Indians or whatever. What the fair maiden was doing where she was always puzzled me, and I was never so lucky. Most of the maidens I came upon were most unfair.

"Wet out there," I commented.

"I can see that, an' I can hear it. No night for man or beast. Come far?"

"Silverton."

"How's things yonder?"

"Pretty good. They were runnin' a raise up from the three-hundred level in one of those mines and struck some mighty pretty rock. Tons of it."

The coffee was hot and strong enough to stand by itself, without any cup. I drank it and liked it.

"Keepin' busy?" I suggested.

"So-so."

"Much travel?"

"Enough."

"Strangers in town?"

He turned his head and looked right at me. "Always is, boy. Mostly folks who travel are strangers. Like you, now. You're a stranger."

"My friend," I said cheerfully, "I just look young because I've lived a peaceful life. I was here when that mountain over yonder was just a soft place in the valley. When I first come here I had to comb grizzlies out of my hair!"

He looked at me out of those cool blue eyes and he said, "Youngster, I come from Arkansas-Missouri country. We seen a heap of windy penny-grabbers down there."

"That why you come west? Where there weren't so many of you?"

He took his pipe out of his mouth and reached for the pot. "Have another," he said. "Who was you worried about seeing?"

"Not worried," I said, "just careful. And it isn't the law." I described Felix Yant and Tobin Wacker.

"Know Wacker," he commented. "Seen the other man around a time or two. I was wondering what he had on his mind. I'll keep an eye out for them."

He leaned over with the pot and refilled my cup. "You ridin' out?"

Why I told him I did not know, only that I was very much alone and needed to put it all into words. He sat back and smoked, listening without comment. He knocked out his pipe when I was finished. "There's money in it, boy. You an' him are some kin, I'd say, and if you live he don't get anything or maybe not as much. He wants you dead out here so he can go back and have it all to hisself. There may be more to it, but that there's the way I see it. Them women now, I can't figure them, least one of them is also in line for that money or whatever it is and wants you out of the way."

"What about the other one?"

"Them's the kind to watch most, boy. She may be a fine woman, and the good Lord put aplenty of them on earth, but you got to know what she wants, what she's after. Maybe it was your pa," he added.

He tamped fresh tobacco in his pipe. "Son, I cotton to you. I like your style. Now I've got a black horse here—"

"I don't want to trade."

"I ain't talkin' trade. I'm talking loan. You got the roan and that's a mighty fine horse, but ridin' the way you figure to do, you'll wear him down to a nubbin'. So you keep your roan, but you take the black, too. You can switch so's you won't tire them too much."

He lighted his pipe. "You take my advice an' cut across the hills to Lake City. Save you time an' distance."

With daylight I was high in the mountains and keeping to Indian trails and the like. Prospectors had been all over this country, and here and there I could see signs of their work. This was high-up country, and without mountain-bred horses a man would get nowhere. It was high but it wasn't lonely. Here and there I sighted men working claims, but I was traveling, not talking. My trail led along Mineral Creek, then climbed the divide up to around 13,000 feet. A body could judge his altitude pretty easy by what grew or did not grow, and vegetation was almighty scarce up that high.

Reining in atop a ridge between two peaks three or four miles apart, I let my horse take a blow and sat my saddle looking over the country. Redcloud Gulch dropped off on my left, but my trail was to the right below Hurricane Basin. From where I sat a man could see a sight of magnificent country, great bald peaks with long talus slopes everywhere about. A big peak off to the southeast was an easy 14,000 feet if ever I saw it.

The air was fresh and clear, and the sky was a vast vault of blue, flecked only here and there with clouds. The roan was eager to go, so we started down, dropping down at least a thousand feet in a mile or so.

Stopping at some marshes where there was water, I let the horses drink, then took off down the canyon to where my trail cut into a trail along Henson Creek.

The trail suddenly turned sharply northeast, and I pulled off under some spruce trees, stripped the gear from the roan, and let him roll a bit. When I saddled up, it was the black. The way I figured it, we had no more than fifteen or sixteen miles to Lake City. From where I rested, I could look back up the trail for about a mile. Then it was out of sight for a ways, and the ridge where I'd topped out was in plain view.

I lay there, just relaxing, watching that ridge. Nothing showed up but a soaring eagle and a couple of whiskey-jacks, who hovered around me looking for something to eat. They were camp thieves and a nuisance, but I kind of favored them for their friendly way.

When we'd rested about an hour, I mounted up, rode northeast until I sighted a couple of cabins, then hit the Henson Creek Trail that took me due east. There were no tracks fresher than a week.

The way I saw it, I was ahead of them, but I daren't take anything for granted. When I rested in Silverton, they might have gotten ahead of me.

The town lay in a pretty little valley among the mountains, and she was booming. This had all been Ute country until 1874, just a short time back, and then the Utes ceded it and miners came in. They struck gold, yet for a time there were only a dozen log cabins or so. Then the boom hit and the town began to build.

Riding down the main drag, I counted seven saloons

and four eating places, several hotels and a couple of Chinese laundries and a billiard parlor or two.

A few days later I rode into Georgetown and put up at the Hotel de Paris.

Chapter XII

The woman who came to the desk was a small, pleasant-faced woman, and I knew her at once. "Aunt Sophie?" I said, and she looked up, startled.

"Why! Why, it's Kearney! Of all people!" She turned quickly and called into another room. "Louis! It's Kearney come back! Kearney McRaven!"

Louis Dupuy, sometimes called French Louie, came in from the kitchen. "Ah! *Mon ami!* But you have grown tall! You were a boy, and now you are a man! And your father, where is he?"

"He was killed . . . murdered," I said. "I do not know why. I have come to you, who were his friend, to see if he left papers with you."

"Come!" He took me by the arm. "It is a quiet morning. We will have coffee in the courtyard." He turned. "Sophie?"

"Of course, m'sieu. At once."

When we were seated in the courtyard, he said, "Tell me. All of it."

So concisely as possible I related the story of the events from my father's death to the moment. He listened without comment until I was finished.

"So . . . it is as he suspected. This Felix Yant. He

knew what to expect of him, and he is, as you suspect, a very dangerous man. Your father spoke of him. He was a duelist, and he has killed several men, but he is not the worst of them. It is *she*."

"Which one?"

"Ah, if we but knew that! This Felix Yant has a sister, an evil woman who loves wealth, power, and cruelty, and the last most of all.

"Your great-grandfather, Kearney, was a ship's captain, and on one of his forays into the West Indies he met a woman on Haiti, a woman of surpassing beauty. Her nationality? Who knows? Perhaps French, Spanish, or Portuguese, perhaps all three, but the other half of her was Carib . . . do you know them? They were a cannibal people who lived in the Indies before Columbus came, a wild, fierce, cruel people.

"Where this woman was born no man knew, and if she knew she never told, nor what or who she was. Your great-grandfather brought her back to Charleston with him, a passenger on his vessel. Shortly after, his wife died . . . very suddenly, for she had always been in good health, and this woman married your great-grandfather. You are descended from the first wife, Felix Yant from the second.

"As is often the case, the two branches of the family diverged sharply. Yours were planters, professional men, and soldiers. Those descended from Serena were wholly committed to evil, yet one and all they had intelligence beyond the average . . . much beyond.

"Your grandfather was an astute businessman who became wealthy through shrewd investments, the acquisition of lands, and the West Indian trade. In the latter case he built upon old established relationships developed by your great-grandfather.

"Unfortunately your cousins were less provident, and moreover there had been a complete break between the two sides of the family. Felix Yant killed your uncle in a deliberately provoked duel, an aunt of yours died from poison . . . nothing ever proved. Your father did all he could to avoid becoming involved, and was serving in the army when your grandfather died.

"There is a plantation of some size. There is property in Charleston, and more of it in Savannah. There is a plantation in Jamaica. Apparently Felix, his sister, and others of his family believed that if your father died, they would inherit. They knew nothing of you."

"My father left some papers with you?"

"He did. He left some evidence he did not wish to use, evidence that would convict one of his cousins of murder, as well as his father's will and deeds to various properties. Other information, I am informed, relates to other properties and the location of other documents you would need to establish ownership."

For a moment there was silence. Then Dupuy added, "As you may have heard, I permit no unmarried, unescorted women to stay in my hotel. I have but a few rooms and I let them to whomever I choose, but only when I choose. Two days ago a woman came here who wished to have a room. I refused her. She became quite furious with me." He shrugged. "As you may know, such things I ignore. I have no time to be bothered with tantrums. But this woman . . . she was very beautiful, and very strong, and I think she is given with hatred of a very special kind. She left, but I do not think I have seen the last of her. What is important is that I am sure she is Felix Yant's sister or aunt. So be warned."

"How could she know to come here?" I wondered.

He shrugged. "My cooking is famous . . . but no, I do not think it is that. Perhaps when here, your father wrote . . . a letter, perhaps to a friend or relative. She might have guessed this was the place to come."

Yet she might have come simply from hearing of the place, for the Hotel de Paris was famous, already a legend, and our friend, whom the miners knew as French Louie, was one of the most renowned chefs of his time. Many noted travelers had gone far out of their way to reach this little mining town in the Rockies simply to enjoy one of his fantastic meals or the hospitality of his hotel.

Lighted with gaslights purchased from Tiffany's, with

black walnut woodwork, books bound in leather in a library of three thousand volumes, and marble sinks in each room, the Hotel de Paris had an elegance peculiar to itself.

The dining room had a yellow and white striped floor —alternating strips of maple and walnut—and the meals served had a Continental distinction. General Grenville Dodge, President Ulysses S. Grant, Jay Gould, Russell Sage, Baron Rothschild, the Prince de Joinville, and many another wealthy and famous man had dined at his table.

There were but ten rooms, each with private bath, a thing scarcely heard of in that time and place. Georgetown was a booming mining camp, but not even Denver had food to compare with that produced by Louis Dupuy, for he was his own chef, with reason to be proud of his skill.

"Louis, do you have a room for me?" I asked.

"For you? I would put somebody out! Yes, I have a room." He led the way upstairs and showed me to a pleasant, sunlit room. "Rest," he suggested, "and then we must talk, you and I."

At the door he paused. "As you may know, I am a man of few friends. Your father was one, a man of true taste and of philosophical leanings. Did you know that he once taught philosophy? Not that that is any criterion. Many of the teachers know nothing. They are parrots of poorly comprehended ideas, but your father . . . he knew. Since leaving France I have met no one whose ideas were so challenging. We talked often . . . and he told me of his plans for you."

"He never told me," I said sadly.

"Ah, I know! You see, Kearney, he had nothing. Much was due him, but he dare not return to claim it. He was a man alone and only with such skills as lacked importance in the West. He was a thinker, and the West was a place where people must *do*. He did what he could with what he had."

"He left me well off at the end," I said.

"So? Then we must talk. You must hear his plans, even if he is gone and though you may not be interested. We will see. In the meantime, stay away from windows, rest, and I will come up later."

He left, closing the door softly behind him. Pulling off my boots, I draped my coat over the back of a chair, and taking off my gun belt, placed it on a chair beside the bed with the gun butt close to my hand.

Occasionally a rig went by in the street, or a rider. Once I heard a subdued murmur of voices. Then I slept, and when I awakened it was night. A reflection of light from the outside kept the room dimly lighted. The walls were dark, but I could see the table and a chair in the corner.

The chair in the corner? I looked again. I stared. A woman sat there, rocking just a little.

For a moment I lay absolutely still, the hair lifting on the back of my neck. What I felt then may have been fear, it may have been sheer disbelief, I do not know.

"I see you are awake, Kearney." The voice was low, a lady's cultured voice, a kindly voice as well. "I hope my being here is not distasteful. I simply had to come. Oh, I know! You do not know me. Your father did, however. He knew me quite well. And you must come to know me, too. After all, we are cousins."

"Are we?" Somehow in that moment when she was speaking, I had controlled my fear. My father had once said, "Fear is a weapon to be used by you if you control it, by your enemies if you do not." I added, "I am afraid you have the advantage of me."

"I am Delphine, Kearney. You have not heard of me?"

"I have not."

"A pity. We could have been such good friends. You see, we heard you had died . . . we even thought your father had passed on . . . some years ago. We were sure . . . well, it was quite a surprise to us to learn that he still lived."

"A shock, I imagine." How had she gotten in here? I knew Louis would not have permitted it, and Sophie would do nothing of which Louis did not approve. Yet she was here, sitting in the corner of my room.

Old tales returned to mind, tales from the swamps

and back country of the Deep South, tales of witches
and witchcraft, of people who came and went mys-
teriously. I shook my head irritably to clear it of such
nonsense, yet I wished I could make her out.

From below came the subdued mutter of voices,
people at supper, no doubt.

"Yes," she admitted, "quite a shock. But now that we
have found you, we must become friends. We must
see much of each other. We are cousins," she added,
"of a sort. Several times removed, that is."

"Louis told me he refused you a room."

"Oh? He spoke of that, did he? Yes, he was tiresome. Very tiresome. A most disagreeable man. The
people about town say a girl refused him and he could
not abide it, so now he hates all women. What a foolish
man!"

"But a wise one," I replied quietly, "a man learned
in philosophy and history, a man worth talking to."

"Oh, I suppose he could be interesting in a way,
but I do not like him. He is cold and abrupt."

"And suspicious?" I suggested.

"But of what? I am but a woman who has traveled
far simply to meet her cousin!"

Fortunately, I had not undressed, planning to go
down for supper later. My boots were beside the bed,
and my gun. I glanced at the chair. It was there, half-
covered by my hat. Had she seen it? I made a mental
reservation not to try to use it until I had checked the
loads.

"Felix will be so relieved, you know." I could not
see her smile but knew it was there. "Somehow he
quite lost you. I must speak to him about that. It is not
good to lose track of one's relatives after having been
separated so long."

Slowly I sat up and swung my feet to the floor. Once
when I was very small, this woman—I believed it was
she—had visited us, and after that my father had been
ill for months. Was there a connection? Or was that
only my imagination?

Picking up a boot, I shook it out, a habit one acquires

when sleeping out where there are snakes, tarantulas, and scorpions. I shook it, and something fell to the floor, something with a metallic sound. Ignoring it, I tugged on a boot, then felt for the other one. It had fallen out of reach, so I stood up and took a step. My foot came down on something on the floor. I gave a sharp outcry, as one will, and Delphine said quickly, "What is it, Kearney? Did you stub your toe?"

"Stepped on something," I commented, tugging on the boot. "Nail or something." I swung my gun belt around my waist and buckled the belt. "Come. We will have supper."

We went down the steps together, and Sophie saw us first. Her lips tightened and her eyes flashed angrily, but she said nothing. "Supper, Sophie? Are we too late?"

"You are in good time, m'sieu. There is roast ptarmigan, hearts of artichokes, and for fish there is trout." She bustled ahead of us, seating us at a table in the warmly lit, pleasant room. Several other tables were occupied. The men, I noticed, all looked at my companion, and so, for the first time, did I.

She was beautiful. As to her age, a factor my father always assured me I should never notice in women, she might have been nearly thirty. I was sure she was older, how much I did not know. She was beautifully gowned, her black hair done in the latest fashion, her black eyes very large and ringed with long lashes.

Beautiful, as I have said, but there was something about her mouth and eyes I did not like, a sense of cruelty and of something else ... something grossly evil.

Or was it my imagination, coupled with some ancient memories of things heard or seen and long forgotten because I had been too young to give them significance?

"You are handsome, Kearney." She looked at me critically. "And quite the young man. I wonder just how old you are?"

"Age is a relative thing," I said. "It is character, as my father always said, that matters. In horses, dogs, men, and women."

"He seems to have been a wise man, your father," she said, a touch of irritation in her tone. "Why then did he not come home?"

"Perhaps because he was a wise man," I said.

"You should come home, Kearney." She leaned toward me. "You should know your own country, your own people. You must come back to Carolina with us. You would love it." She put her hand over mine. "Please, Kearney? You will think of it? We need you there."

She said "we" but she meant me to think "I." The fashions of the time were suited to her, and she used them well. The gown she wore suggested what it concealed, and although all the men in the place were giving her their attention, she ignored them, devoting herself completely to me.

"We have been searching for you, you know," she said.

"We traveled a lot," I said, thinking of nothing better.

"This man, this Frenchman . . . he was a good friend of your father?"

She suspected, or perhaps from some means she knew, that whatever my father had might have been left here. I shrugged and waved a careless hand. "Father always liked good cooking, and Louis is the best, the very best. They talked of books, too, but friends? I think no more than acquaintances. If my father had a friend," I said thoughtfully, "it was that man in Denver . . . the one on Larimer Street. I was too young," I added, "when we were there, but the man was from somewhere in the South. New Orleans, I think. I know they had much in common."

Whether she was believing me I had no idea, yet she listened attentively as she ate.

Why had she come west when Felix was already here? Did she not trust him? Or was there some deadline, some date that made speed imperative? Somehow I must be rid of her and talk to Louis again, and I must see those papers, whatever they were.

"This man in Denver," she said, "you knew him?"

"I only saw him. I was a child. My father was back this way alone, later. I was working at the time and he traveled east by stage. I only know that he spent some time in Denver, doing what I am not sure."

That was true, and remembering it, I wondered. What *had* my father been doing? He left me but rarely, as if knowing there was a danger that threatened us both, but on that occasion he had gone to Denver and had been gone more than two weeks. Had he come to Georgetown then? It would not have been out of his way . . . at least not much.

"The food *is* good!" Delphine was saying. She looked at me oddly as she spoke, almost as though she were examining me, expecting some effect or reaction from me. "You must talk to him. He will listen to you. I do want a room here, Kearney, a room just like yours." She looked at me. "Close to yours."

"He listens to no one," I said. "Louis makes up his own mind, and if he dislikes someone, he tells them to leave. No matter who they are."

"But surely—"

"I would not even try," I said. "I know the man."

"Not even for me?" She put her hand on mine again, her fingers caressing my wrist.

I was embarrassed, yet short of breath too. She was a beautiful woman, and I had been long in the mountains and never in all my life had met such a woman, so seductive, so beautifully gowned. "I . . . I'll try," I said. "I'll see."

And at the moment, I meant it. After all, what harm could it do? This was the most comfortable place to stay, and she was very much the lady . . . or appeared to be.

I started to rise and in my haste put my foot down wrong and fell back rather awkwardly into my chair. It was nothing but clumsiness, but as my hands dropped to the chair arms to push myself up again, my eyes met hers.

In them I surprised an expression such as I had never seen in the eyes of any human, and only once in the eyes of any living thing. Rising once from a stream where I had been drinking, I had looked right into the eyes of a mountain lion, all poised to leap.

Suddenly I knew I had to get away, to be alone, to recover what was left of my good sense. "I am afraid I . . . I think I had better go lie down," I said. "I am feeling unwell."

"Do that, Kearney. Go lie down. I will see you another time."

Excusing myself, I got up hastily and went to my room.

Chapter XIII

Scarcely was I back in my room with the gaslight lit than Louis appeared. I sat down on the bed.

"Are you all right?" he asked sharply. "How did she come to be with you?"

When I explained, he shook his head irritably. "She must have come in while I was in the garden. Damn the luck! Kearney, you must avoid her! She is the one, I am sure, whom your father warned me against."

Moving my boot, something rattled on the floor and I looked down. A carpet tack. It must have been that which I shook from my boot . . . but how would such a thing get into my boot in the first place?

"What's the matter?" Louis demanded.

Reaching down, I picked up the tack. It was an ordinary carpet tack except that the point was covered with a hard, shiny substance of a yellowish brown color. "This," I said. "It fell out of my boot."

He took it from me, very carefully, and studied the point under the light. Briefly, I explained how I shook out my boots as I always did and the tack fell to the floor, and that it must have been that I had stepped on when I stood up.

"Get your sock off!" he said. "Let's see that foot."

"I must have stepped on the side of it," I said. "It would have hurt much more had I stepped on the point."

There was no puncture or scratch on my foot. Louis examined the point again. "You've been very lucky," he commented grimly. "I am sure this is a poison, and I am sure it was meant to kill you. She must have placed it in your boot while you were asleep, never imagining you'd shake out your boots."

"We all do it," I said. "You learn quickly out here."

"She must have believed you stepped on it when you stood up. She believes you are poisoned."

He was still examining the tack. "I know something of this sort of thing," he commented. "When I was studying at the seminary in France, there was a professor there who was making a study of plant poisons—arrow poison and the like which had been used by primitive peoples. It resembles pakuru, a poison made from a tree of that name. If my memory serves me correctly one staggers, becomes clumsy, is apt to lose control of some muscles, then one dies. Depending on whether one gets a little of it or much, it can kill in anywhere from fifteen minutes to several hours, but usually the quicker time."

"When I started to rise, I almost fell," I said. "It was pure clumsiness, but—"

"Of course, she believed her poison was working. Very well, the thing for you to do is be gone before morning. Be out of here and away into the mountains."

"I came to see the papers my father left," I protested.

"And so you shall. How long will it take? An hour . . . less, surely. In the meanwhile I shall see your horses are made ready."

He took up the tack. "I shall get rid of this. It must not be left lying about, and I am sure you do not want it." He looked at it. "An ugly thing . . . murder is the answer to nothing. It invariably creates more problems than it eliminates. A dozen times in my life I have thought of it, and of course did not do it. I am a civilized man. However, a year after, the person I would cheerfully have murdered was no longer of importance to me, and in many cases of no importance to anyone. Time eliminates so many problems. It is a good thing, I think, to save newspapers, then read them months later. One soon discovers then what is important and what is not. Many a crisis that seems about to shake the earth and bring down governments turns out to be no more substantial than those dust devils which one sees in the desert or plains. They spin furiously for a few minutes, then fall apart, leaving not even a ghost of themselves."

There was a tap at the door, and when Louis opened it, Sophie was there holding the familiar buckskin case that my father had so long carried.

He took it from her and passed it on to me. "There! I know nothing of what it contains, and only what he told me of his story. I think you should read these, but please, *mon ami,* before you do anything, consult with me. And with Sophie."

"Sophie? I thought you did not like women?"

"Most of them I dislike. Not woman . . . women. Silly creatures, most of them. Sophie is different. We have been friends, Sophie and I, and although she does not know it, when I am gone this will become hers. Sophie is a jewel, Kearney, a jewel of the purest water. She is a philosopher, a true philosopher with a sense of reality far better than mine. She sees much and says nothing, a rare quality in a man, let alone a woman. Most women sparkle beautifully as young girls. These are the robes nature puts on them to help trap the unwary male, but once the game is trapped the bait disappears, and most of them settle into dullness."

The idea was amusing, but I objected. "You can't say that of her . . . of Delphine," I said. "It seems to me the bait is still there."

He shrugged. "Of course. She is a huntress. She is not looking for a man. All men are useful to her, none really important. Many of the famous courtesans of history were such women. Sex was not important to them. They simply used it as a tool in reaching for wealth or power. Such a woman usually controls the situation because she herself does not care. I think Delphine, like her brother, if such he is, wants wealth because it insulates her from people. She has an inborn hatred and contempt for people. They are like spiders with webs, not to trap prey necessarily, but simply as a place to *be*, where the world cannot brush against them. Apparently whatever they have is not enough to insure this, and what is yours would be enough. But beware, my friend! Such people are intent, they are relentless and single-minded in their purpose, whatever it may be."

"I cannot always run from them," I protested.

"You cannot. What you must do is go east, establish your claim to the property, and settle the fact once and for all that there is an heir and you are he. If you wish to take possession, do so. If not, sell the property and return here, away from them and all they mean, buy yourself a ranch, and make your own place in the world. Your father avoided the issue because he wished to avoid the family feud, he wished to be free of all that, but there was a final killing. It disturbed him very greatly, and to return would have meant more killing. Also, there were others between him and the property. That, apparently, is no longer so. You are a shrewd, intelligent young man, Kearney, but I would suggest you move quickly to assert your claim while they are still looking for you here. I have friends, and I can arrange for you to move very swiftly indeed, so go east, see a man whose name I shall give you, and take possession. The rest is up to you, and now I shall leave you with these things," he said, tapping the buckskin case, "but do you study the contents carefully."

The room I had overlooked the street, and I sat near the window but at one side of it so that I might survey the approach to the hotel. I could not see directly down into the street without pressing my face against the glass, which caution told me would not be advisable. Delphine was not likely to take a shot at me, but I did not believe for the moment that she was alone. And if she had come alone, she would not long remain without recruits.

Louis was right in suggesting that I slip out of town. One attempt had been made to kill me, but when it was realized that the attempt had failed, they would surely make another. It was this that was irrational about them, that they seemed to want to gain possession of what papers my father had left and to kill me also, but so impatient were they that they could not seem to wait until I came into possession of the papers they wanted. They would kill me first and take their chances on the papers ... or that seemed to be the case. What I had surprised in the eyes of Delphine was simply that, an eagerness for the kill.

First, to read and understand what my father had left. It was only a small packet of papers, including a very skillfully drawn map showing the locations of several pieces of property, two plantations, one quite large, and several patches of pasture and woodland in other parts of the state. Accompanying them were the deeds to two of the smaller parcels.

There was a letter, folded and sealed, addressed to me. I broke the seal.

My Son:

When you read this I shall be dead. Since your mother died I have lived for you and you alone and now that I am gone the decisions will be yours to make. If you decide to go back, know that you must see Old Tolbert. He will know best how to proceed.

For three generations there has persisted in our family a deadly feud which has resulted in seven duels, four of them fatal. There have been other deaths attributed to one cause or another, but some at least were from poison.

Twice I was myself embroiled in duels, twice I was victorious, and after that efforts were made to use poison or to way-lay me. I had enough. I simply disappeared. Then I met your mother, married, and you were born.

There was no honor among them. They wasted their inheritance and wanted the rest. At last count there were thirteen of them and but three left of us. Their name is Cabanus although some have used the name of Yant. If something happens to us they will be the closest and can claim any estate, and this, as much as hatred, is behind it.

Do not take them lightly. They have intelligence of a high order, and they have courage, yet they will stop at nothing, and will kill from ambush or with a knife in the dark, or poison, and it is said the women are skilled and practiced poisoners with poisons brought by them from Surinam, where they frequently go.

I had hoped to keep you from all this, had hoped to win by gambling enough money to send you to school, to set you up somewhere in a business or profession, and have done with all that. Then word came to me that they were seeking me out.

The most skillful and deadly of them all is Joseph Vrydag, a cousin of theirs, lately of Surinam. He would now be a man of forty years and spent some years before he was twenty in the goldfields of California and Nevada. I have no idea as to his appearance.

There was a little more, but there lay the gist of it, and it seemed I should have no recourse but to lay claim to what estate there was, if only to defeat them. When one is very young, death seems remote. I thought of the poisoned tack in my boot. I should have to be wary.

Joseph Vrydag . . . no idea as to appearance, but a man of forty years. I must walk with caution, and alone.

There remained one more document. It was another map, but an ancient map, drawn upon beautifully tanned deerskin. On it were located a river, a small fort or what appeared to be so, and an Indian village. Trees were indicated and a cliff, nearby a deep canyon or ravine, and at a point in the wall of the canyon, a cave was indicated, or what appeared to be a cave, behind a waterfall.

What it meant I had no idea, but somehow I got the idea that it might be the most important item of all. Why was it enclosed here? Obviously it was very old, obviously a part of my legacy, if such it could be called. There was no indication as to the location of the map, no names were given, nothing beyond the few terrain features. The map was meant to be used by someone who knew the area to which the map applied.

On a sudden inspiration I opened my bedroll, where I sometimes carried a few extra items of clothing, and got out my old buckskin hunting shirt. It had been patched a time or two but was still useful. On the inside of the back, just above the waistline, I stitched the buckskin map, the face of the map toward the back of the shirt so it was not visible.

When I had finished the stitching, I stood up and stretched, and as I did so I glanced out of the window. There was a man standing across the street, somewhat in the shadows. As the night was cold, he wore a heavy coat. Moving to the side of the window, I drew the shade, then went to the door, glanced into the empty hall, and in two quick steps was at the door of the room next to mine. It stood open, as the room was empty. Closing the door after me, I went to the window of the dark room and peered out.

The man in the heavy coat was still there, his shadow obscured so I could not make him out. Another man came up the street and joined him. I saw the white of his face as he looked up. So then, I was being watched for.

Returning to my room, I put the last of my possessions together, rolled my blanket roll tighter, and lay down on my bed to wait, with the light turned off.

A hand touched my shoulder. It was Louis. "No light," he warned, "and come now!"

Rising, I took up my rifle and blanket roll and followed him down the dark hall. How he expected me to leave the hotel without being seen I had no idea, for the

front entrance opened upon the street and the back
door upon what I remembered as a wide, vacant area.
Yet I had not had time to examine it.

He led the way to the back door and paused. Outside
I heard a confused mumbling and what sounded like
a drunken argument, then a rather confused medley of
voices singing "Jeanie with the Light Brown Hair."

"Step outside," Louis whispered, "and join them.
Say nothing, just go along with them."

The door opened a crack and I slipped out and men
closed around me. Almost at once the door opened
again, but this time the hall was lighted and a shaft of
light fell over the group.

"Come on, boys," Louis was saying, "be reasonable! I've got some sleepy, tired people inside!"

"Aw, look!" a drunken voice said. "There's French
Louie! Good ol' Frenchy! Come on, Louie! Have a
drink!"

"Too much work," Louis said affably, "but I'll tell
you what I'll do. You go sing somewhere else and I'll
give you a couple of bottles!"

"It's a deal!" the man beside me shouted. "Good ol'
Frenchy! 'Member when we worked the graveyard shift
together?"

"Now, now, boys," Louis said. "Here, take these
bottles, and you boys just drift along. My guests are
tired people and need their rest."

"We were just serenadin' 'em," another miner said.
"Come on, Louis! Come along with us!"

"Some other night," he said. "You boys get along
now!"

He closed the door, and staggering and singing, waving a bottle or two, they started off across the lot, singing "Tenting Tonight on the Old Camp Ground."

The man who had draped his arm around my shoulders now whispered, "Your hosses are under them cottonwoods yonder. When we get to 'em, you just slip
off and you're on your own."

"Sure . . . and thanks."

"Forget it. Any friend of Louis's is a friend of ours."

They staggered on singing, and I stood under the trees for several minutes watching the hotel. Nobody followed the "drunken" miners and nobody came toward me, so evidently the ruse had worked. Mounting and staying behind the trees and buildings, I found my way to the edge of town, taking bypaths until well clear of it. Then I rode off along the trail to the south, following Clear Creek.

From time to time I paused to listen, but there were no sounds of pursuit. Nevertheless, I decided to leave the trail at the first opportunity.

By moonrise I was on the dim trail that led to Chicago Lakes. There was a good chance they would not guess what I was doing, and I had told no one. Had I been going west, the route was by way of Silver Plume and Bakerville, and east the logical route was that toward Idaho Falls and Denver. Instead I had gone south into some very rough, wild country. By daybreak I was crossing a shoulder of Chief Mountain, and looking back could see no sign of pursuit. After a brief stop to switch gear to my other horse, I rode on down to Cub Creek and followed it to Troublesome.

Coming out of the mountains with the Hogback in front of me, my belly was fighting hunger and my horses needed a rest if I intended to push them as hard as planned. Ahead of me there was a low house built of flat rocks, a corral with a couple of horses, and some cultivated ground. I rode into the gate and stepped down.

A man came to the door. " 'Light an' set," he said. "We're just at table."

"I'd be obliged," I said, and led my horses to the trough for water. When they'd had their fill, I picketed them on a patch of grass, and dropping my gear in the shade I walked in.

There was a blond young man and a woman just as blond. Neither of them were much older than me. The house was far cleaner than most.

"Come far?" he asked.

"A piece."

"Out of the way here," he commented. "We see mighty few people."

"Been workin' the other side of the Divide," I said. "Goin' to see my folks in Kansas."

We talked idly as we ate, about grass conditions, rainfall, and the price of silver and beef, always top subjects in Colorado at the time. News was scarce and they were hungry for outside talk, so I gave them what I could, as I'd covered a sight of country one time and another. They hungered for me to stay, but the road was calling and the distance great.

When I topped out on the rise, I looked back. They were still standing in the yard and they seemed to be waving, so I waved as well, although I knew they could not see me. They were tough young folks, the kind who made do, and they would get along all right until there was sickness. It's then you need folks around you, and a woman needs womenfolks.

Denver lay off to the north, but I made no show of going there, just taking out across the prairie and putting the Front Range behind me.

This was Indian country I was riding into, Comanche, Cheyenne, and Arapaho country, with Kiowas further east and Utes all about. Pa had been friends with the Utes, knew both Ouray and Shavano, or Showano—I'd heard him called both. Why they took to pa as they did I'd no idea, but they surely did. Somewhere along the line he'd done them a service or proved himself to them somehow. They were a strong, courageous people, and I hoped I could avoid them, for they did not know me and I wanted to kill none of them, nor to be killed by them.

That night I camped on Willow Creek, made me a spot of coffee and finished the cold meat and bread Louis Dupuy had given me to travel on, then turned in, dead beat.

My eyes opened on a damp, foggy morning. Everything was dripping and wet, and much as I was wishful for a hot meal and coffee, I decided against it. Bringing in the horses, I saddled up and taken out.

It was spooky, riding in that fog. A body couldn't see beyond his horse's ears, and although I was riding a dim trail, I'd no idea where it went or what lay ahead of me.

Suddenly it seemed to me I heard other sounds than my own. I pulled up sharply, listening.

Sure enough, there was somebody . . . or something . . . out there in the fog.

Chapter XIV

Somebody—and more than one rider—was moving out there in the fog, and not far away. I whispered to my horses, trusting to my own, worried about the other. Their ears were pricked but they seemed as nervous as I, and neither made a sound.

Hoofs coming nearer. It would be close work for a rifle, so I drew my pistol and waited. Closer and closer, and then they were passing by, not more than fifty or sixty feet away. There was only a sound of hoofs, one irritable curse, and they had passed me by, pointing toward Denver. For several minutes I waited, then holstered my pistol and started off, at a walk first, then a canter.

Whoever had passed me might have no interest in me, but they were dangerous times, with Indians riding the war trails and any number of men willing to take advantage of any unwary traveler. The old-timers never shot until they could see what they were shooting at, but the greenhorns might blaze away at anything that moved.

As the fog lifted, I slowed my pace to look around. It was wide-open country, a distant butte showing here or there and not two hundred yards off a herd of antelope, heads up to see what manner of a creature I might be. Uneasily they moved away, not running, just fading into the landscape.

At noon I made a stop on Box Elder Creek. The creek was not running but there were pools of water here and there. After stripping the gear from my horses, I gave them a chance to roll, watered them, and then saddled the other horse and got a fire started for coffee. The place I'd chosen was under the edge of the creek bank with brush growing along the edge, so my smoke—what little there was from dry wood—dissipated in going through the branches.

By simply standing up I could survey the country without showing myself, so I looked it over carefully now and again, ate, drank several cups of coffee, and dozed a little in the sun. By the time an hour was past, I was moving out over the prairie again, holding to low ground and changing my angle of travel from time to time so anybody watching me could lay no ambush.

The afternoon was hot and still. In the distance heat waves danced and shimmered, and in a far-off basin lay a vast blue lake that was not there at all. A lone buffalo bull, looming black and ominous against the sky, seemed to have legs enormously long, and he seemed but a short distance away, but I knew he was well over a mile away. This was a land where mirage was usual, and I had seen them before this.

Eastward I rode as the day was waning, eastward while the shadows gathered, and nowhere did I see any rider or any moving thing but occasional buffalo, antelope, and a few stray cattle, yet I was haunted by uneasiness. By now my enemies would be moving to prevent me from reaching Carolina. They would know Delphine's attempt at poison had failed, and they would be coming east to find me.

Some of their clan remained in the East and they

could be reached by telegraph. The wires had been in
for several years now and were frequently used by
cattlemen and other businessmen. I knew about them,
and their existence made me uneasy, for by now word
could have reached others of the clan, who might even
now be moving west toward me. I had no reason to
doubt that the others had remained in the East to await
word from Delphine or Felix.

Now I rode into a rough and broken land, sand hills
and washes, sparse growth of any kind, yet riding up a
wash I came on an undercut bank where the remains of
old campfires were. Charred ends of sticks and brush lay
about some of the fires.

Dismounting, I put together a small fire from the
ends of charred sticks and whatever was around, needing only enough to make coffee. It was very still. No
sound but my own movements, the slight jingle of
spurs, the occasional scuffing of my boots, and the
crackle of the fire taking hold, and my eyes kept straying
to my horses, trusting to their natural alertness.

I did not like being hunted. It kept me on edge, irritable and restless, yet these very qualities were needed
now, for to relax too much might mean the end of me.
Well I knew the caliber of the men who sought me.
They were ruthless, relentless, without scruple. I was
something in the way of what they wanted and so to be
erased, rubbed out, dismissed with a gunshot or a knife
blade. Yet there was hatred for me and what I had
come from, so there would be a measure of satisfaction
in destroying me.

They were several . . . how many I had no idea. I
was a man alone.

My water bubbled and boiled. I dropped in the coffee, then after a bit a few drops of cold water to settle
the grounds, although I did not much care.

Several times I stood up, letting my eyes sweep the
country around, yet my horses cropped at the sparse
grass contentedly. I was filling my cup when I saw the
roan's head come up, ears pricked.

Well, it taken me a minute, no more. I scooped sand

over that fire and gulped coffee whilst standing up to
have a look-see.

Nothing.

The roan was looking off to the southwest, nostrils
dilated. "Watch 'em, boy," I said.

Taking up my rifle, I walked a bit higher up the
draw, my cup still in my left hand. I was going to get
me a bait of that coffee come hell or high water, and it
looked to be all of that. One thing I was sure of. When
trouble came, it wasn't going to be something picayun-
ish.

Nothing in sight, so I went back, filled my cup again,
emptied out the coffeepot, rubbed sand over it to take
off the worst of the soot, then fitted it into my gear.
Shoving the rifle back in the boot, I straddled my horse
and led out of there.

My mother never raised any foolish children, so I
rode down that wash for a half mile before I decided
to come up out of it. Taking a draw that ran off the
wash to the northeast, I followed it until it shallowed
out and I rode up on the plain.

Several times before I topped out, I pulled rein to
give myself a look around, but I could see nothing. It
was twilight on the plains, or as much twilight as a man
ever sees in a land where darkness comes quickly.

A star hung in the sky like a lonely lamp in a widow's
window. The air was cooler now, and fresh with a wind
off the western mountains. The horses stirred restlessly,
eager to be off, so seeing nothing, I turned my face
eastward and rode away toward the coming night.

Behind me the sky was weirdly lit, a magnificent sunset with clouds tinted rose and red, with golden arrows
shot upward by the archer of the sun. Sometimes I
looked back, but not only to see if I was followed. In
part I looked toward the setting sun because terror
may ride with beauty, and a man needs to milk his
hours of the precious things.

To ride fast, to travel far, these were empty things
unless a man took the time to savor, to taste, to love, to
simply *be*. That much I had from pa, and some from

Louis Dupuy, who for all his cynicism was a senti-
mentalist under the skin.

Into the coolness of the night I rode alone. Onward,
eastward.

There was a railroad at Dodge City. Maybe it was
further west, for they'd done a sight of building. The
steam cars would carry me fast to where I needed to
go.

For an hour after darkness fell, I pushed on before
I began watching for a place to camp.

When the moon was rising, I rode into a tree-
bordered hollow in the prairie where there was a good
spring and a pool of water. My horses gave no sign
of anything, so I rode in, gun in hand for trouble, but
hoping the way was clear.

First off I saw a pole corral, then a lean-to barn,
and beyond it a dugout faced with rock slabs built into
a good wall. The horses wanted water and I let them
have it, ears pricked for sound, my nose for any smell.

No wood smoke, no fresh manure, no fresh-cut
wood. Walking over to the dugout, I rapped on the
door. When no response came, I lifted the latch and,
keeping well to one side, opened the door.

All quiet. The place smelled empty, so I struck a
match. A bunk bed, a fireplace, a table, cooking utensils,
and on the wall a piece of paper nailed up.

Lighting a candle I held it up to the paper.

NOTISS

This here place belongs to me, you are welcome.
Just leeve it like you fond it. My wife's buried yonder
under the trees, an our baby beside her. I am a
lonely man. Can't take it alone. I hev gone back for
another woman.

A.T.T.

P.S. If there's flowers about, put sum on the graves.
She was a good woman. She done her best.

There was a fire laid on the hearth and the floor was
swept.

Going outside, I stripped the gear from my horses
and turned them into the corral. Then I went back to

the house and bedded down for the night. Several times I awakened to hear the coyotes howling. It must have been a lonely place for the woman, too. He would have been gone much what with hunting for meat and working.

At daybreak I was out and saddled the roan, led both horses outside, and tied them to the corral. Then I went in, laid a fresh fire, and swept the floor. After closing the door carefully, I looked for the graves. They were both on a low knoll somewhat shaded by a huge old cottonwood. The two graves were side by side and both were covered with withered flowers, obviously left by several different hands.

There were a lot of yellow and some purple flowers about, I didn't know what kind. I put them on the graves, stood beside them with my hat off for a few minutes, then I mounted up and rode out of there.

The date on that notiss had been two years old. Had he made it out? Would he find his woman? I had an idea he would be back, and if not, another like him would come along eventually. Over thousands of miles of western lands where pa and me went riding, we saw their burned-out cabins, their burned wagons, their graves, and sometimes their bones, but nothing stopped them. There were always more. Not the wildest of the Indians nor the army itself could keep them back. There was a hunger in them to blaze new trails, to farm new land, to watch the sun rise up over their own acres.

The Indians were magnificent warriors and they themselves had once come from out of nowhere to take the land from those who held it, and to hold it for a while themselves. Guns and arrows may stop an army, but they cannot stop men and women with their dreams.

Three days later I rode into Dodge City and left my horses with Bill Tilghman, who was marshal there. "Turn them into the pasture," he said. "They will be safe there."

"Tilghman?" I said. "My pa knew some Tilghmans back east. There was a Tench Tilghman who was an aide to Washington, back in Revolutionary times."

"We were related," he replied.

He was seated in a chair outside the office. I squatted on my heels. "I'm Kearney McRaven," I told him, "and headed east to claim some property that's been willed to me. There's some coming along who would like to keep me from it, and they are kinfolk, but distant. I am wanting no trouble, but if they come hunting me, I got to stand up to them."

"You planning to be in town long?"

"I'm riding out on the steam cars," I said, "and it will be in the morning. Best I can do."

"Would you leave tonight if I can get you on a train?"

"Sooner the better."

"I believe in avoiding trouble, Mr. McRaven. I will put you on the train tonight."

"They said—"

"I know what they said. I know what they would say, but I also know a man who is going east who would just as soon leave tomorrow. One way to keep the peace in a town, Mr. McRaven, is to recognize the possibilities of trouble beforehand."

"Why I spoke to you. This here is your town, and I am of no mind to make trouble."

"Thank you." He got to his feet. "Leave your horses here and take what you need with you. I'll see they are cared for."

My blanket roll and saddlebags were what I needed. I slung them over my left shoulder, and carrying my rifle, I went along with him. In a matter of minutes I was fixed to leave on the evening train.

"Buy you some dinner?" I suggested. "I am obliged."

"It looks like a busy night," he said, "but thank you, just the same." He turned away, but when he had gone only a few steps, he paused and turned. "McRaven?"

When I stopped, he said, "Those men looking for you . . . what are they like?"

"Those I know are tall, slim men. Favor black frock coats and black hats. Long-faced men who don't smile very much, and they always stay together."

When the steam cars rolled out of town that evening,

I was riding the cushions, setting back there like a king, letting the locomotive take me along. Last thing I saw as I rode out of town was three men riding in. Three long, tall men in black coats.

They were riding side by side and they did not turn their heads toward the train.

Maybe it was them.

Chapter XV

We had ridden the steam cars a time or two when pa and me were traveling, but not enough for me to get used to it. When I came into the car, I dropped into one of the seats upholstered with red plush and I settled back for the ride.

The train was mixed, two freight cars, four cattle cars, a mail car, and two passenger coaches. Hooked on behind was a caboose. The folks in the car with me were a plump young woman, very blond, and two younger versions of her, maybe six or eight years old. There was a stern-looking man with a chin whisker who looked like he had just bitten into something that tasted bad.

A man of about forty sporting a heavy gold watch chain across his vest with an ivory toothpick dangling from it sat in a seat ahead of and just across from me. On the seat right opposite there was a sleeping cowhand. Like me he had a rifle stuck down beside him, and I suspected his belt gun was stuck into his waistband.

There wasn't much to see outside the windows but the wide grasslands and the smoke streaking past. After a while I dozed off. The train was going almighty slow most of the time. This was track that had been laid fast, so they were cautious with it. Once we stopped while several hundred buffalo crossed the track. The towheaded children stared wide-eyed, and even the sour-looking gentleman with the chin whisker leaned forward to see. The cowhand took a look to see what was happening, then went back to sleep. The train whistled and began to inch forward. Over on the trail I saw a stagecoach passing us. A few minutes later, we passed them, the engineer whistling derisively at them. Most places the stages had been put out of business by the railroad, but here and there they hung on, mostly serving off the right-of-way towns.

Sometime during the afternoon we slowed again and stopped. I was half-asleep and did not open my eyes. After a bit the train moved on, bumping and groaning between whistles.

We stopped at a station. There were three or four houses, a big tent with a hotel sign on it, and some large corrals. We ducked out of the train and ran for the eating place, first in, first served. I found myself sitting next to the cowhand.

"Goin' fur?" he asked.

"Carolina . . . if I'm lucky."

He sized me up quizzically. "Expectin' not to be?"

I shrugged. "There's some don't want me to," I said, "mostly back yonder."

"I'm with the cattle," he said: "S'posed to be ridin' the caboose, but what the hell? I never rode no cushions before, so I slipped in here."

"Conductor say anything?"

"Naw. Hell, my boss ships five, six thousand head a year. He ain't about to complain."

The food was antelope steaks fried in rancid grease, but I'd eaten worse. The coffee was good, the bread dry and crumbly. I gulped more coffee, wiped my mouth with the back of my hand, and sprinted for the train. It was whistling, and when we grabbed hold of it we had to run, for it was already moving. I was first on the steps and gave him a hand.

"Thanks," he said. "The boss will be waitin' when we hit Kansas City. Wouldn't want him to find me missin'.'"

"Tough?"

"Tougher'n a boot. Pays well, feeds well, expects to get two days' work for one day's pay."

We both went to sleep. We rumbled over a bridge, slowed down for some reason, and I looked out to see the sun was down, the sky streaked with red, and a herd of antelope keeping pace with the train.

The cowhand looked over at me. "They catch you, what'll they do?"

"Shoot me, or try to. You see, there's money in it for them."

We dozed, and the train rumbled on into the night. There was a smell of coal smoke and cinders in the car. I turned around, trying to find a comfortable spot on a seat that had long since ceased to be comfortable.

He glimpsed the butt of my pistol. "Can you use that thing?" he asked.

"Uh-huh," I said. And after a minute, "Hope I don't have to."

We slowed down again, traveling no faster than a man could walk. "I'm Billy Jenkins," he said suddenly.

"Kearney McRaven," I said, and we shook hands.

"Punch cows?" he asked.

"I have. Held a bunch in the mountains all last winter. Rode down out of the hills an' found they'd killed my pa."

"Same fellers?"

"Uh-huh."

"You get to Kaycee, you see my boss. He's Ben Blocker. Tougher'n a boot, but a good man. You tell him about it. He's tough but he's square. Knows folks."

"Not much anybody can do."

"You just think there ain't. You talk to ol' Ben. He's got him an answer for everything. Mostly he's right."

"Thanks."

The train rumbled on, and we both slept. It was the same, slowing, stopping, picking up speed.

We stopped at a station to take on water. "Got to see to my cows," he said, lurching erect.

"Give you a hand," I said.

We walked back along the cars. Only one was down, and with a couple of long poles we prodded it erect again so it would not be trampled.

"I can't afford to get in no fight," Jenkins said. "I got to think of them cows."

"Ain't askin' you to. It's my fight. Anyway, I think I'm ahead of them . . . unless they wired ahead."

"How many is there?"

"Too many. Maybe a dozen. So far's I know, there were only two or three out west. There's some women-folks, too."

"Young?"

I shrugged. "Young enough. Beautiful . . . like a desert rattler is beautiful."

The train moved out and we dozed again. I awakened with the cold nose of a pistol against my temple, and out of the corner of my eye I saw a tall man in a black coat and black hat standing over me. "Get up," he said. "Get up easy."

A moment I hesitated. Might as well be killed fighting as taken out and be butchered like a sheep. And then I thought of that blond woman and those two youngsters.

"All right," I said, "just take it easy."

Slowly I got to my feet. Billy Jenkins was asleep, or seemed to be. The woman was staring at us, wide-eyed. So was the man with the chin whisker.

Carefully I got up. Another man stood in the end of the car and he had a shotgun in his hands. This was it, then. Even if I tried, they'd blow me apart with that scatter-gun and probably kill or injure the others as well.

"Walk to the back of the car," the tall man said, and when I turned my back to walk, he jerked my six-shooter from my belt and tossed it on the seat.

The man with the chin whisker straightened up. "Here! What are you doing to that man?"

The tall man's voice was deadly. "Pull in your horns, granpa. We're just takin' him for a walk."

"An' set still," the other man commanded. "Set right still."

The train was slowing again. Teetering a little with the uneven movements of the car, I walked back toward where the man with the shotgun stood. He had piercing blue eyes, high cheekbones, and a thin mustache. There was a scar on his chin.

He stepped aside to let me go through the door to the platform that separated this car from the caboose. I stepped onto the platform at the very instant the train shuddered to a stop. Instantly, I moved. My left hand slashed back to hit the gun wrist of the man following me, and at the same moment my right shot up, taking the man with the shotgun under the chin and smashing his head back.

Taking a wild leap, I sprang from the platform into the night. I hit the ground with my knees bent and went head over heels down the slight embankment. I rolled over and came up holding my waist gun, which they hadn't got.

"Kearney!" Jenkins yelled.

I glanced up quickly, and he threw me my other gun. A deft catch and it hit my hand just as one of the men came down the steps. I shot him as he hit the ground. He threw his hands up, and I shot him again, and he turned halfway around and fell, rolling slowly down the bank not a dozen feet from me.

Up at the front of the train I heard curses and the fall of something heavy, like a timber. Evidently the track had been blocked to stop the train, so that meant there was another man out there somewhere in the dark. The train whistled. In a moment I was going to be alone on the plains with one dead man and two who wanted me dead.

Jumping up, I sprinted for the front of the train. A bullet whined past, and I heard the report of a heavy rifle, and then the train beside me was moving. I shoved one gun into my waistband and then the other, hoping they would stay where I put them.

Another shot that kicked up gravel under my feet. The train whistled, and I leaped at the ladder on the end of a cattle car. A bullet ricocheted off the car above me, but by then I had swung between them. Clinging with one hand, I drew a pistol with the other and waited. The train was rolling faster now, but somewhere up ahead there was another man.

I caught a flash of white from a shirtfront and then the red orange blast of a shotgun. Sheer reflex action saved me for that fleeting glimpse of white, and I swung my back against the car following and shot.

It was a waste shot. I hit nothing, but where I'd been that shotgun charge hit, and one of the cattle gave a frightened lunge, smashing against the side of the car. And then we were rolling down the grade ahead. Slowly I holstered my gun and felt for the other. It was still there, behind my belt.

Clinging to the ladder, I tried to catch my breath and slow my heart from its pounding. The train rumbled on into the night.

A long time later I climbed to the top of the train and walked along the top to the car behind. When I reached my car, I climbed down the ladder, swung to the platform, and went in.

Billy Jenkins sat up when he saw me, and the blond woman turned around and stared, as did the two little girls. I walked back and dropped into my seat. "Thanks," I said to Billy.

"Thought you'd need that," he said.

"I did." No need to tell him I carried a spare.

"You get one of them?"

"Uh-huh."

"You didn't see him after?"

"Didn't have time. Didn't need to. I shot where I was looking. He's dead . . . twice."

"One down," Jenkins said.

"Yeah . . . and too many to go."

"Like I said, when you get to Kansas City, you talk to Ben. He always knows what to do."

The man with the chin whiskers no longer looked

sour. "That was fast work, young man," he said, "mighty fast. Who were they?"

"Doesn't matter much," I said. "The name they use isn't their own."

I slipped out my gun and fed three cartridges into it to replace those fired.

"Billy," I said, "when we get to a station, wake me up, will you?"

He nodded. "I will. You go ahead an' sleep. I'll keep watch."

"May have hurt one of your steers," I said. "I think the crosspieces caught part of the shot, but not all of it. You may have a dead crittur on your hands."

"You get some sleep," Jenkins said, "and don't you forget that telegraph. We passed a station back yonder."

Suddenly I could scarcely keep my eyes open. I curled up in the seat, trying to make myself comfortable. Under me the car rumbled and bumped over the rails. The train whistled, a long, lonely call into the darkness.

And then I was asleep.

Chapter XVI

He was seated on the top of the corral watching his cattle when Billy Jenkins led me to him. He wore corduroy pants stuffed down into laced boots, a corduroy jacket with the belt hanging loose, and a narrow-brimmed felt hat. His mustache was dark and streaked with gray. There was a touch of gray at the temples.

"Mr. Blocker? This here is Kearney McRaven. He's got problems, and I told him you could help him."

Blocker rolled his cigar in his teeth and glanced over at me. "Looks like a man who could take care of his own troubles," he said. He motioned to a seat beside him on the corral. "Climb up and sit down."

He glanced down at Billy. "Your report says you're one head short. What happened?"

"That was my fault, sir," I said. "That steer was shot with lead intended for me."

"You catch any of it?"

"A couple of pellets. Done me no harm. Don't know where they picked up that shotgun, but they taken it for granted it was loaded with slugs. It carried bird shot."

"Tell me about it."

So while Billy Jenkins went off about cattle business, I sat on the corral bar and told Ben Blocker about what happened and what I had to do about claiming my property. He listened, rolling his cigar a time or two but making no comment.

"They're a-hunting me, Mr. Blocker," I said, "and I can handle the fighting part of it. Maybe I can handle it all. Trouble is, pa ain't with me no longer and I'd nobody to sort of talk it over with. Billy, he surely sets store by you. He figures you can do anything."

"He's wrong, Kearney. I can't, nor can any man. Looks to me like you're in trouble, all right. But maybe I can help. What you need is a good lawyer."

"Pa always fought shy of lawyers. Said they caused more trouble than they ever settled."

Blocker laughed. "Well ... sometimes. But a good lawyer can save you a lot of trouble. For instance, I know one right here in Kansas City who was born in Carolina. He knows folks down there. More than that, he's figuring on taking a trip home right soon. We'd better go see him."

"No, sir."

"What?" He looked around at me. "Did you say no?"

"Yes, sir. I don't want to get him killed. Or tangled

up with them women, either. Maybe we could get him to come to you . . . not me. Maybe I could sort of drop in on you, like."

"You think you'll be watched? And if you went to a lawyer's office they'd guess why?"

"Yes, sir. And they'd kill him. I mean that, sir. This bunch are like wolves. They kill first and ask questions afterward. Killing the wrong man doesn't mean *that* to them. I've been watching and I've seen nobody around, so they don't have me located yet, but by nightfall they will."

Blocker took out a heavy gold watch and glanced at it. "All right. These stockyards are in what is called the West Bottoms. You meet me at six o'clock in the Livestock Exchange, at Twelth and State Line. We can talk there."

He paused, looking at me again. "Have you got walking-around money?"

"Yes, sir. I have enough, sir."

"See you there." Blocker dropped off the fence. "Keep out of trouble now. This here is a fast town."

Carrying my rifle, saddlebags, and blanket roll, I headed uptown, keeping off the busy streets. Mostly I was worried about all that money I was carrying, so I headed for the Wells Fargo office.

Now, coming in off the street I looked pretty rough, but Wells Fargo had done business with rough-looking men since the gold rush in California. "I want to make a deposit," I told the man in the office.

He looked me over carefully. "All right. How much?"

"Have you got a private office? I want to get in out of sight."

He looked at me again. "Come right along," he said, and indicated that I should walk ahead of him.

Seated in his office, I taken up my saddlebags and began taking out the money. He never turned a hair. In those days a man never knew who was carrying money and who wasn't, and there were men selling stock down in the Bottoms or at the Exchange who looked a lot rougher than me.

It came to nine thousand seven hundred and fifty-two

dollars. "I'll keep the seventy fifty-two," I said. "I'll need some walking-around money."

"That should do it," he commented dryly. "Now, your name?"

"Kearney McRaven." I hesitated, "Anything happens to me, this here is to go to Miss Laurie McCrae of Silverton, Colorado Territory."

"My name is Eliot," the Wells Fargo man said. "This is quite a large sum of money."

I pocketed my receipt. "If it's all right with you, I'll leave my rifle and my gear with you. I've got some running around to do, and it wouldn't look right to be packing a rifle."

"Stay away from gambling, Mr. McRaven," Eliot suggested.

"Thanks," I said, "but I'm not inclined that way. Do you know Ben Blocker?"

"Of course." Eliot's interest was obvious. "We all know Mr. Blocker and we have all done business with him. I had no idea you were an associate of his."

Well, I wasn't quite sure what he meant by associate, but it sounded right so I didn't argue the point. "Look," I said, "there's been some shooting trouble back down the line, so if a couple of men come hunting me, you don't know anything about me. It won't be a lie, because you surely don't know much, but above all don't tell them where I went. I don't want any trouble in Kansas City."

"Is the law involved?" Eliot asked. "We cooperate with officers whenever we can."

"So would I, if they seemed to need it. So far the law has taken no interest in what's going on, and I don't think they will. Seems to me most officers right now are more concerned with what happens in their own town without hunting trouble outside it."

He noticed my holstered gun. It was barely covered by my coat, but the tip of the holster showed. "You can be arrested in this town for carrying a weapon," he said. "You know, this isn't Dodge City."

I grinned at him. "I surely know it, Mr. Eliot, but

I'd sooner be arrested than killed, which is what I have to think about."

At six o'clock I was at the Livestock Exchange, and the first person I saw was Ben Blocker.

"Good! I was getting worried. We have an appointment at the House of Lords." Then he added, "It's a gambling house, but you can get the best food in town there . . . if they know you."

"All right," I agreed, "but I don't gamble. Fact is, I was just warned against it by Mr. Eliot over at Wells Fargo."

"A good man," Blocker said. "We've done business from time to time."

As we walked up the street, he explained a little about his business, buying cattle in Texas and driving them north to the market, sometimes holding them on good grass until they were well fattened before bringing them to market. I had worked with enough stock to know competence, and had been impressed by the way people responded to his name.

"Mr. Blocker," I said hesitantly, "when you buy cattle, do you ever have partners?"

"Almost always. Cattle buying isn't as lucrative as it once was. Prices for cattle bought on the range in Texas have gone up, and so have the expenses of making a drive, but there's still money to be made."

"I'd like to get into something like that," I said, "but I've been thinking of ranching, too. There's mighty fine grass in the mountains out Colorado and Wyoming way, and the cattle can winter on the range."

"I've heard of that." He glanced at me. "You've experience with that?"

"Yes, sir. I held a herd on grass all last winter, and they came off in fine shape. The grass cures on the stem, and you won't find any better feed anywhere. The trouble is that most of them are so hungry for profit they overgraze. Seems to me from what I've seen that small herds of mixed longhorn and Durham or longhorn and Hereford do the best."

We stopped outside the door of the House of Lords.

I was looking around warily. I'd seen two men following us and I said, "Mr. Blocker, there's two men behind
us who've been following right along. You'd better get
inside."

He smiled and put his hand on my arm. "Son, don't
worry about it. Those are my men ... just in case. Billy
Jenkins is one of them, because he saw those men who
attacked you. The other one is Carlin Cable."

"I've heard the name."

Blocker chuckled. "So have a lot of others. He's a
good man with a gun."

When we were seated at a table in a quiet corner,
Ben Blocker ordered dinner. "Charlie will be along
soon. His name is Attmore. Good man, with connections in the South. He came from the Carolinas or
Georgia, I'm not sure which, but he will know what
you're talking about."

He paused for a minute, his eyes sweeping the crowd
in the gambling hall below. "You spoke of investing in
cattle. How much money are you talking about?"

"Two or three thousand dollars," I said.

"That isn't all you have, I hope?"

"No, sir."

"Good! Never put all your eggs in one basket, to re-
peat an old saying. At going prices, two thousand dollars will buy and deliver at the railroad about one
hundred head of steers. No one can be sure what the
market will be, but this year I brought them to Dodge
City for eighteen dollars a head and sold for twenty-
eight. Last year I started three herds over the trail. Indians stampeded one of them and managed to drive off
about two hundred head. We lost a half dozen swimming a swollen river, and two more were killed in that
stampede. All that cuts into the profits, as you can see."

A short, fat man suddenly appeared at the table. He
wore a gray suit, obviously tailored for him. His face
was florid, his shock of white hair carefully combed. He
carried a wide-brimmed hat in his hand. "Ben! It's good
to see you! And this," he said, turning to me, "will be
Mr. McRaven? How do you do, sir? It's a pleasure, a
great pleasure!"

"Sit down, Charlie, and order. Then we can talk."

When I left my gear at the Wells Fargo office, I had kept with me my father's buckskin case. Now I took it out and spread the papers before him.

He glanced at the map first. He looked at it, looked again, and swore softly. "Yes, yes! Well, I'll be damned!" He looked up at me and tapped the largest plantation marked on the map. "You know the story about this place? They say it's haunted."

"Considering some of my relatives, I'm not surprised."

He chuckled. "Met them, have you? Met Delphine? Oh, she's a pretty one!"

He turned to Blocker. "Yes, I know the story, know the area, and that's not surprising, because a lot of people do. That plantation has a bloody history, right from the beginning, but it's a valuable piece of property."

Briefly, I explained the circumstances of pa's death and what had happened since.

"You killed one of them? You're sure?"

"Yes, sir. I know where I put my shots, sir. Either one would have killed him."

"They're a bad lot, Ben, a bad lot. I've known them or known of them since they were boys. Yant isn't their name. It is L'Ollonaise. Whether they were related to the pirate of that name, I do not know. One of the boys was reared by a very decent family named Yant, but he ran away and left them. They have used the name intermittently ever since, as well as others."

"The one with the scar on his chin?"

"Elias, and one of the most dangerous of them. A dead shot and a master with any sort of weapon. He killed a man in Charleston when he was but fourteen. He got off because he was so young and the man he killed was a notoriously quarrelsome man. Later he killed a man in a duel at Mobile, another in New Orleans. It is a question between he and Felix as to who is the most dangerous."

"Not a pleasant family," Blocker said wryly.

"You are right. Nobody ever wanted to cross them,

because sooner or later, on one pretext or another, there would be a challenge. Nowadays a lot of us have forgotten how prevalent dueling was in the old days."

Attmore glanced at me. "What is it you wish me to do?"

"Take the necessary steps so I can inherit," I said.

He had been glancing through the papers as he talked, and now he shrugged. "Nothing so very difficult here. You may have to actually go there to take possession."

"Then I shall go."

"If you do, please remember an attempt was made to poison your father, and at least one attempt to poison you. They will not give up, even after you have inherited, for they will still be next in line."

Suddenly I glimpsed Billy Jenkins coming across the room, weaving through the crowd of gamblers and sightseers. "Boss," he said to Blocker, "they're coming up the street now. There's four of them, alike as peas in a pod."

Chapter XVII

Attmore glanced at them, then at a nearby table, lifting his hand to his hat as he did so. "Rest easy," he said to me, "nothing will happen."

Jenkins had fallen back a few steps from the table, and I saw Carlin Cable come moving up behind the L'Ollonaise men.

They moved up to our table and ranged themselves

before it, staring hard at me, then glancing at the other two. "Sit tight, gentlemen." It was Elias, he with the scar. "We only wish to talk to McRaven here."

"I doubt if we have anything to talk about," I replied, "and whatever it might be, you are wasting your time."

"I think not," he said, and brushed his coat back. He had a gun in his waistband, a hand resting on it. "If you will come along with us there need be no trouble."

A quiet voice spoke from behind them. "Gentlemen? I am Tom Speers, the city marshal. Is there something I can do for you?"

It was the man to whom Charlie Attmore had gestured. Beside him were two other men, both tough, competent-looking men. Elias glanced over his shoulder and saw Billy Jenkins and Carlin Cable. Two more men, obviously Texas cowhands, loitered near the door.

Elias let his hand fall. "No, I am afraid not, Marshal. We wanted to talk to Mr. McRaven here, but it can wait."

"Of course," Speers replied quietly, "but not in Kansas City. Do you understand?" He gestured about him. "In this room now and before the night is over there will be twenty-five of the most noted gunfighters in the West. All are my friends, all of them avoid trouble in Kansas City, and all of them would be very upset if anything happened here to disturb the situation. They come here to relax when not handling cattle or hunting buffalo. They know how much I enjoy a quiet town."

He took a gold watch from his pocket. "Nearly eight o'clock, gentlemen. I've just had your horses brought up outside. By eight-thirty you should be outside of town and moving away. I might add that if you are not, a posse made up of the men I mentioned will apprehend you, and sometimes it takes eight or nine months to bring such a case to trial. I know," he said, gesturing with a careless hand, "it isn't very efficient of us, but that's the way it is."

Elias L'Ollonaise shrugged. "Of course. We understand perfectly and would no nothing to disturb the tranquility of your fair city." He smiled thinly. "Thank you for bringing our horses around. We came in by train and weren't aware we had any."

"You have now," Speers replied cheerfully. "I can't offer any promises as to their quality or disposition, but they are horses."

Elias glanced at me. "We'll be meeting again, I think."

"Of course," I replied cheerfully, "but didn't we meet before? On a train?"

The only visible signs of anger were in a tightening of the lips. "We remember," he said coolly, "and we won't forget. When it is something like that, we never forget."

They were escorted from the room, and Attmore shook his head. "Had me worried there for a minute, but I'd told Tom what might be expected."

"You're giving them horses?" I asked, skeptically.

"I am," Blocker said. "They are four of my remuda on the last drive. They either made trouble or didn't stand up to the rough work. I'm well rid of them."

"Saddles?"

Blocker shook his head. "I didn't go that far. They will ride bareback with rope hackamores." He smiled. "One of those horses is a bucker, a very mean, deceptive bucker. He will go along quietly until something startles him or he takes a notion."

Attmore tapped the papers before him. "Lucky Ben caught me when he did. I leave for Charleston tomorrow, and I'll see what can be done about this. In the event that I need you, you will be here?"

"I'll be in touch with Mr. Blocker and with Tom Speers as well. One or the other will be able to locate me at any time. I'll get my mail at the Livestock Exchange."

"Fair enough." We shook hands. "One more thing. Do not imagine you have defeated them."

Nobody needed to tell me how lucky I had been, and how lucky I continued to be. We ate our supper and I talked almost none at all, leaving that to Ben Blocker and Attmore. Sitting there, wrapped in my own thoughts, I thought about all that had transpired since that day when I came down from the mountains to find my father had been killed.

Whatever I might inherit was still a vague dream that did not seem quite real to me. Never until pa died and left the money he won gambling had I had even a penny I had not worked for, and worked hard.

A few things I had learned. A poor man gets little respect from strangers. If he is a good honest workman who does his job well, even if he is poor, he will get respect from those who know him.

I'd never known a thief who was what you would call a poor man. The thieves I'd known, and knocking about as pa and me had, I'd known aplenty, were always folks who had a little and wanted more ... without working for it.

They stole because they wanted money to spend on women, gambling, or flashy clothes. They weren't willing to earn their way into affluence, but wanted to steal from somebody who had earned it.

Using the effort spent in tracking pa and me down, the Yants or L'Ollonaises or whatever they called themselves could have been well-off. Of course, they were a special kettle of fish and there was vindictiveness involved in their pursuit of us.

"About those cattle," I said to Blocker. "I want to buy a hundred head of steers to sell, and I want to buy a hundred head of young breeding stock to drive to Colorado."

"I've a man in Beeville who is buying stock for me. You write me a draft on your Wells Fargo account, and he will do the buying for you as well."

He turned to the lawyer. "Attmore, this young man has been herding cattle in Colorado and Wyoming. He knows the country. He says the grass cures on the stem and cattle will fatten on the range there. I think we should pool our resources and locate a ranch—"

"Two ranches," I said, "one at a lower elevation to which we can drive in bad winters. I know some good locations if nobody has moved in since I left."

"We would need somebody to handle the ranching operation," Attmore said.

"I could do that," I said, thinking of Laurie. "I've been thinking of locating out there, somewhere on the western slope of the Rockies."

We talked for an hour or more, discussing all aspects of the problem, and I surprised myself. Never before had I had to come up with answers, but my hard work on the range with cattle and horses, and in some cases sheep, had taught me more than I'd realized. At the time I had not been thinking of going into the cattle business but only doing the job at hand, yet in the process I had learned a lot. For the first time I began to think of settling down, ranching, and the problems involved. "We'd need more than my hundred head of young stuff," I said. "We should start with five or six hundred at least."

"We will start with two thousand," Blocker said. "Attmore and I will provide the stock, other than your hundred head, and we will provide the working capital. You will handle the project on the ground itself. You will get one third—"

"Fifty percent," I said.

"What?" Blocker stared at me.

"I get fifty percent, each of you get twenty-five percent. You will provide the capital, but I will be working every day of the year to see that our investment pays off. I will have to check range conditions and water, handle any rustlers, deal with Indians, and either do or take charge of all the work involved. Furthermore," I said, "I will have to scout the country for a suitable ranch site, which will take a good deal of doing in itself, and then hold it against others who might fancy my location."

Blocker glanced over at Attmore. "He's got a point, Charlie."

"Yes," Attmore agreed reluctantly, "so he has. Neither of us could afford either the time or the energy to explore that country, while he probably knows right where to go."

"Each of us has to sell what he has," I said, feeling a little smug, for it was the first actual business deal I had ever made for myself.

"It's agreed then?" Blocker said. "And as soon as you've finished this business in Carolina, you'll go west?"

"I will."

We talked on for another hour and then, growing tired, I stood up, suddenly realizing I had no place to sleep and my bedroll was undoubtedly locked in the Wells Fargo office.

"No problem," Blocker said, when I explained. "Right down the street there's a hotel . . . a good one, too. At this time of night Sam Dean will be on the desk. You just tell him Ben Blocker sent you."

Tired as I was, I was glad it would be no further. On the street I stopped for a minute, looking around. Several men stood on the curb, talking and chewing tobacco, and further down the street was another saloon and a crowd of men stood before it. Beyond it I could see a hotel sign. It must be the one Blocker mentioned.

Turning, I started going along the street. Suddenly a voice spoke almost at my elbow. "Sir?"

She was small, seemed scarcely more than a girl, and sedately dressed, but well dressed. She had big dark eyes and a lovely clear complexion. "Sir? Would you walk me past those men? It is very late, and I—"

She took my arm. "Please! My father would die if he knew I was on the street at this hour, but Amy had so much to tell me and we hadn't seen each other in so long and the time just *flew!*"

As we spoke, we were walking along. She did not look like the sort of girl who would accost a man on the street, and I was going that way anyhow.

"It isn't far. Just around the corner. Oh, I am so glad you came along! I didn't know what to do, and some of those men looked so *rough!*"

"Is this your home?"

"Oh, dear, no! My home is in Virginia, but papa had to come out here to buy *cattle*. And he is selling some horses, too. We *raise* horses, you know, and papa said these cattlemen are getting so they want fine stock and not just those grubby Mexican horses . . . mustangs, they call them."

I was accutely conscious of the fact that I was still wearing a shirt I'd had on for three days and that my suit was needing a good brushing. With my free hand I straightened my tie.

Suddenly we were passing my hotel. I glanced inside and glimpsed a man behind the desk wearing a green eyeshade and sleeve garters. "This is my hotel," I said. I was dead tired, and pretty or not, I needed sleep. In another few minutes I'd be flat on my face.

"Please? It's just around the corner."

"All right," I said, "but I'm just about all in. I—"

We turned the corner and suddenly her hands gripped hard on my right sleeve. "All right, here he is, *kill him!*"

Chapter XVIII

Had there been time to think, I would have blessed my father. "Someday," he told me when I was very young, "you may not have the use of your right hand, if only for a few days, so learn to use your left."

Boxing, where a left is of first importance, helped a lot, but I had deliberately used it for many things, becoming able to use it with saw or hammer as well as my right. Of course, I learned to use a pistol as well.

My left hand drew the pistol without even thinking, and I fired. They were close together and coming at me, and I must have hit something. Jerking my right arm free, I sent her staggering toward them, fired again, and dodged around the corner.

Thrusting the gun into my waistband, I stepped into the hotel. The night clerk was on his feet, spectacles in his hand. "What's going on out there?" he asked.

"Damned if I know," I replied. "Ben Blocker told me to come to you and you'd fix me up with a room. I was almost to the door when the shooting started. I ran."

"Wise," he said. He pushed the register toward me. "Sign right there. It will be number twelve, upstairs on the right."

People were running in the street outside, and there were shouts. "Crazy!" I commented. "A man's a fool to go where there's shooting. It's a good way to get killed."

"You're right," he said, "but the world is full of rubbernecks. They want to see everything."

Locking the door behind me, I reloaded the empty chambers and put the gun on the dresser. Then I took off my coat and shirt, washed my hands and face, and pulling off my boots, I lay down on the bed.

Just what happened out there I did not know. They had been close together and coming at me, but even so I might have missed. They had fired, but obviously I had not been hit. I had seen the girl fall, but that might have been from being off balance as I jerked free. In any event, Tom Speers was not going to like it.

There was much confusion in the street below, but I had not lighted a light, wishing to attract no undue attention. For a long time I lay awake, thinking. Attmore would discover what must be done to claim my inheritance, but that would take time. In the meantime there was nothing to be done here. I could go to Carolina myself or go back west and wait to see what was happening.

If I went west, I could scout the location for our ranch. I had a few ideas, but I'd be looking at the country with new eyes as it is one thing to ride through a country, another to plan a ranching operation, and the right location would be important. We had only discussed cattle, but I was also thinking of sheep as a possibility. Although I'd herded cattle and worked on ranches here and there, I'd never picked up the average cattle rancher's dislike of sheep. Given the right area and management, they might be better and steadier money than cattle, but that needed some looking into.

Lying there on my back, I considered all aspects. Finally I got undressed and into bed, but with a pistol at hand. Getting shot at was no pleasure, and although they were hunting me, I was not hunting them. I wanted to get out from under and I felt safer out west.

That girl now, the one who grabbed my arm . . . was she one of them or somebody they hired for the job?

It wasn't until I got dressed the next morning that I found the bullet hole through the side of my coat. It had been hanging open, and the bullet had made two holes.

That had been close . . . much too close.

For several minutes before going down the stairs, I studied the street outside. There was only a little I could see of my own side of the street, but across the street there was nobody.

When I reached the lobby, a place with hide-covered chairs and several buffalo and elk heads on the walls, there were men standing around and talking. The air was thick with cigar and pipe smoke.

"Shot," somebody said. "They found her on the street after that shooting. She's not dead, but she was hit twice."

"Who did it?"

"Who knows? It was some more of that night shooting that has been going on. She was a new girl over at Mary's place."

"Why would anybody want to *kill* her?"

"Speers believes she got mixed up in something that did not concern her. Right now he's looking for a wounded man. He found some spatters of blood on the walk about twenty feet from where she fell."

Ben Blocker was at the Livestock Exchange when I came in. He waved at me to come over, and I crossed the room to sit with him. There were at least twenty men scattered around the room but nobody who looked familiar.

Ben threw me a sharp look. "Shooting last night," he said.

"So I heard."

We had some bacon and eggs, and I told him I was leaving. "My problem," I added, "is getting out of town. Obviously they are watching me."

Blocker took out a fresh cigar and removed the band. He glanced at it, then bit off the end and spat it out. He reached for his vest pocket and lifted out his watch. He glanced at it. "Steamboat," he suggested, "to Leavenworth. I can arrange for you to pick up a horse there. You can catch the steam cars further west, if you like."

"My problem," I explained, "is that I don't know who to look for. Some of them I know, some I don't, and there are so many they can hire."

Blocker shrugged. "Know what you mean. There's a good fifty men within a dozen blocks of here who would kill a man for fifty dollars."

He glanced at me. "That shooting last night. Were you involved in that?"

Briefly, I told him what had happened. "It was dark around that corner. I don't know whether there were two or three of them. She grabbed my arm, and when I threw her off she must have staggered toward them, and they shot. At least one of them shot at me." I showed him the holes in my coat. "And I shot twice at them, nicked one of them, I think. But my bullets didn't hit her. She was well off to my right. I am sure they shot her by mistake, or she fell in the line of their fire."

We finished our coffee. "That steamboat ... when does it leave?"

He glanced at his watch again. "You've got an hour."

I got up. "That girl ... where would she be?"

"Down the street ... at Mary's place."

"I want to see her."

"Stay away from her. You're in the clear. Not a thing to tie you to it, and there may be an inquiry. Will be, I should say."

"Take me a minute."

He shrugged. "I'll go with you then." He glanced across the room, motioning to Billy Jenkins and Carlin Cable.

She was fully conscious when they showed me to her room. She was lying in bed, her face very pale, her large brown eyes, really beautiful eyes, seeming even larger now.

She was scared when she saw me. Blocker carried such an air of authority that she was sure he was an officer.

"I'm sorry you got hurt," I said. "I didn't mean for that to happen."

She was very cool. "I tried to get you killed," she said. "They paid me."

"How much?"

She flushed. "I was to get fifty dollars, which they paid me, and fifty more if you were killed."

"Is it so easy to get a man killed?" I asked.

She shrugged. "I've seen them killed for less. What do you want with me?"

"Nothing . . . except to say I am still sorry. And you earned your money, even if it didn't work."

"You're very good, you know," she commented. "Nobody so much as thought about you shooting with your left hand. I was to keep your right hand in a tight grip and press against your gun."

"They really didn't care about you, did they? Standing that close, there was every chance you'd get shot."

"I mentioned that. They said they couldn't miss at that range." She turned her eyes back to mine. "If you say I said any of this, I'll say you're a liar."

"You're a cold-hearted little devil," I replied, "but I am not going to say anything. I am just sorry you got shot."

Taking fifty dollars from my pocket, I gave it to her. "Get well," I said. "And if you hope to live long, stay out of such things."

She took the fifty dollars. "You are a fool," she said, "but if you wish to remain a live fool, watch out for the blond one."

She would say no more, and we left, and when the

steamboat left the landing, I was upon it. Standing by
the rail, alone in the darkness, I asked myself why I
had not gone east? Was I afraid? Perhaps, I admitted,
but mostly it was distaste at what I might find there.
The country itself I knew I would love, but I wanted
no more to do with the L'Ollonaises. After all, my
future lay in the West. I liked Blocker. He was a solid,
simple-man, but a shrewd man of business and just
such a one as I needed. The cattle on the range I could
handle, but the business I would leave to him.

My thoughts kept returning to Laurie, in Silverton.
On a sudden inspiration I went below and sat down in
the main cabin and wrote her a letter.

There were few passengers aboard, and I kept to myself. So much had happened since the death of my
father that there had scarcely been time to take stock,
but I felt that now was the time to stop roaming about
and to make something of myself. All about me the
country was growing, expanding, developing, and I
wanted very much to be a part of it. Also, Felix Yant's
questions as to what I intended to make of myself had
irritated me. He had left me feeling inadequate, and
less than I should be.

What had become of him? Where was he now? The
man was dedicated to killing me, yet there was something about him that I liked. Was it his resemblance to
my father? Or to myself?

Suddenly I looked about me. How did I know he
was not near? Or some of the others? And what had that
girl meant when she warned me against 'the blond
one'? She would say no more, having said that, and I
knew not who she meant, or whether it was man or
woman.

At Leavenworth I took a room at the National Hotel,
bought a newspaper, and scanned it. There was a presi-
dential election coming, and with shame I realized I
knew nothing of either man, nor had I ever taken interest in politics or government, unusual in my time, for
politics was the chief subject of conversation wherever
one went.

My world was too narrow, too involved with myself

and my own problems, and this when I lived in the land where government was the business of every man and such a government could only do well if each of us voted with intelligence. I shook the paper irritably. My father had talked of such things and I had listened with only half an ear, yet at the Livestock Exchange men had talked of little else.

Determined to become more than I was, I read the paper through, each item betraying to me how little I knew. My father had tried to give me something of an education, but since then I had done nothing to further it.

When morning came, I ate a quick breakfast in the hotel's dining room and then went down Delaware Street to Sidney Smith's Book and Stationery Store.

Although I'd never done it myself, being too busy herding cattle, cutting railroad ties, or whatever, I knew that most men spent a lot of time in courtrooms. The popular heroes of the West were less likely to be stage drivers or gunfighters than lawyers. To hear one of the best-known lawyers plead a case, men would ride for miles, and when court was in session a western town was crowded with people. Most of those frontier lawyers were handy with quotations from Alexander Pope, from Shakespeare, Milton, Gray, or Francis Bacon as well as the Bible.

The lawyers knew the public came for the show, and they usually managed to put on a performance. There were always a few men sitting around the cracker barrel in a store or on a bench in front of a saloon or the post office talking about trials. It was the theater of the West, before there was any theater. Lawyers were much admired, their quotations recognized like old friends, and their arguments analyzed. Nobody had to ask if court was in session in a western town, you only had to notice the number of rigs tied to the hitching rails, the number of men in black broadcloth, and the women in their Sunday-go-to-meeting clothes. They came from miles out in the country and they brought picnic lunches. Many of the lawyers knew but little law, but they were long on common sense, the logic born of the frontier

itself coupled with a shrewdness in reading people and
juries. The emotional appeal was important, and they
wasted no opportunities.

Time and again I'd heard them quote, but I'd never
read the books they quoted from, although a surprising
number of the courtroom followers had.

The bookstore was well stocked, but I didn't know
where to start. I ended up buying copies of Appleton's
and Blackwood's magazines, *The Wealth of Nations*
by Adam Smith, and *The Lady of the Lake* by Sir
Walter Scott. I knew nothing of either book except that
pa had often talked about Scott and he had read me
most of *Ivanhoe*. Once in a while when we were riding
out across the country pa would recite poetry, of which
he knew a lot. One I remembered was *Lochinvar,* by
Scott. It was very popular all over the West. In a saloon
one time, I heard a drunken cowpuncher recite most
of it.

There was at least one more bookstore in town, operated by a Mr. Morgan, but I had no more time. The
longer I remained, the greater were my chances of
being located, if that had not happened already.

At the bar of the Star of the West Saloon I found my
man. He had been described, so I knew him on sight.
He was a slim, dark man with a hawklike nose wearing
a derby and a black broadcloth suit.

"Hobie Jackman?" I asked.

He gave me a quick, hard look. "It is," he said.

"Ben Blocker sent me." I paused. "He said you'd
give me a horse . . . or provide one."

"A horse, is it? A fast horse?"

"Fast is all right," I said. "A stayer is more important. I am riding west. I might need him as far as
Abilene."

He paid for his drink and turned toward the door,
and I followed. "Have you eaten?" he asked suddenly.
"I was just about to have a bite next door at Delmonico's."

I'd been browsing in the bookstore longer than intended, and it was nigh time for a noontime meal. "All
right," I said, not knowing if there was some other pur-

pose in his suggestion. He was a sharp-looking character, not the sort of man with whom to trade horses.

Delmonico's was in a two-story brick building not exactly next door, but close. We got a table near the wall, where I could watch the door. He let me choose my seat, and when I chose the one where I could watch the door, he smiled for the first time. When he sat down, I saw he was packing a gun in a shoulder holster. I had not seen many of them, but heard of them.

"Play cards?" he asked suddenly.

"I don't know enough about them," I replied.

He smiled again. His teeth were white and even, and when he smiled he was an attractive man. "Nobody does," he said, "only some of us think we do."

We ordered beef stew, mashed potatoes, and coffee. He said suddenly, "Got the rigging? I mean, do you have a saddle?"

"Not with me. I came east on the cars."

"All right." The food was served and we ate. "Where are you staying? The National or the Planters?"

When I told him, he nodded again. "If you've got any gear, get it and pay your bill. Don't waste any time. I don't know what the trouble is and don't want to know."

"It isn't the law," I said.

He shrugged. "That's what I figured. I know Ben Blocker and he's a straight shooter. Saved my bacon once, but that's awhile back." He looked at me quickly. "Anybody I should be looking out for?"

So I told him about the L'Ollanaises and about the women. He flashed his teeth at me over that. "Beautiful as that? I'd let 'em catch up."

"You wouldn't," I said. "They fancy poison and have no hesitation about using it."

"Come down Fourth Street," he said. "It will be the old red barn setting back off the street. Better move fast."

At the National I picked up my blanket roll and my rifle. A quick glance around the lobby showed no familiar face, and nobody was paying attention. As I had paid when I took the room and had nothing more to say, I walked swiftly into the street and headed for Fourth. There had not been time for them to get here, yet I was worried. Suppose they had guessed which way I'd run. And expected me to run.

Hobie Jackman was standing outside the barn and he had a saddled sorrel horse standing ready. It was a handsome animal, looked to have some Morgan strain, which spoke well for him.

"What do I owe you?" I said.

He waved a hand. "Any friend of Ben's is a friend of mine. The hostler at the Drover's Cottage will take the horse. If you need him further, keep him."

Swinging into the saddle, I shoved my rifle into the boot. "Thanks," I said.

"One more thing. Stay off the trail when it gets close to the railroad. They can see you from the cars and be waiting up ahead."

Turning the sorrel, I rode out of town. Glancing back, I saw Hobie Jackman standing there, looking after me. I wondered about him. There was something quiet, sure, and deft about him. Whoever he was, he was a dangerous man, a skilled man at whatever he did. There was no waste motion about him, and no wasted words.

The saddlebags were stuffed. Opening the flap on one, I saw it was packed with food. A square of bacon wrapped in brown paper, some coffee, some biscuits. In the other bag was about four handsful of .44 cartridges. Mr. Hobie Jackman was a knowing man.

Twenty miles west I made camp under some cottonwoods in a hollow off the road.

Abilene was no longer a cow town. The trail drivers had long since worn out their welcome, and the railroad had gone on west. Turning into the street, I glimpsed a slim, blond man in a black, flat-brimmed hat standing on a corner. He wore a tied-down holster with no gun in it. Abilene no longer cared for pistol toters. Turning the sorrel around, I rode into an alley and along it, and then I simply rode out of town. That night I stopped at a farm well off the road and out of sight.

Probably that man was an innocent stranger, but I was taking no chances. That he was not a resident was obvious from the holster.

He just might have been the blond man I was to watch out for. If that girl had been telling the truth, and if it was a man she had meant.

Chapter XIX

At the livery stable in Hays City I asked the hostler if he knew Hobie Jackman. He looked at me, tamped tobacco in his pipe, and said, "I know him."

"He loaned me this horse. Will you hold it for him?"

"Surest thing. You need never worry about no horse of Jackman's, not in this country." He spat. "Hobie Jackman's knowed all up and down the country, mister. Minute you rode in I knew that was a Jackman horse. Even before I seen the brand."

"I'll need another horse."

"Got me another Jackman horse here, young man. He's a black . . . fine horse. Do you?"

He indicated the horse, and I nodded. I should not have needed to look, for I was beginning to understand that a Jackman horse could not be bad.

"You know Bill Tilghman?"

"Everybody does, mister."

"He'll have the horse, if there's any question."

"I never answer questions of that kind, mister. Who rides through here passes in the night as far as I'm concerned. Anyway, any friend of Bill's is a friend of mine."

On impulse, I asked, "How about Hobie?"

"He pays his bills. Takes good care of his stock."

Switching saddles, I stopped by the store for a few odds and ends, then rode down Big Creek toward the southeast for a couple of miles, then skirted a clump of brush and a few trees and headed off to the southwest. That night I made camp in Longout Hollow. Riding out before the stars faded, I was crossing the Smoky Hill when the sun came up.

It was a long riding country with nothing anywhere you looked but distance, miles upon miles of grass with nothing in sight but occasional herds of antelope. Once I sighted a prairie falcon, and jackrabbits aplenty. There'd been scattered showers, so we made no dust, and I was thankful for it. I rode west, then turned up Wildon Draw, skirted the Round-House Hills, and made camp on Big Timber.

Since the buffalo had grown fewer, the grass was growing up. This was mixed grass country I was in, western wheat-grass mixed with bluestem and patches of crazy weed, whose blossoms made great patches of pink and rose on the low hills.

It was a fine country for riding, but I was riding wary of trouble. Felix Yant was somewhere about, and like all of that L'Ollonaise crowd, he had a gift for showing up when least expected. Yant had apparently not come east at all, just setting back there in Colorado waiting for me to come back like he knew I would. Yet if he was expecting me to visit Teresa, he was wrong. I'd put her from my thoughts, not liking the way she cottoned up to Yant while I was westward.

Nobody needed to tell me I'd had the breaks. Sure, I could shoot and I could get into action pretty fast, but I'd been lucky, too, and I could not expect to be lucky all the time.

Bill Tilghman was on the street when I met him. He recognized me at once. He smiled as he noticed the horse I was riding. "I see you have met Hobie. Well, you will be able to tell your grandchildren about him. Do you mind my asking how you met?"

So I told him about Ben Blocker and Mr. Attmore, and also about the trouble on the railroad and the further trouble in Kansas City. He listened without comment until I finished and then he said, "I can have your horses brought in tonight."

"Thanks. I want to leave by daybreak."

"The men you mentioned," he said, "came in shortly after you left. One of them went back toward the west. I have not seen them since."

"And I hope *I* don't. I am not afraid of them, but I want no trouble I can avoid. I'll get my horses and ride out. I'm heading for the western slope of the Rockies."

"I've heard of it." I thought he sounded a bit wistful. "I doubt if I will ever get so far."

In the morning my horses were there, and I mounted up. My roan gave me enough of a workout to let me know he hadn't lost anything, and then with a good pack of grub I headed west. At noon I had miles behind me, so I took a short rest and switched horses. That night I camped in a draw just back from the Arkansas River.

In the middle of the night, I awakened suddenly. All was still, but the horses had their heads up and were looking down toward the riverbed.

It took me only a minute to get my boots and pants on. I swung the gun belt around my waist and drew it to the right notch. A glance at my fire showed it was still holding a faint red glow, and I swore softly. If the wind was right, they could smell that . . . or at least I would.

Moving like a ghost, I got my horses in close, rolled my bed, and saddled up, taking a moment every now and again to listen.

A glance at the stars told me I'd slept about two hours. If that was Yant down there, he had been watching Dodge. Probably spotted my horses and figured I'd return for them.

Careful to make no sound, I sifted dirt over my fire

and rode out of there, walking my horses where I knew
the soft grass was. Not until I had a quarter of a mile
behind me did I start to run for distance. Turning
southwest past the sand hills, I headed for the Cimarron. Striking another area of soft sand, I held to it until
there were no tracks for him to find and then I rode due
west.

After a bit I turned sharply south along a shallow
stream-bed and made dry camp that night in a buffalo
wallow. Next day I came up to the railroad.

A dozen empty cars, picked up from sidings here
and there. The train had stopped at another siding, and
they were coupling up to another empty freight car.
There was an earthen ramp there for loading, and I
rode up to the trainman. "How's for a ride? The horses
an' me?"

He glanced at me. "Cost you a couple of dollars,"
he said.

"Three," I said, "if you let me off this side of La
Junta."

We led the horses into the empty boxcar and tied
them at one end. Then I went back outside and scuffed
out the horses' tracks. He watched me skeptically.

"You dodgin' the law?"

"No. But I'm dodging."

He chuckled. "Better get that boot track yonder,
then. No railroad man wears high-heeled boots."

When I was aboard, he gave the signal and the train
slowly pulled away. I closed the car door so it was only
open a few inches. Then I went into the corner of the
car away from the horses and stretched out with my
folded coat for a pillow.

The train rumbled and bumped over the track, occasionally whistling like some wailing monster. From
time to time I went to the door and peered out. It was
night, and the stars were out. I talked to the horses a
little bit and went back to sleep. In the chill of dawn
I awakened. The train was stopped.

When I reached the door, I heard the crunch of footsteps alongside and the trainman came to the door.
"Ready for some coffee?"

"Ready and willing," I said.

Swinging down, I walked along to the caboose with the brakeman. "Recognized you," he said. "You went east with the Blocker cattle. He ships a lot of stock over this road."

A huge pot of stew was on the stove. He waved at it. "We killed a buffalo calf a couple of days ago and saved the meat. That's the last of it."

"You grew the vegetables, I suppose?"

"Nope. You'll find that stew long on spuds. We gathered up a few off the top of several carloads we were carrying. The onions and carrots we picked up here and there."

The stew was excellent, the coffee black and hot. I drank a cup, and at their invitation had another.

"You shoot mighty quick," the brakeman commented.

"I had to. They were fixing to kill me."

"Who were they?"

"Relatives of mine," I said, "distant relatives, but not distant enough to suit me."

"Place this side of La Junta," he said, "where there's a loading platform and a chute. Like back yonder. Be the best place to get off."

We were silent for a while, and then the conductor asked me, "Known Blocker long?"

"Not long. We're partners in a cattle deal. Ranching."

"Money in that, I hear. I heard a lot about it from a German baron who had some fancy racing stock in Colorado. Before I took to railroading I worked for him a spell. His name was Baron von Richthofen. He had some of the finest trotting horses in the country, but he was always talking about the money to be made from cow ranching."

We yarned away the hours until the train slowed for the stop where I was to unload. I jumped the horses over the little gap between the earth platform and the car and sat my saddle waving as they pulled away.

For a few moments I waited and watched the train pull away toward the westward, and then I came down off the ramp and headed southwest. Over there beyond the Spanish Peaks was the Wet Mountain valley, and I wanted to look it over before going on west.

My enemies, I was sure, were far behind and had lost my trail. If they looked for me now, it would be in Denver or Georgetown . . . or maybe in Rico, where Teresa was.

Nevertheless, I checked the magazine in my Winchester and the chambers of my pistols.

A man couldn't be too careful, and I remembered only too well the cold blue eyes of that man with the scar.

And there was always Felix Yant, a cool, thoughtful, dangerous man who made few mistakes.

Alone I might be, and maybe they were far away, but I pulled up and took a careful look around the country. It was mid-morning and already the heat waves were shimmering out there.

It was going to be a long, hot day.

Chapter XX

Topping out on a ridge, I stood in my stirrups and looked all around the country. It was typical plains country, slightly rolling and here and there some staghorn cholla, a variety of cactus typical of this country. In the distance some mesas loomed against the sky, and the dark spots on them would be juniper.

Settling back in the saddle, I came down off the rise and immediately turned down a draw, then up another one, and cut across a low divider between two more.

It looked like nobody was out there, but I did not feel that way. I just had a hunch, and it kept spooking me . . . somebody was closing in on me from somewhere.

Again I switched back and rode up a draw in some soft sand, then out upon the plains, where I let the roan run for a bit, then slowed him down. The country ahead was rimrock country, low hills rimmed with sheer faces of rock, some of them no more than four to six feet high, while the hills themselves varied around forty or fifty feet. There was a lot of juniper here and more cholla. The Purgatoire River was off to the west.

My trail led me up on the mesa again. It was very hot. Wiping the sweat from my brow, I looked all around. Empty . . . not even an antelope. Heat waves shimmered and danced. Mopping my face, I rubbed my hands down on my pants to dry the palms. No tracks but animal tracks. I drew up at a little seep and let the horses drink. Trotting the horses down the draw, I wove around through some juniper and then went up on the cap-rock for another look around.

Off to the southwest there was a plume of dust, and it seemed to be coming my way. Walking my horses toward it, I suddenly sighted a well-worn trail and beside it a stone corral and a building. There was a faint suggestion of smoke rising from the chimney.

Pulling up in a clump of five or six junipers, I stepped down, and rifle in hand, walked closer. There were several horses in a corral, and a harnessed team waiting.

A stage station! Sitting down in the shade of the junipers, I watched the stage come in, saw some dusty people get down to stretch their legs, and watched the teams changed. I saw nobody whom I knew, but there were two horses at the hitching rail near the station.

After a bit the stage pulled out, but nobody came near the horses. I was hungry and there would be food down there I did not have to fix for myself, and fresh coffee.

Mounting up, I rode around the corral and down to the stage station, coming up on its blind side. I

shucked my Winchester from the scabbard, tied my
horses in what little shade there was, and walked
around the corner.

It was a low-roofed building with two windows and
a door. The door stood open and I stepped inside.

There was a man behind the bar with no hat on, and
two men on the business side of the bar who wore hats.
Both had been and were drinking. One was a stocky,
barrel-chested man with thick legs and worn-down boot
heels. The other was lean and tall, slightly stooped.
He turned his head slightly and peered at me. Crossing
to the one table, I pulled back the bench and sat down,
laying the Winchester across the bench beside me.

The man without the hat looked at me and asked,
"What'll it be?"

"Coffee," I said, "and whatever you have fixed to
eat."

"Give you a chunk of pot roast," he said, "if you like
buffalo."

"I could eat a wolf," I said. "Let's have it."

The tall man looked at me again. I knew trouble
when I saw it, and did not meet his eyes. "I'm a wolf,"
he said.

Under my breath I swore. The last thing I needed
now was a quarrelsome drunk. I was hungry and I was
a little tired and my patience was running short. The
heavyset one had not even given me a glance. He was
pouring another drink.

"I'm a wolf," the tall one repeated.

Ignoring him, I watched the man bring in the meat
from the kitchen. He put it on the table in front of
me and said, under his breath, "Watch yourself."

The tall man had turned his back to the bar and was
looking at me, a hard, ugly stare. I'd seen the kind before. Give them a drink and all their natural meanness
comes out and they'll pick on anything handy, prefer-
ably an Indian or a Mexican.

"I'm a wolf," the man repeated. "Let's see you eat
me."

The meat smelled good and I started to eat, ignoring

him. Yet I'd had no more than two bites when he loomed over the table.

"When I talk, damn you, pay attention!" He grabbed at me, and I knocked the hand aside and shoved the table into him. He staggered and went down. I walked around the table, and when he came up off the floor I hit him with my left hand.

As I did so, I moved so that he was between me and the man at the bar, who had not even turned around. That way I could see them both. The tall man was four inches taller and had longer arms, but loudmouthed as he was, he knew nothing about fighting. He took a long, clumsy swing at me, and I grabbed his sleeve and jerked him toward me, kicking his feet from under him. He hit the floor hard and for a moment sat there, shocked and suddenly sober . . . or nearly so.

"I'll kill you for that," he said, matter-of-factly.

"I'd give it another thought," I told him. "You haven't done very well so far."

Without taking my eyes from him, I said to the stage tender. "You got a graveyard out here?"

"We have. Nothing but Injuns in it, though."

"If you want to be remembered," I said to the tall man, "you'd better tell him your name before you reach for that gun."

"Think I'm scared?" he demanded, and I knew he wouldn't fight unless the odds were all with him.

"I don't think you're scared," I said, "and I hope you're smart."

He stood there, and I backed off and sat down at the table. When I picked up my fork, it was with my left hand. He looked at me and he wanted to kill me, but he simply didn't have what it took. "To hell with you!" he said.

He looked at me, and my right hand was resting on my thigh close to my gun butt. It was even closer to the gun in my waistband, but I didn't believe he had even seen that. It was also within two inches of my Winchester, which was pointed toward him under the table.

"To hell with you!" he repeated. Then he turned to

the man at the bar. "Come on, Shorty. I'm leavin'."

The man at the bar still did not turn. "You go ahead, Slim, I'll stick around for a while."

"You what?"

Shorty turned his back to the bar. "We ain't known each other long, Slim, but I reckon it's long enough."

Slim stared at him, unbelieving, then he went out and slammed the door behind him. Shorty looked after him, then turned back to the bar.

After a minute I said, "Shorty?"

He turned his head to look at me. "Have you eaten yet? This pot roast is pretty good . . . if you like buffalo."

"I've et it a time or two," he said.

"Sit up, then," I said. "I'm buying."

He walked over with his drink and sat down across the table from me. He had a broad face and a thick neck, and he looked like a fighter and a stayer.

"Him an' me," he said, "we rode for the same outfit. We quit at the same time, just naturally drifted off together. I never saw him when he was drinkin' before."

"He'll get himself killed," I said.

"And I'd be his partner. I'd have to stand with him," Shorty said. "If a man has to die, it should be for something worthwhile, not a two-by-twice loudmouth trouble-hunter."

We ate and we talked very little. When I'd finished my third cup of coffee, he said, "You goin' far?"

"Huntin' a ranch out on the western slope. Figured to look over the Wet Mountain country first."

"Mind if I ride along?"

"You hadn't better, Shorty," I replied. "I've got trouble on my trail, but it's my trouble, not yours, and I want to handle it alone."

"Too bad," he said, wistfully, "you're the kind of gent I'd like to ride along with."

"Shorty," I said, "my name's Kearney McRaven. I'm headed for the upper Colorado River area on the west slope. I'll be hunting ranchland. I'm going partners with Ben Blocker and a lawyer named Attmore from Kaycee. We could use a good man."

"I heard of Ben Blocker," he said. "He any relation of Ab Blocker, the trail driver?"

"Not that I know of," I said, "but they're cut from the same mold."

"Those fellers you got trouble with . . . are they close by?"

"I have a feeling they are, but I don't know. It's an ugly fight, Shorty, but it's my fight and I have to make it. I don't want a good man to die because of me. If you see two or three long, tall, slim men wearing black outfits, you fight shy of them. They are mean, and they are trouble. They will face any man living with a gun, but they'd just as soon shoot him in the back, dry-gulch him, or drop poison in his soup. So stay clear . . . but I'd like it if you showed up out west there, rustling a job."

"I can use a gun."

"Not this time, Shorty. You come west and you've got yourself a partner, but this is my fight. There's another thing, Shorty. I'm keyed for this fight. I'm ready to handle it alone. If I start depending on somebody to help, it will take the edge off and I'll be less careful. There are times when it is better for a man to be alone and dependent on nobody but himself."

"Your funeral."

"It may be." I paid for my meal and his and then walked outside. After a careful look around, I switched the gear to my other horse and rode out of there. When I topped out on the ridge, I glanced back and Shorty was standing there, looking after me.

Most western cowhands rode partners with somebody, and often they stayed together for years, but I had ridden with nobody excepting pa, and when I was a youngster, with Pistol.

When I pulled out of that stage station, I didn't plan on going far, but I found a good horse trail that led toward the south and took it. This was country I'd been through a time or two and I held to a good pace. I knew where I was going now, for it was a place where pa and me had holed up once a long time ago.

It was coming on to dark, with a few stars already

in the sky, when I unsaddled and picketed my horses. There was water there, and grass. There was a good stand of juniper around and a place where a fire could be lit and kept out of sight. By day a man could see for miles, for we were a good thousand feet above the rest of the country. The view to the north was especially good.

There was plenty of dry wood around that would give off no smoke, so I had a fire, a hot meal, and some coffee. I took the horses to water again because I hadn't let them have much there at first, then picketed them again.

Leaving the coffee on the coals, I took my rifle and picked my way through the rocks and the juniper to the edge of the cliff . . . or as near as I needed to go.

Above were the stars, a million or two of them, it seemed like. Below was a vast empty blackness, blackness without a break for miles and mi—

There was a fire down there. It was a long way off, a pinpoint of light was all, but a campfire nonetheless. Nobody needed to tell me who was at that fire. Of course, it could be somebody else, but I knew it was not, and at the same time I had a sort of strange premonition that a showdown was before me.

I didn't mean a showdown on some far-off day, I meant now . . . soon . . . within hours.

Walking back to the fire, I laid out my guns, and one after the other I cleaned them, checked the action, and then reloaded them.

All right, then. They were asking for it and they could have it.

Unrolling my bed, I banked my fire a mite and laid some sticks close to hand, for the night was cold. This country was like that. Hot as it might be in the daytime, a man could always use a blanket at night . . . and I was at an altitude of about sixty-five hundred feet.

Twice during the night I awakened to listen, and each time I checked my horses, but they were eating quietly, unworried by anything.

Lying awake that last time, I tried to come up with some scheme that would give me the advantage, but the trouble was, I would not go hunting them, and that gave them the choice of a battleground. Think of it as I would, I could come up with no bright ideas.

I was going to have to face two or three tough, dangerous men, and I would have to do it alone.

The Mesa de Mayo, where I now was, was a lookout point long favored by Indians in the area. From one position or another atop the mesa, a man could see for miles in any direction he chose. Before daylight I was up, saddled the roan, and packed my gear as soon as I'd had some coffee. There was no need to make fresh coffee. I just drank what was left in the pot.

Somehow they had managed to stay with me, losing the trail now and again, but generally aware of what my destination might be. I could be sure they would have a man in Silverton and probably one in Rico, and they would be watching the railroads and scouting the main routes west.

Coming down off the east end of the Mesa de Mayo, I crossed the Cimarron, taking time to water my horses as I did so. Then I doubled back to the west, keeping the mesa close on my right.

By noon the coolness of the morning was gone, and once again the heat waves were shimmering, turning the horizon and the plains before me into a dancing, liquidlike air. The Spanish Peaks, which I knew were far away, suddenly stood in the sky before me.

There was no water that I knew of close by, although there were creeks that ran into the North Canadian. However, I did not want to turn from my trail and pushed on. Turning off might have saved me a lot of grief.

There was a dim trail led between Sierra Grande, a huge peak lifting thousands of feet above the country around, and Capulin Mountain, a sort of tower. I started some antelope, and they went bounding away, taking my attention with them. When my eyes returned to the trail, I pulled up sharply.

Riding toward me through the shimmering heat waves were three immeasurably tall black figures. They were spread out and riding right for me, walking their horses.

There was no way I could escape. My only choice was to fight. Yet there was a chance . . . a slim chance.

To reach for my Winchester would invite a bullet. Trusting their picture of me was as indistinct as mine of them, I slipped the six-shooter from my waistband and held it alongside the pommel of the saddle as I rode toward them.

It was them. I'd had no doubt of it, and now there could be no more running, no more evasive action. My heart pounded with slow, heavy beats, and even the roan seemed to sense the tension that was in me, for he began to step with short, quick steps, alert for an instant movement. It was well that he did so.

They came toward me, and the distance narrowed. I made no attempt to get away, just kept my horse moving right at them. One of them spoke to the others under his breath, and they all started to pull up. It was the moment I had been waiting for.

Just as their horses began to pull up, I slapped the spurs to mine. Rarely did I use spurs on a horse, but this time the signal was instantaneous. He gave a great bound, and as he leaped my pistol came up. I saw one of them grab wildly for a gun, and then I was among them, through them.

There was time for one quick, chopping shot as I brought the gun down. The man who was drawing threw up his hands, and as his horse leaped wildly, he toppled from the saddle, and I was off and running.

I heard a shouted curse and then a clatter of hoofs as the horse whose rider I had shot started to run away. Glancing back, I saw one of them going after the horse and the other swinging for a shot at me. Yet before he could get his horse turned and steadied for a shot, I had put at least four horse-lengths between us, and before me was a dip in the trail. I heard the angry whip of a bullet and then the report and turned the roan at right angles down the hollow, my other horse running neck and neck with my mount.

Behind and above me I heard the pound of hoofs of a running horse and knew a rider was cutting across-country to head me off. He was closing in on me, and suddenly the shallow wash along which I had been riding petered out and I was facing a lava field close on my left. Yet the trend of the lava was forcing me toward the east and closer to those in pursuit of me. I was trapped . . . unless there was a way through the lava.

A gap opened on my left ahead, and gambling it was not a blind passage, I swung my horses into it. Yet my horses had put scarcely their length into the opening before I was struck a wicked blow on the shoulder.

Almost, I lost my grip on the pistol I held, but somehow managed to get it thrust back behind my belt. The opening in the lava took a sharp turn, and I was racing north again, but somehow I had lost my grip on the lead line, and my other horse was running free. The mountains before me danced weirdly, and I felt a strange lightness and giddiness. Losing my grip on the reins, I grabbed wildly for the saddle horn and fastened both hands on it. Yet suddenly my horse swerved, and I felt myself falling.

I fell . . . hitting hard and bouncing, then lunged to my feet and made the edge of the lava in a plunging run, where I fell once more. A moment I lay there, then I crawled deeper into the lava, keeping my head down and using every bit of skill I knew. Twice I got up and ran for short distances, working deeper and deeper into the ferocious-appearing lava. There were jagged edges everywhere, but I crawled wildly to get some distance behind me, then tumbled into a gap where the lava had been forced to either side by a huge boulder. I lay there, gasping for breath . . . listening.

My own horses ran off somewhere, and the riders swept by, following them. Within minutes they would realize I had fallen and would come back, searching for me.

Careful to make no sound, I worked my way through a narrow gap in the lava, and keeping to my belly or knees, I wormed my way through it. There were spaces where the flows had parted to go around some obstruction, others where it had piled up, and there were abrupt drop-offs of eight to ten feet. Coming upon a few feet of grass, I lay still for a while, listening.

How far had I come? Less than a hundred yards so far. I heard an angry shout, then swearing. The clatter of a horse's hoofs, then the horse drew up, not far from where I was. I lay perfectly still, careful to make no sound.

Over me the sky was blue, scattered with a few puff-balls of cloud. Almost due south of me loomed the tower of Capulin Mountain. Beyond it was the still greater mass of Sierra Grande, over two thousand feet above the surrounding country.

Somebody spoke, and in the clear air I could hear their voices. "Got to be near." Another voice said, "I hit him. Hit him hard."

As if on cue, my shoulder began to hurt. I remembered that savage blow on the shoulder. I had been shot then. Moving slightly, I felt a dampness on my side, below the shoulder.

Blood . . . I had been hit.

I must get away. If they began to climb over the lava, they would find me. Desperately, I tried to recall how wide this flow had been. Not much over a mile, I thought. Avid as they were to kill me, I doubted if they would cut their boots to pieces hunting me. They would look, probably not for long. They knew I was wounded but they also knew I was armed.

Rolling over on my knees, I started to crawl. A voice stopped me.

"How's Corley?"

"Bad. We've got to get him to a doctor. He was hit hard and dragged. Elias is with him."

"Wait until I get my hands on that McRaven!"

"Hell, he's dyin' now. I got him. I know I did."

"We thought we had him two or three times. He's harder to kill than a 'possum. Every time you think you've got him, he crawls off. I d'clare, next time we get him, alive or dead, I'm a-goin' to *bury* him. Bury him deep an' pile the grave with rocks."

"He's afoot, and he's bad hurt. Leave Elias to take

care of Corley. You an' me, we'll scout both sides of
this lava bed. Sooner or later he's got to come out, if
he lives. Then we'll get him."

I sat up and felt up under my shirt. I found the hole.
Could see it by craning my neck. The bullet had gone
through my shoulder, leaving an ugly blue hole where
it went in, and it had come out at the back. Tearing
my handkerchief, I plugged both holes, barely reaching
the one back of my shoulder. The shoulder moved, so
I didn't figure I'd broken any bones, yet I had lost
blood. I crawled a little further, following the way
that seemed easiest, then stopped. My shoulder was
really hurting now, and my throat and mouth were dry.
My head felt heavy and my eyes did not seem to focus
properly. Shock, maybe, as much as the bullet. What
I needed was a hole. Someplace to crawl into, someplace where they couldn't find me.

A shadow crossed my face. I glanced around, then
up. A buzzard!

They would not have to look for me now. The
buzzards would point the way.

Chapter XXI

Hot was the sun above me, slow the circles of the
waiting buzzards, silent the rocks about me. I lay flat
on my back, and I closed my eyes. Only to lie still,
only not to move, only to wait!

Wait for what? For death? I was a fool. Many a

man had recovered from worse wounds than I had. A bullet through the shoulder, what was that? Yet I did not move.

The wound was probably not too serious. The loss of blood was, and the lack of water. My horses were gone. I had my pistols and what ammunition remained in my cartridge belt. Around me was a bed of broken, jagged lava, which would cut my boots to ribbons in no time. There were pitfalls and cracks, and nowhere a man could run except in those occasional places where the lava had run around an area because of some obstruction or chance. Here and there were long aisles between flows. In some of them grass grew, in some there was only sand. Water, if it was to be found at all, would be caught in some natural tank or hollow in the basalt.

A boot scraped upon stone, and the sound shocked me into awareness. Pushing myself up, I broke into a stumbling run down the little avenue between flows.

My wounded shoulder hurt abominably when I ran, and I could feel the dampness of blood. I ran clumsily, staggering, stumbling, bumping into rocks. My feet seemed to come down in erratic patterns. I swore bitterly and plunged on until I fell.

For a long moment I lay still, heart pounding. Then I got up and ran on until suddenly my way was blocked by a jagged wall of basalt. Finding a break that gave access to the top, I climbed up. Instantly a bullet smashed the rock beside my head and the report of a heavy rifle boomed in my ears. I tried to run over the broken lava, risking a broken leg at every step. A jackrabbit burst from the ground at my feet and went leaping along over the rocks and down another crack. Turning sharply, I followed it just as another bullet whapped against a rock and then went whining off across the lava.

The crack where the rabbit had gone led to another of those breaks in the lava field, and I went down it, hearing another shot as I did. This time fragments of rock stung my cheeks and one good-sized piece rapped me on the skull.

For a moment I thought I was hit again, but the flying rock had merely broken my scalp. At the bottom I turned sharply down the space between the flows and came to a drop-off of some six feet. Down I went, half-falling, bringing up at the bottom in a cloud of dust.

For a moment I stood still, my lungs gasping for air, my head spinning dizzily.

No further, I told myself. I'd make a stand here. I simply could go no further.

Yet I did go on. Only now I walked, peering this way and that for some hiding place, some spot fit for defense.

Let them find me. I'd rather fight than run. I told myself that, but all the while another part of my brain sat in judgment on my actions, telling me that I did want to live, and not only to live but to defeat them. They must not profit by killing. My father was gone, and probably others, but I would not—

I fell.

Even as I fell, I knew that I was falling and there was nothing I could do about it. I did not feel myself hit the ground, but when I got my eyes open and my brain clear for an instant, I was on the ground.

Getting my hands under me, I pushed myself up. There was blood where my head had been. There was blood where my shirt pressed against the sand. On my hands and knees I knelt, staring at the bloody sand. Slowly the idea percolated through the fog in my brain. I had to get up. I had to move. I had only my pistols and they had rifles, and they would not be likely to miss again.

Shelter . . . a hideout . . . someplace, just anyplace. Lava fields are of many kinds, and lava flows proceed to cover everything. Sometimes the outer skin of a flow would cool and solidify while the lava kept flowing within, as water through a pipe. But I could find no such place.

Then, when I had given up, suddenly the narrow aisle along which I had been walking opened on the bank of a small stream. Kneeling, I scooped up water, splashed it over my face. Then I drank a little, and then a little more. I crossed the stream, which was very small, and kneeling to face the direction from which I'd come, I drank some more. Then taking off my hat, I threw a double handful of water on my head. It stung a little where it touched the cut on my scalp.

Finally rising, I walked up the slope and onto the trees.

It was late afternoon now. The sun would be gone soon. I sat down close among some junipers and waited for somebody to come after me.

Surprisingly, I felt better. It might have been the water. It might have been the moment of rest. From where I sat I could see the edge of the lava and the opening from which I'd come. Gun in hand, I waited.

A rattlesnake crawled from some rocks into the grass near the stream, just at the place where I had crossed. "Let them come now," I told myself. "I have an ally." But they did not come.

Suddenly I awakened. It was cold. The stars were coming out, and the lava field lay flushed and sullen in the last reflections from the vanished sun. I put my gun back in my holster. I had dozed, slept, and not for a little while but at least an hour. Or so I thought.

For a few minutes I looked all around. Directly to the south of me was the vast bulk of Sierra Grande. To my right front the lesser tower of Capulin, and off my left shoulder a peak bulked large.

My shoulder was stiff and sore, and I was afraid to move for fear of starting the bleeding again, yet if ever I was to escape it must be now, under cover of darkness.

If only I could find my horses! The roan would not go far and would try to find me. I knew this because he had done it before. Often he followed me like a dog, and sometimes I would deliberately hide, but he always found me. A horse, particularly one that has run wild, has a nose almost as good as a hound.

The other horse would undoubtedly stay with the roan. They would also want to feed and they would want water. The creek where I had drunk and which lay before me, just down the slope, probably was a feeder for the Cimarron River.

Grasping a branch with my right hand, I pulled myself erect. For a moment I stood still, bracing myself. I had lost blood and was weak, but under the circumstances was not in bad shape. Less bad than after the beating I had taken in the cabin. It seemed a long time ago.

Keeping to the slope, slight as it was, I started to work my way downstream. Suddenly I saw a light. It was far off, perhaps two or three miles, and it was on the slope of that other big peak. At the base of that peak, rather. And it was not a campfire.

Slowly the stiffness left my legs and I walked more easily. After a bit I thought I saw another light, near the first one.

A ranch?

Skirting a bunch of trees, I got a better glimpse. It was a town. But what town? Further east, maybe thirty or forty miles—I was unsure of the distance as I'd never been there—was Robber's Roost, where Coe hung out with his outlaws, but this was too far west.

A half hour or so later I was crouched in the darkness at the town's edge. My head was aching and I was exhausted. Kneeling on the ground, I studied the buildings, which were few. A blacksmith shop, now closed, a saloon, a general store, and a couple of other buildings. There were several dwellings built of logs or stone, and one that I could see was adobe.

At the hitching rail before the saloon, three horses were tied, the horses of the L'Ollonaise brothers.

So they were here before me. Carefully, I moved my arm to a more comfortable position. Without doubt they had brought the wounded one here for treatment, and also without doubt they would spend the night here and would be eating here. The thought of food made my stomach growl.

First, I must discover where they were. I started to rise, and just at that moment someone said, "What's the trouble? Have you been hurt?"

My hand went to my gun, but it had been a woman's voice and she was speaking from a darkened window close by. I could see the vague outline of her, and of something white, a curtain, no doubt.

"I've been shot," I said, straightening up. "I need some care and some food. I can pay."

"Come to the back door," she said. "I would rather no one saw you enter."

When I reached the back door, she had it open. For an instant I hesitated. This woman knew nothing of me, yet she was inviting me in. I started to speak, but she interrupted. "Please! Come in!"

Once inside, she drew the blinds and then lighted a lamp. She was young, quite pretty, and simply dressed. "Sit down right here." She indicated a chair. "I'll get some hot water. Luckily," she said, "I was just about to make tea."

She poured the water into a washbasin and then put more on the stove. She came to me with the washbasin and a cloth.

"Let's have that shirt off."

When I took the gun from my waistband, she held out her hand for it. "Let me put that down for you."

"I'll just keep it," I said. "I feel better with it close by."

She put my shirt aside, and with many *ohs* and *tsk, tsks* she began to bathe my shoulder. Dried blood had caked around the wound and stained my side. Carefully she washed it away, then bathed the wound with a solution of carbolic and water.

"You were lucky," she said. "It broke no bones."

While she was bathing and dressing my shoulder, my eyes strayed around the room. There were a few pictures, a thick carpet on the floor, a bed, and a dresser. The stove was in an adjoining room and visible through the door.

When she had finished with my shoulder, she went for the tea and brought it back with a thick sandwich. "You'd better eat," she said. "I don't have much to offer." She smiled suddenly. "I wasn't expecting anyone."

"You live alone?"

"Yes . . . my mother died. I work in the store sometimes."

"What place is this? I had no idea there was a town
anywhere near."

"It's Madison. Named for Madison Emery. The
mountain out there is Emery Peak, and that's named for
him, too. It's quiet, usually, unless some of that crowd
over at Kenton come in here. That's Robber's Roost,
Kenton is. Sometimes a dozen of them will stop here
when passing through. We all know them."

She watched while I ate. "You were hungry!" she
said. "I wish I had more. In fact, I was going over to
the store when I saw you. I just . . . well, I just knew
you were hurt and couldn't stand having you out there,
needing help." She got up, putting a shawl around
her shoulders. "You lie down when you've finished
that. I'll be right back."

"There are some men out there," I said, "who are
looking for me. Don't tell anyone about me."

"I won't," she promised.

She glanced at me again. "Please lie down," she said.
"It will be all right. There's another bed in the next
room, so you can stay the night if you want, right where
you are."

She went out and closed the door behind her. For
a moment I sat perfectly still. She seemed nice, but . . .

I was worried, and trusted nobody. One after the
other I checked my guns and reloaded the empty chambers. Then I poured a fresh cup of coffee.

Desperately tired as I was, I could not trust myself
to sit down on the bed. To sit down would be to lie
down, to lie down would be to fall instantly asleep.
Suddenly I got up and put on my shirt, difficult as it
was to do. Taking my coat, still stiff with dried blood,
I went outside and closed the door behind me. Then I
walked swiftly along the back of the buildings toward
the general store. I glanced in.

It was empty except for a balding man with glasses
behind the counter. Glancing across the street from the
dark alley where I stood, I saw the horses, still tied to
the hitching rail.

As I stood there, two men came to the door. One of them was a L'Ollonaise. The other was saying, ". . . wants to speak to you. Right here a minute ago."

They stepped out on the boardwalk, and she came from the shadows, the shawl over her head now. She was speaking. "Can tell . . . where . . ."

There was some subdued talk and then L'Ollonaise said, "Fifty dollars? Are you crazy? I can find him myself!" He turned to the man beside him. "Where does this woman live?"

She grabbed at his sleeve and he thrust her roughly aside, then stepped to the door and spoke to someone inside. Another L'Ollonaise came out, and following the third man, they started down the street. The woman screamed something at them, then began to run . . . straight toward me.

She came into the narrow space between the buildings, and there was no way we could avoid coming face to face. She stared, wild-eyed. "You! I thought—"

"Thanks for fixing my shoulder," I said. "Now you know how Judas felt."

"I'm sorry! I really am! I wanted to get out of this place! I want to *live!* I want to get away from here and never see it again! I hate everything about it!"

"You will hate the next place, too," I said. "What you are you will carry with you."

I brushed past her and walked across the street. At the hitching rail I untied their horses and mounted one of them. He humped his back a little at the unfamiliar touch, but I turned him sharply around and, letting the others do as they would, I rode out of town.

The rough road sent my shoulder to throbbing, but I followed a trail up the creek, then cut back through the hills toward the area where I had last seen my own horses. It was beginning to cloud over, only a few stars showing when I reached the creek again about at the place I had crossed it to reach the town. Starting back along my trail, I rode at a rapid clip toward the lava beds.

The horse I rode was restive, sensing the unfamiliar rider and not at all pleased. Coming through a scattered clump of trees, I came suddenly upon my own horses. Pulling up, I called out to them, then swung down and caught the roan's reins. Swiftly I changed horses, then turned and rode into the night.

Westward now, my shoulder throbbing, and so tired I could scarcely sit a saddle.

All night long I rode, dozing in the saddle, and at daybreak I rode into the streets of Trinidad.

First off, I found a corral and a bait of hay for my horses. Then, packing my gear, I headed down the street. There was a hotel alongside Davis and Barraclough's store and another across the street and further along. At the Colorado Hotel I got a room, and stripping down to my belt, I bathed my shoulder in hot water. It was stiff and sore and I took my time getting cleaned up. I washed some of the blood out of my coat and shirt and hung them to dry, digging into my blanket roll for a fresh shirt. It was rumpled but clean.

There was a drugstore run by a man named Beshoar, who was also a doctor, but he was in Pueblo on business, so I bought some carbolic and went back to my room and stretched out on the bed.

I'd only seen three riders coming up on me out there, but there had been four of them . . . and that fourth man worried me. He had not been in Madison, apparently . . . so where was he? Anyway, one of the four had been wounded and dragged. He was down and probably out of the picture.

After a while I dozed off, and when I awakened it was sundown. I looked out of the window and along the street. There was a rig standing in front of the Davis and Barraclough store and a couple of horses tied to the hitching rail. Neither horse nor brand was familiar. My room was on the ground floor, so I drew the shades a little tighter and pulled on my boots. My coat was almost dry. Checking my guns, I belted them on and then donned my coat. I was hungry and still tired, and my mouth tasted awful. My head ached and I wanted no trouble from anybody. Leaving my Winchester and gear, I went out on the street.

The air was cool and pleasant with a faint smell of sagebrush and cedar, mingled with the wood smoke of cooking fires. For a few minutes I just stood there, enjoying the evening and the quiet of the place. Trinidad was on occasion a pretty wild place, but at the moment it was tranquil, and that was the way I hoped it would stay.

Fisher's Peak loomed black and huge beyond the town. There was a restaurant sign down the street, and I went in. There were two long tables where a half dozen men were eating family-style and some extra tables. I was in no mood for conversation but didn't want them to think me uppity, so I dropped down at the end of a bench.

A bald-headed man, quite fat and sweating, walked over with a coffeepot. "Two bits," he said, "an' all you can eat. If you want somethin' you don't see, don't bother to ask. We ain't got it."

I put my two bits on the table and reached for a plate loaded with thick slices of beef. There was a mound of mashed potatoes into which somebody had been digging and a bowl of beans. I helped myself.

"One thing," the fat man said, pausing across the table from me, "there's fresh apple pie. You ask for that, you get it. One piece to a customer. I don't dare set that out or these cow nurses would eat the whole thing. Leave nothing for nobody."

"Now, now, Slats," a tall, redheaded cowpuncher said, "you'll make this gent think we got no manners, although I do allow you make a mighty fine apple pie."

"That still won't get you no extry piece," Slats said.

Red looked over at me. "He used to cook for the old BB4 outfit. When he quit, the whole crew quit an' follered him."

Red's eyes hesitated a moment on the hole in the shoulder of my coat, and undoubtedly he had noticed the stiffness with which I moved my left arm, when I did.

"Good cooks are hard to find," I said.

He passed me the meat. "Eat up," he said. Then he

added, "This here can be a troublesome country, but we're lucky. We got us a good sawbones. He's a mighty decent man," he added, "closemouthed, too."

"Thanks," I said, "I hope I won't need him."

He gave me a long look but said nothing more. The others talked among themselves, seeming not to even be aware of me. My seat left me a view of the door, and had been taken with that in mind, which I am sure Red noticed.

The view of the street was a good one, so I lingered over my coffee. Red stayed on, too, seeming to ignore me. We watched the others leave, and then he turned around toward me, pushing his hat back on his head.

"I'm a kind of friendly gent," he commented, casually. "I punch cows when the job's available. Come up the trail from Texas."

"I've been there."

"Seen your horses when you come in. They've covered some country."

"They're good stock."

"None o' my business," he commented, "but I surely hate to see a man walk into a trap."

Something inside me chilled. For an instant even my heart seemed to stop. "A trap?"

"Uh-huh. Seems to me you're a man runnin' from something or runnin' at it. Maybe this here ain't my business, like I said, but I sort of cottoned to you, and I surely didn't to those others. Not even their woman."

"How many of them?"

"Two . . . three, countin' her. The way I figure it, you better count her."

"You are right, *amigo*," I said quietly, "she may be the worst of the lot. They're here?"

"They surely are, and they seen you come in. They know where you are right now. They have staked out your hotel. In fact, they staked out Sherman's, too, not knowing where you'd go."

There was a door to the street, the one where I had come in, and there was a door out through the kitchen. Both would be watched by now, I was sure.

"What made you think they were watching for me?"

He chuckled. "Mister, you come into town on two hard-ridden horses, you leave them at a corral, you get you a room. You got blood on your coat when you come in, you favor one side of you. You're watchful as a cat huntin' mice, an' besides—"

"Besides?"

He grinned, both hands flat on the table. "I been waitin' for you my ownself."

Chapter XXII

My coffee cup was in my right hand, but my left was in my lap close to my belt gun. "You? Waitin' for me? Well, looks like you found me. If I'd known you were waiting," I added, "I'd have come along a little faster."

He smiled. "From all I hear, you've been ridin' a rough trail to trouble these last months. How could a pleasant-lookin' gent like you get so many folks mad at him?"

"They chose up sides before I was born," I said. Carefully, I put down the cup.

He had a taunting, whimsical look in his eyes, not at all an unfriendly one. "Family fight?" he asked.

"Sort of. Since they killed my pa, I'm the last one to stand between them and all they want, and from the way they act, it must be plenty, although they are said to be good haters. I never even knew they existed until just awhile back."

"You got a friend knows all about it."

"A friend? Me? I don't know anybody in this part of the country."

"This here friend, he sent a man ever which way to flag you down an' get you to set still until he caught up with you. He'll be along soon, if you can just abide here."

Someone was coming along the walk outside, and then the door opened and a man came in. It was Felix Yant.

He stopped just inside the door and looked straight at me. He was wearing a holster, as always, but he carried a sleeve gun, too. That was what I thought of now.

"You cover a lot of country," I said. "Pull up a bench and sit down."

He crossed to the table and sat opposite me, which put him around the corner from where Red was sitting. If he so much as glanced at Red, I did not see it. He was totally concerned with me, totally concentrated. He was like a bull snake facing a mouse . . . only I didn't feel like a mouse.

He turned and looked at Red. "This will be a private conversation, do you mind?"

Red got up. "Nope, I surely don't." Then Red looked at me. "*Abide* is the word," he said.

"Thanks," I said, and he walked over to the bar.

Yant studied me. "You've grown up," he said. "You've come a long way."

"Things been sort of pushing me," I said.

"You didn't make it to Carolina," he said, smiling with that chilly little smile he had.

"I didn't have to go," I said. "It's all taken care of without me."

That startled him. "What? What do you mean?"

"Made a tie-up with Ben Blocker," I said, "who is a big cattleman. With him and his lawyer. I didn't have to go east, because I sent my lawyer to look after things."

It shocked him. Obviously he had known nothing about Attmore, nor apparently had he had any idea of my using a lawyer. There are those, and we were both of that sort, who handle such matters on a one-to-one basis. The intervention of third parties is unpleasant and not to be considered. There are people who live out their entire lives in such a manner, and Yant was probably one. Essentially a loner, a cold, distant man, he probably had few contacts away from his immediate family, and it was possible they saw little of each other unless drawn together by some mutual need.

"I am going into the cattle business," I added, "and just did not have time, and this lawyer was from that part of the country and understands the situation."

Obviously it was something they had not bargained for. They had centered their attention upon me— eliminate me and the field was clear.

"Now," I said, and this I did not know, "the matter has been settled. If anything happens to me, the estate goes to my heirs, and you folks aren't among them."

"You're lying." I am sure that made him feel better, but he was obviously worried. "Nothing can be done that fast."

"It can," I said, "when the man doing the fixing has the right connections. He's related to a judge and some other folks. He looked over the papers and didn't figure it would take long."

He sat very still. Slats came over with a pot of coffee. "One for my friend," I said, "and for me."

"You're cool," Yant said at last. "You have guessed that we have you trapped and you're trying to talk your way out of it."

"No," I replied, after a minute, "I am not talking my way out of it, and I don't want to." Surprisingly, I realized what I had said was true. I'd been too busy running and protecting myself to think about it all, but now I was getting mad, and the more I thought about it, the madder I became. "You and your folks have been begging for trouble. You've hunted me and hounded me, and it stops here. By this time you should have learned better. You've lost one man—"

"Two," Felix said. "For that alone we would kill you."

"I skinned up a few others," I added.

He looked at me, and for a moment there was a shadow of something else in his eyes, almost a wistfulness. "I am sorry it is this way," he said then. "Maybe if—"

"You murdered my father," I said.

He shrugged. "He was in the way, as you are now. I am not alone in this. It involves all of us, and our futures. We were so sure your father was dead... had been killed. And then you..." His voice trailed off and he was silent.

Not for an instant did I relax. This was a dangerous man, and perhaps he was trying to get me off guard. My ears were alive to the slightest sound, too, although I observed Red standing at the bar in such a way that he could watch both doors. What we were expecting never happened, for suddenly the bat-wing doors were shoved aside and two men came into the room. Both men wore badges. The first one was a small, gray-haired man, but with a look about him that called for no nonsense.

They came right to our table. He looked at me, then at Yant. "I understand you two and some of your friends out there are having difficulties."

"Not really," Yant started to say. "I—"

"You," the gray-haired man said, "are riding out of town. You are leaving now, and I mean right now. I will tolerate no shooting in our streets. I don't give a damn what your troubles are, but settle them somewhere else... not here."

"Officer," Yant said, "I do not think we need listen to any more of that. Outside are—"

"I know," the marshal replied grimly, "several more of your murdering kind, and right now they are being watched by six good citizens armed with shotguns and buffalo guns. Get out now—and fast!"

When Yant had gone, I sat very still, waiting. After walking to the door with Yant, he came back to me. "All right, I am giving you one hour to clear out. Let them get on their way and then you go."

Red spoke up. "He's supposed to meet a man here, Marshal. It is important."

"That's his hard luck," the marshal said. "You get your gear and your horses and get out, do you hear me? I've nothing personal against you, don't even know who you are, but I want no shooting in my town. Do you understand?"

"Of course," I replied. "In your place I'd have taken the same action. I will be gone within the hour."

As I rose he noticed my belt gun and smiled grimly. "Ready with it, were you? Well, I don't blame you. They're a bad lot. There's a way down the Picketwire that Red here can show you. In your place, I'd keep off the trail and along the river and cut off up Burro Canyon toward the Spanish Peaks."

His cold gray eyes warmed a little. "Been on the dodge a time or two in my younger days. Know how it feels."

Red took me down the lanes between barns and corrals, along a muddy little street overhung by trees to the riverbed. For a while we sat there, looking over the country ahead of me.

"On your own," Red said. "I got to wait for your friend."

"If he figures to traipse along after me," I said, "he'd better pull his head down into his collar, because I've no friends around that I know of and I am going to be looking out for Yants or L'Ollonaises or whatever they call themselves. I'll be right edgy about the time he catches up to me . . . if he does."

"He will."

"I'm cutting out for Apishapa Pass right now, yonder west of the Spanish Peaks. If he's so anxious to get himself into a shooting fight, tell him to come on . . . whoever he is. I'm going to be needing all the help I can get, but tell him no more running and dodging for me. From here on I'm hunting scalps."

Red turned his horse around, lifted a hand, and loped off. Me, I just sat there a mite, studying the country without anybody around, and then I took off toward the west, keeping to cover.

Nobody needed to tell me this was a showdown. They wanted it and I wanted it. All of a sudden I realized I wasn't at all scared. I was wary and I was ready.

The way they indicated was a good one, and holding to the river bottom of the Purgatoire, I rode westward until I was about opposite Reilly Canyon. Riding up out of the riverbed, I found my way into the trees and cut across the hill to Burro Canyon.

When I came down into the Burro Canyon trail, I found none but old tracks, and started up canyon, riding at a good gait.

The mountain air was cool and pleasant, with a smell of pines and wood smoke from the fires of a few prospectors working along the canyon or small draws opening into it. There was no sound but the hoofs of my own horses. Looking up the slopes around and before me, I could see the lighter green of aspen thickly massed along the mountainsides.

Checking every trail that came in from a branch canyon, I found nothing, yet I knew my enemies were not far off and would be making every effort to locate me.

Before me loomed the towering Spanish Peaks, clouds gathering around them. "Rain, boy," I said to the roan. "She's going to rain. I think we'd better hole up."

High above on the slope ahead I glimpsed what looked to be a small bench tucked into a corner of an aspen grove. Riding past it and looking for a way up, I found what I wanted and rode a switchback route up that steep slope.

It was not all I'd hoped, but I could get my horses back far enough so as not to be seen from below. Stripping their gear, I picketed them on the meadow and went to work to build a shelter. From the ominous look of the clouds gathering over the mountains, I did not have much time.

At the near edge of the aspen were dozens of small trees from six to eight feet tall, and going among them I cut off a few of the smaller ones close to the ground, then bent the tops of four of the eight-foot trees together and tied them, adding others where their position made them useful. Working swiftly, taking only time to glance at the lowering clouds from time to time, I gathered spruce boughs and thatched the dome-shaped frame, working from the bottom up with each successive layer overlapping the one below.

Gathering other spruce boughs, I made a bed for myself, and in a relatively sheltered place outside the shelter I laid a fire and a crude reflector made of some great slabs of bark from a deadfall.

After building a fire, I dipped water from a stream and started my coffee. Then I returned to my thatching. By the time I had water boiling, a few spattering drops of rain were falling. Running out to the meadow, I brought my horses in close to my own shelter, for there was much good feed to be found under the aspen. Then I added fuel to my fire, hustled my gear into the shelter, and was all snugged down for the night.

Frying the last of my bacon, I ate a chunk of biscuit and drank what amounted to three cups of strong black coffee. Hungry as I was, it tasted good. The rain had increased to a steady downpour, and here and there large drops fell inside my shelter, but not enough to worry about. I'd taken the trouble to build where no water ran, and where it could not gather in pools. Outside my horses stirred from time to time.

Lying on my back in the darkness, my face carefully situated between places where large drops occasionally fell, I stared up into the blackness of night and thought how little it took to really satisfy a man.

Shelter, a small fire, food, and a time to rest. It wasn't much, but I'd been so many times with less. This, I reflected, might easily be my last night on earth. Whatever else I was getting into, one thing was sure. It would be a fight with nobody to stop it and no getting away.

Momentarily I wondered who the "friend" might be of whom Red had spoken. Who was there? I shook my head in the darkness. It had to be a mistake. Pa was dead and I had no friends close enough to help, certainly none who could send men out to watch the different routes I might have taken.

For a long time I lay awake, mostly thinking about Laurie and wondering how she was. The movements of my horses were reassuring, for that roan would let nobody come near without snorting, blowing, or showing his anxiety in one way or another.

Sitting up, I added a few sticks to the edge of my fire to keep it smoldering. Then pulling my blankets around my shoulders, I went to sleep.

Snug and warm I slept, but I awakened to dampness and cold. Turning on my back, I looked up at the spruce boughs overhead. Much of the rain had run off due to my thatching, but some had come through. Sitting up, I put on my hat, shook out my boots, and tugged them on. Then I got to my knees and put on my gun belt, thrusting my spare into my waistband.

My fire was cold and dead, but I dearly wanted a cup of coffee, so I started the fire again and put the coffee closer. It was the remnants of last night's coffee and so would be strong enough to float an ox, but right now that was what I needed.

With all tracks washed out, they were not going to find me unless by accident or the smell of my smoke, and I wanted my coffee enough to take the risk. Brushing off any twigs or leaves I'd picked up, I carefully rolled my blanket and groundsheet.

It was still raining but it had settled down to a fine, gentle rain. Building up the fire a bit, I warmed the saddle blanket a mite and then saddled up, wiping away most of the water on the roan's back before I put the blanket on him.

If my friend found me, he was going to have to be good. Still, he would know I was directed to Burro Canyon, and the rest might follow from there. But this was not a much-used trail, and I believed it would drop off to the west and let me down into White Creek or at the head of Echo. I'd never been up this far before. I was a mite southwest of the West Peak of the twins, and they towered above me. The nearest one was over thirteen thousand feet and the other only slightly less. There were several lesser peaks, including Saw-tooth, just west of them.

Stepping into the saddle, I turned off along the bench I was on, keeping the aspen between me and the trail below. Now I was through running. They were some-where about and I meant to find them.

From time to time I paused to listen. Sounds carry well in the mountains, although a peak or a shoulder of mountain can screen them away from a man. Yet I heard nothing.

The trees grew thicker. The bench fed onto a small plateau between West Spanish Peak and the White Peaks. It offered a way north, skirting some slide rock by a very rough route.

Topping out on a low ridge, I pulled up at the edge of the spruce and looked back the way I had come. It was well that I did, for they were there, maybe four or five miles back. Four, I counted, following right along the way I had come. And there very easily could be more of them somewhere around.

Above me loomed the naked rocks of West Spanish Peak, and I sat my saddle, watching them come, only specks along the trail, unrecognizable as anything but men on horseback at this distance. Turning, I glanced up at the peak that towered above me.

This was Huajatolla, the double mountain, often called "the breasts of the world." There were dozens of legends about them and about their being the home of the highest gods. Years ago pa had told me stories of the gold that was said to have been taken from them by the Aztecs and carried away to Mexico. Legends, or the stuff of legends. If mines there were, they have been long since covered by slides. Sun worshipers were rumored to have had a temple on the eastern peak.

Wind ran a ripple through the aspen just below me, moving across them like a small wave in a sea. The rain had stopped. Here and there the sun threw a shaft of light down from the clouds.

On my left staggered platoons of spruce advanced up the steep sides of the West Peak, platoons broken by inroads of slide rock weathered from off the peak. Here and there pockets of snow remained, clinging to shadowed places. The pass swung westward here to descend to White Creek, but I turned north, planning to cut over to the head of Echo. And then I saw the knoll.

It was low, covered with spruce, some of them fallen across and among some moss-covered boulders. Long ago someone, Indian or white, had camped there, for a little circle of blackened stones indicated where fires had been. Behind it on the slope there was grass, then scattered spruce, and a dim trail through the spruce seemed to point toward Echo Creek. Riding up the knoll, I turned in the saddle and looked back down the trail. From this spot one had a perfect field of fire.

Dismounting, I led the horses back to that grassy slope and picketed them there. Taking my Winchester, I walked back to the rocks and brush atop the knoll and sat down in a comfortable place.

I was tired of running, tired of wondering what came next, ready for a showdown. They were many and I was one, but before this day was over, I told myself, I'd lessen the odds.

Warm sunlight came through the broken clouds. Far-off rain still obscured the distance. I nibbled at a cracker, and a curious whiskey-jack hopped close, watching for crumbs. Breaking off a piece, I tossed it to him, and he accepted it quickly and hopped nearer, either trusting too much or secure in his ability to fly quickly up and away.

They were closer now, coming on without seeming to worry, sure no doubt that I was still running. The rifle felt good in my hands, my position was excellent, and I had a getaway route at the back. Nor was the knoll isolated. If need be, I could move to either direction under partial cover.

My shoulder was still stiff and I moved carefully, sparing it. Good health, natural strength, and the clean, fresh air of the mountain country healed wounds quickly. I took a sight on a turn in the trail. It was a good four hundred yards off. To the right of it a splash of scarlet gilia ran down the slope, the flowers red as blood.

Pushing my hat back on my head, I placed my rifle on the tree trunk I intended using for a rest and got out another cracker, sharing it with the whiskey-jack.

How did a man feel, living his last hours? Was I, now? The air was fresh off the peaks, cool with a chill of snow and the icy cold that was up there, only a couple of thousand feet above me.

A bird flew up down by the trail, and the first rider appeared. They were hunting me and they had shown they would kill without hesitation, so I shot him.

My sight was purposely low, for they were coming up the mountain, but my bullet went where intended, a flickering light on his vest, a medallion, perhaps, or a gold nugget on his watch chain.

He must have convulsed at the moment the bullet hit him, spurring his horse by accident, for the gray horse leaped forward, the rider swaying loosely in the saddle, then falling.

He toppled from the saddle, hitting hard beside the trail, falling in that splash of gilia while the gray horse came running on up the slope and past me, stirrups flopping.

The rifle shot slapped against the rocky peaks and echoed off down the canyons, and then it was still. The whiskey-jack rustled impatiently among the leaves, and far overhead an eagle soared.

My eyes went from the trail, where the others might appear, to the fallen man. A man shot so is rarely killed at once but dies slowly, yet to aim at a man's head when the body presents so much the better target was foolhardy. There was no movement. Either the fallen man was still in shock, was shot through the spine, or was lying still to deceive me. In any case, I remained where I was.

For a long time nothing happened. Yet I was wary. Perhaps they were talking over their next move, yet perhaps one of them had already gone to the ground and was now trying to encircle me. If so, he had several bare or almost bare patches of ground to cover, of which I had already taken note.

The sun was warm and comfortable. On the trail

below nothing moved, but I was not deceived. They were somewhere along that slope, edging toward me no doubt, watching for a shot. Carefully I eased myself further down behind the logs for better protection.

Another man gone. Was anything worth the death of so many strong men? They could draw off . . . I could not. I had only myself on whom to depend, and it was I they were trying to kill, so I had no choice but to fight. If they were to pull off now, it would be the end of it as far as I was concerned, but beyond this point I was not going to run. No longer could I stand to live with death hanging over me and about me.

Suddenly a flicker of movement caught my eye, and a man darted from behind some rocks and ran for cover. Briefly he was in full view, but it would have been a scratch shot and I did not fire.

Then there was a time of waiting. Soon that man would have to move, and when he went for the next cover, he would be in the open for a good thirty steps, time enough and more.

Uneasily, I looked all around. It was too quiet. A glance at my horses, and they were cropping placidly at the grass. Suddenly I had an urge to get out, to get on my horse and get out, as fast as I could.

Moving along deeper into the grove, I took another careful look around. Of one thing I could be sure. They were neither the kind of men to quit nor the kind to sit waiting, so I knew that somewhere, somehow they were moving, trying to get to me or get around me.

Worried now, I swept the slopes of West Spanish Peak but saw nothing.

Turning swiftly, I went back through the trees overlooking the meadow where the horses were. I started to step out and go to them, but hesitated. Softly I called. The roan looked up and took a couple of steps toward me, and I called again. He took a bite of grass and drifted my way, the other horse following. When they were near, I spoke softly again. "Come on, boy, right over here."

He came, taking his time, ears pricked, yet playing a game with me. He was not going to make it easy. He would have to be coaxed a little. Again I spoke, more softly, and he took a step toward me, then another.

Glancing back along the trail, I saw nothing. Carefully I scanned the slope that rose on the east. Nothing. Westward the ground fell away toward Sawtooth and the canyon of Chaparral Creek. There was a trail a mile or two west that dropped off toward the Cucharas River. The other trail, along which I had come and which led past my temporary base, led northward and then dropped off into Echo Canyon. To the eastward, which was on my left, there were patches of slide rock in among the trees. Timberline here was about eleven thousand feet, I figured. Judging by the plant growth, I was a mite below ten thousand feet.

Nothing stirred.

Worried, I moved up a little, keeping low to the ground. They weren't just setting there waiting for me. They were the hunters and I the hunted, and they were coming at me from somewhere. Higher up on my left those patches of slide rock left them open spaces to cross, and that slide rock could sound like a lot of bottles rattling against each other when you crossed it. From my right they had to come up slope through the trees to get at me.

My position was good, but I didn't like it. I never liked being stalked. A cool wind came down off the West Spanish Peak, and overhead a lone buzzard swung lazily down the sky, then hovered over the trail to the south. That man I'd shot ... well, that was three of them gone.

I wondered if Yant was out there. Elias surely was. And suddenly I realized they were in no hurry. They had me. No doubt even now they were moving to get behind me, to hold me here until I was dead.

They knew I could shoot. They knew now that I wasn't going to be easy, and they also knew that they could not afford to lose more men.

Again I looked around, trying to imagine how they planned to come at me, but I could see no way. My position, such as it was, was good.

To hell with them! I wanted some coffee and I was

going to have it. Snuggling close under a spruce with low-hanging boughs, I built a small fire, never taking my eyes from my surroundings for more than an instant and always ready to catch any movement from the corners of my eyes. The rising smoke would dissipate itself upon the spruce boughs. They would smell smoke and wonder.

For the first time the thought came to me that I might not get out of this alive. In the rush of action there is small time for thought. Now there was. These people wanted me dead, and they had killed before this. They were out there, how many I did not know. There might be four, and there could be a dozen. I put the coffeepot on the fire. Then I smiled to myself. They would smell the coffee and they would wonder.

Felix Yant would like that touch. He had enough of a sense of irony to appreciate it, and it would make them think I was not afraid.

Was I afraid? Yes, I guess I was. I was scared to death.

"Kearney?" The call was low, a woman's voice. "Kearney, come here, I want to talk to you . . . alone."

I'll just bet she did.

"Kearney? We haven't had any trouble, you and I, and we mustn't have any. Why don't we just ride out of here? Just you and me?"

Reminded me of that story pa used to tell me about Ulysses putting wax in the ears of his crew whilst he had himself tied to the mast so's he could hear the song of the sirens. Only I didn't need any wax. I recalled that brad loaded with sticky poison and left in my boot.

So I sat right still and said nothing at all. Yant, I knew, was an impatient man. I hoped the others were, too. What was the name of the one I'd been warned was most dangerous? Vrydag, Joseph Vrydag. I wondered if he was out there.

That was the trouble. I was alone and there were several of them, all of them shrewd, conniving people.

Were they waiting for dark? Hoping I'd try to get away? The little knoll on which I'd taken refuge was

only a few feet higher than the country close around
me and covered not over a third of an acre, if so
much. There was a tight grove of trees, mostly spruce,
and some boulders, several of them waist-high. There
was considerable brush. The chance that they could hit
me by just shooting into the area was a hundred to one
or better.

Going out of here, my only way was north, but I'd
heard much talk of this area and knew from that and
my own experience that there were three ways I could
take. Due west past Sawtooth there was a trail into
Chaparral Canyon and down to the Cucharas. Right
behind me was the trail down Wade Canyon and another that branched off it and led to Echo Canyon.

Trouble was, I was sore. I was tired of running and
ready for a showdown. Or so I told myself. Probably
I was a damned fool, seeking a showdown when there
were so many against me. So far I'd been lucky, too
lucky for it to last.

Suddenly they began shooting, searching fire aimed
at driving me into the open. Hugging the ground, I let
them shoot. Only a ricochet could get me where I lay,
but there were a couple that came too close for comfort.

Right then I was wishing pa was with me. Then I
was glad he wasn't, only I was a mighty lonesome boy
with all those men shooting to kill me and me here
alone without a soul to help.

The fire was still showing coals and the coffee was
hot. I poured and drank a cup, hunkering down under
that ol' spruce. A couple of hard biscuits in my saddle-
bag provided all the meal I was likely to get, but they
tasted good.

It was clouding up, clouds gathering real heavy
around the Spanish Peaks. Unless I missed a guess,
it was going to be one of those thunderstorms that scare
the living daylights out of a man. Up this high, every
bit of lightning in miles would be drawn to those towering peaks above me like to a lightning rod. I'd heard
folks say that aside from the Lone Cone out in western
Colorado, there was no place like the Spanish Peaks
for lightning. A magpie who had been fretting and

scolding around evidently figured the same way, because he flew off and left me there alone. I finished the last of my biscuit and brushed off the crumbs. A bullet clipped a bit from the spruce and dropped it to my shoulder.

Those folks out there now, those Yants and L'Ollonaises or whatever their names were, had they ever been through a thunder and lightning storm up this high? If they hadn't, they were going to get a surprise, I could tell them that.

When the lightning starts striking around within a few yards and the thunder starts rolling and banging down those rock-walled canyons, it's enough to make the hair stand on end . . . but the electricity in the air takes care of that.

How many of them were out there? Four? Or a dozen? And that woman . . . she was out there.

Where was that Joseph Vrydag, said to be the worst of them?

Emptying the grounds from my coffeepot, I packed it up. Suddenly I was thinking that when darkness came, or in the midst of the storm, I was taking out of there. I was going to run like a scared chicken. Right then I just didn't want anybody shooting at me again.

The storm came with a rush of wind and a crash of thunder. Lightning struck that peak above me, and the air was filled with the smell of brimstone. The rain was a solid wall advancing toward me on the breast of the wind. I made a run for my horses. To hell with it! I was—

And there they were, three tall Yants, or whatever they called themselves. They stood facing me and they had guns and the next thing I was shooting.

Chapter XXIII

The sun was gone but its bloody light lay splashed upon the Sawtooth Rocks, and upon my left enormous masses of black and ugly cloud thrust like Hercules between the pillars of the twin peaks, cloud shot through with lightning that lit up the bare pink slopes of Wahto-yah, the Breasts of the World.

And facing me, three tall dark men, their faces reflecting the red light of the dying sun like light from the fires of hell.

No word was spoken, nor could one have been heard. The sky in that moment was weirdly lit, and then the rain swept on us and our pygmy guns made tiny sounds against the crash and roll of thunder.

Their eyes were on my rifle in my left hand, and the surprise for them had been as great as for me. Only I dropped the rifle and opened fire with my six-shooter and I saw a man spin and drop, and firing again I saw a blood-red face turn to blood itself as my bullet smashed him back.

Desperate, alone, fighting for life and for the death of my father, I triggered the gun empty, then grabbed the second from my waistband. Then another gun was firing on my right. I saw them fall, and a man at whom I had not fired spun and dropped with the rain driving down upon him, and then it was that all three were gone, and for a moment I stood in the driving rain staring at their crumpled bodies, and a hand fell on my shoulders and a voice said, "That was for pa, Kearney," and turning around I saw it was Pistol.

His battered hat was rain-soaked now, but he was smiling and his teeth showed white. He grabbed my hand and put an arm around my shoulder. "Let's get out of here, boy," he said, "there's a better place close by."

It proved not to be so close by, but it was a better place. It was a log cabin at a place called the Gap on the Cucharas River. We followed the Peaks Trail down along the slopes and then cut across a saddle to come down to the cabin. It was warm and pleasant inside and there was a good smell of frying meat.

A bald-headed man turned around from the fire. He had a fringe of red hair around his ears and a wide red mustache, waxed at the ends that stuck out beyond the sides of his face.

"Set up, boys!" he said. "The steaks are fried and the beans are on the way!"

We'd been soaked through before we got our slickers on, so we were wet now. We backed up to the fire, and steam began to rise from our clothes, but the smell of the food was too much for us and we sat down on the homemade benches and ate, and while we ate we did not talk.

When we had eaten and the coffee was poured, Mustache put more wood upon the fire. Outside the wind whipped the house with lashes of icy rain, but we sat snug within, and Pistol and me, we looked at each other. At that moment I was proud of my broad shoulders and the strength I had, for Pistol had been a boyhood idol for me.

"Ah, lad," he said smiling, "you're a man now!" He turned on the others. "Would you believe it? He had two of them down and was working on the third before I could get a shot in. This kid is hell on wheels!"

"You taught me," I said.

"Not me." His face was sober. "It was your pa taught

us both, and a better man never lived." He looked at me. "It was them killed him, wasn't it?"

"One of them," I said, "shot him in the back of the head."

By the firelight in the old log cabin, I told them of the judge and how I recovered my money and of the fight in the snowbound cabin. The words I used were stark and simple words, for these men had lived such things and they needed no dressing up. What was not said they could supply, for they knew how such things went. They were lonely men, hard men, men who had lived by the gun. One of them was Red.

"I wanted to tell you, McRaven," he said, "but the name I'd have used wasn't one you'd have known. He told me to tell you to wait, and if the sheriff there had known Pistol was close by, he'd have killed horses trying to get him."

Our eyes met, and surprisingly he was embarrassed. "Yeah," he said, throwing the dregs of his coffee into the fire, "your pa tried to steer me clear, but somehow I was just headed down the outlaw trail. He was a good man, your pa."

"When this is over, I'm going to ranching, Pistol. I'm going to need good men who can handle cattle." I told them about Ben Blocker and the deal we made, and Mustache said, "I rode with Ben. I rode up the trail to Kansas with him, and on to Ogallala, and a squarer man I never knew, nor one more loyal."

"You can ride for him again," I said, "and for me."

"You settling down?" Pistol looked at me, and I nodded.

"I've got a girl in Silverton, and when this is over I'm riding back that way."

"When it's over?" Pistol looked up at me from where he sat by the fire. "It's over now. That was the end of it."

"No," I said, "I saw their faces there in the last sunlight. Felix Yant was not one of them. So he's left, and so is the woman."

Red shifted his feet, and his boots grated on the

sandy floor. "There's another, too. He did not come with them. He told them they were fools, that they must wait for you to light somewhere, but they wouldn't listen."

"Felix stayed?"

"He didn't say why. He just stayed." Red paused. "It was the woman got it out of him. I'd followed them and I listened outside the wall, pulled mud from the chinks and listened. She told him he'd gone soft.

"Felix, he looked at her and said, 'He's one of us, after all. He's kin.'

"'Wasn't his father kin? You killed him.' That was what she said.

"'This is different,' he said. 'Why, he could be my own son! If I had a son—'

"Then she laughed, she just laughed at him and said, 'Felix, you'll never have a son! You couldn't have one if you wanted one!'

"Well, he just looked at her. He said, 'Delphine, if somebody else doesn't kill you, I may.'

"'Stop it,' this Vrydag interrupted, 'just stop it. We've troubles enough. Our strength has always been because we worked together, and we must work together now. We must destroy him.'

"Felix Yant smiled. 'And suppose he has established a legal claim to the estate? What then?'"

Red waved a hand. "That was the way it sounded. Anyway, it isn't over. There's three of them left." He paused. "That's a mean lot of folks, believe me. In all my born days, and I've ridden the trail for years, I never seen such a poisonous lot."

"I'm going to Silverton," I said, "and they can follow if they like. I want no more killing."

"Sounds like this Felix Yant likes you," Pistol suggested.

For a minute I considered that, then shook my head. "It's just a notion. It won't stop him, believe me. That's a hard man yonder."

Outside the rain came down in a drenching downpour, and I knew the canyons would be running neck-deep with floodwater. It was no time to travel.

Pistol had aged and seasoned, but there were laugh wrinkles at the corners of his eyes and his face was leaner and harder.

"When you ride, boy," he said, "I'm riding with you."

"It's been a long time," I agreed. "We've got a lot of ground to cover, talking about pa and all." I glanced around at him. "You knew more about pa than I did."

He nodded. "He helped me when it was needful, and I was a good listener. You were young, Kearney, and he didn't like to burden you with all of it. Me, I could listen and keep my mouth shut, and much of his talking was just sort of thinking out loud."

"Wherever you go," Red advised, "watch your back trail."

We ate the steak and beans, and we ate doughnuts that Mustache made, and we talked of cattle, horses, and mines as such men will. Each had a tale to tell of a horse or a place or a time, and the cabin was warm and pleasant, with the storm outside.

Often I just listened, and sometimes my thoughts would wander back to the Spanish Peaks and the three dead men who lay together there, their bodies washed by rain and the hate they carried dissipated by the bullets that took their lives. They were strange men, born to hatred and motivated by little else. Even the desire for the estate, which was strongest in Felix and Delphine, seemed less a motivation than that blazing fire of hatred and the lust to kill.

These men were riding the outlaw trail, but all of them had punched cows in their time, and no doubt would again.

There were things to be learned by listening, and I was always one for learning, yet I could not forget Felix Yant and Delphine. That other one, with whom I'd had no contact, was not quite real to me. A danger . . . but a quantity unknown and therefore not to be judged.

Where were they now? They had not followed, but soon they would know something had happened if they did not know even now.

Suddenly I became worried about Laurie. Suppose Delphine learned of her?

Yet how could she? I had walked along a street with Laurie, I had spent an evening in her home—was that so much?

Did I dare go to her now? Might I not attract the vindictive spite of Delphine to them?

"Storm or no storm," I said suddenly, "I'm riding out at daybreak."

"And I'll ride with you," Pistol said.

Mustache packed grub for us, and when the first light came, we took out down the trail. Red was outside with Charlie and Mustache, and they said, "Don't you worry none about anybody along this trail. We're going to stake it out."

Well and good, but they could not watch all the trails.

We had two packhorses now and we took off down the Cucharas River, and Pistol led the way up a narrow game trail along the east slope of a north-south ridge to Coleman Canyon, then down to the head of Rilling Canyon, following that for roughly a mile, then cutting through the forested hills to Indian Creek.

It was a lonely route, and we were whipped by wind and rain, the rocky trails often slippery underfoot.

We camped near a rainwater pool in rocky country surrounded by cedars just shy of La Veta Pass. We had pushed hard, but that night we sat by the campfire and remembered the days when we were boys together and wandering with pa.

"You saved my bacon that time," Pistol said suddenly. "That man would have killed me. And you just a youngster, too."

"It was our fight you were fighting."

"Mine, too. When your pa took me up and helped me, I got to feeling I was a son to him, too."

"And we felt the same," I said.

"It's been a rough ride since," he said. "I came upon trouble here and there, so I got to riding the wrong trail, just like Red did."

"In every town in the West there's men who got off into rough country a time or two," I said, "but it's their own fault if they stay there. The way I see it, every time a man gets up in the morning he starts his life over. Sure, the bills are there to pay, and the job is there to do, but you don't have to stay in a pattern. You can always start over, saddle a fresh horse and take another trail. Now look at it straight. I've come upon some money from pa's winnings. Perhaps there'll be more from that estate back east. Anyway, I've bought cattle and I'm going into the Rockies to locate in some high country I know, and I'll need help. There will be a job for you, and one for Red, and Mustache . . . well, I could eat his cooking forever."

Pistol added fuel to the fire. "Kearney, since I taken off from you and your pa, I've never rightly had no home. I've been holed up with those outlaws over east of here lately or further north along the trail in Brown's Hole or at Robber's Roost over on the San Rafael Swell. I surely would like to cut loose from all that."

"Looks to me like you've cut loose," I said. "We'll say no more about it. You'll have a working interest in my share, because part of this money was pa's and he would have wanted it so . . . and I do too."

We let the fire die and rolled up in our blankets, watching the stars play peekaboo through the cedar branches and the clouds drifting. I was almost asleep when Pistol commented, "Well, he died winners, anyway. Not many of us do that."

Silverton lies in a basin something over nine thousand feet up with mountains all around. Otto Mears had built a narrow-gauge railroad up from Durango, winding through a deep gorge that engineers had told him was impossible as a route. The town was booming. The mills and the mines were working, and there were a lot of miners working small operations in all the canyons close by.

We rode into town just shy of sundown and I got a room at a hotel for the two of us, and Pistol, he said,

"Kearney, I'm not a trusting soul. You go see your girl. I'm going down to the Tremont and ask around a little. If there's any of that lot in town, there's a man down there will know it."

First I rode over to the livery barn, and Chalk got up when he saw me pull up outside.

"Howdy, son! Looks like you kept your hair so far!"

"So far," I agreed. "Any trouble with Henry bothering the McCraes?"

"He come back around, but two, three of us, we sort of read him the riot act. We also told him how healthy it was down Arizona way and how men of his stature and disposition were about to come onto hard times in Silverton. He slung his pack and started leavin' tracks behind him. Judgin' by the speed at which he taken out, I expect he's nigh to the border by now."

"Thanks. I'm beholden."

"No trouble. We don't cotton to his kind. One of those gamblers down on Blair Street, he was all for shootin' him on general principles. 'Men like him,' this gambler said, 'contribute nothing but trouble.' "

When I'd stripped the gear from the horses, Chalk indicated the black. "Seems familiar. Get him from the man over to Ouray?"

"I did."

"He must have cottoned to you. Not often he lets a body take that horse . . . and you've had him awhile."

"I'll buy, if he'll sell," I said. "That's a good horse." Then I told him about my ranching plans and who I was doing business with.

"Reminds me," he said, "I've been holding a letter for you . . . from Kansas City."

It was from Attmore. The matter of the estate was settled, my ownership proven, and the title delivered free and clear. There were a few papers to sign, which Blocker would bring west with him. From what Attmore suggested in his letter, the surrounding neighborhood breathed a sigh of relief to know the Yant-L'Ollonaise family had not inherited.

So that was over.

Somewhere down the canyon a train whistled.

"There she comes!" Chalk said. "The Durango train's comin' in!"

Pistol had gone over to the Tremont, and I decided to follow. I'd collect him and we'd eat at the Bon Ton, as I always did.

A cool wind was blowing down the gulch when I turned into Blair Street. The train was chug-chugging up the track and there were lights in the cars, and lights were starting to appear in the buildings, although it was early. The train was running late, I gathered, and would be starting back almost at once.

People were spilling from the train as I came abreast of it, and I paused to watch. Seeing a train come in was still a novelty in most western towns, and there was always the chance of seeing someone one had known.

Coming down the steps, the people trooped toward the street or scattered toward their homes or places of resort. A fair lot of them headed for the Tremont, where Pistol was.

The last of them came off the train, and I turned to walk away when something caught my eye, and I turned sharp around.

Felix Yant stood on the platform facing me, and out at the edge of the platform, maybe fifteen feet from him, was a short, rather heavyset man with a wide face wearing a derby. His black coat was open, and I could see a gold chain from which were suspended several objects indiscernible at the distance.

Behind them a woman was descending, and at a car yet further along, a rather stooped old man wearing a white planter's hat. All this I took in at a glance.

From the direction of the Tremont someone was coming toward me also, but my eyes were upon Felix.

On my left the locomotive was still gasping steam after its long climb up from Durango, on my right, space and some buildings, but I did not look. My eyes remained on Yant but held within their range the others as well. The woman I knew. Was one of the others the mysterious Joseph Vrydag?

This was the end. My hat brim was pulled low. It

was pa's hat, one of the few things of his own that he'd left me. I wondered if Felix recognized it.

There was not hate. He had hated pa and killed him, and yet I had no hate in me, but just the grim acceptance of the inevitable. Yet it was Delphine who worried me. What would she do? What if she produced a gun and began to shoot? Could I shoot a woman? Of course, if she attacked me, yet I wanted only to have her out of it.

"Yant," I said clearly, "you can get back on that train. You've still got time."

He had stopped, a good thirty yards off. The heavy-set man had stopped too and had turned half toward me. Only Delphine continued to move toward me, and suddenly I was swept by panic.

What was she doing? What—

"Kearney," she said sweetly, "it has been such a long time! Such a very long time! We're so-o-o glad to see you!"

Men and women stood around watching, people who knew none of us, people who would only see a beautiful woman approaching a young man with endearing remarks, a woman who seemed to be welcoming a long-lost friend or relative, and with every step she was drawing closer.

She was speaking loudly enough for all to hear, and now she said, "Kearney! It has been so long! I want only to hold you in my arms again! I want—"

She meant to kill me, or to hold me while the others did, and I dare not fire, I dare not resist. I could turn and run or I could be killed. I—

Suddenly someone ran past me. I heard a voice that I knew. "Delly! Of all people! What a thrill to find you all here so far from home! I do declare, Delly!"

Laurie!

I started to yell to warn her, but she was not stopping. She ran up to Delphine, who tried to avoid her. She made a desperate effort to turn aside and keep coming at me, but Laurie caught at her arm.

"Delly! Just like you used to be! Always out chasing the young men! And so much younger, Delly! Why, he's young enough to be your son! Maybe your grand-son!"

Delphine jerked angrily, but Laurie clung to her arm. And suddenly the men started to move. Their ruse failing, they were coming at me, and I saw the man in the derby reach inside his coat.

Not many in the West were familiar with a shoulder holster, but I'd seen them in Kansas City. As his hand came clear, I drew and fired.

There was no thinking. In that instant everything inside me was icy still. My gun came from my waistband and I fired. Then without looking, I swung my gun toward Felix Yant. It had to go past the struggling women, and his gun was coming up. He was taking aim, duelist-style, but even as my gun swung to cover him, there was a shot and I saw his knees buckle.

Pistol was suddenly beside me, and he fired again as Yant tried to lift his gun.

Then we both walked in.

Felix Yant was sitting sidewise on the platform. There was blood on the planks beneath him and there was blood on his shirt, and his gray trousers were soaked with it.

"From the first," he muttered, "from that first day in Rico, I . . ." He stopped talking and simply stared vacantly at nothing. "I knew, I . . . Kearney, I . . . I'm glad it wasn't . . . you."

People were coming up. They were standing around. "Evil," he muttered, talking to no one now, "evil! All of us! Cabanus, L'Ollonaise, Yant . . . evil! All of us."

A hand slipped into mine, and Laurie was beside me. "Let's get away from here," Pistol suggested.

Behind us the train whistled and began the slow chuga-chug as it backed away from the station. I glanced back. A few people were clustered around Yant, and now someone walked over to the man who must have been Vrydag.

"Delphine!" I pulled up suddenly. "Where—"

"She got on the train," Laurie said quietly. "I put her on the train along with an old man who had been following her, a man in a white hat. He said to tell you his name was Tolbert. I don't know why, but when he told her to get on the train, she said never a word, but did just as he said."

"My father mentioned him," I said. Vaguely I remembered something about going to Old Tolbert if there was trouble . . . or that he would help me.

"They're gone," Laurie said. "Come home with me. You, too," she said, turning to Pistol. "You're one of the family now."

Burns was sitting on the edge of the porch when we walked up to the house. "Your mother invited me in," he said to Laurie, "but I thought I'd better wait out here."

"It took me longer than I planned," I said, "but I came back."

"So you did," he agreed, "and brought trouble with you."

"No way a body can account for other people's notions," I replied cheerfully. "I came back because of my promise to you and another to Miss Laurie McCrae. Now, tomorrow Miss Laurie McCrae and me, we have an appointment with a sky pilot who will make it proper for us to travel in double harness. And there's one more thing you can do, if you're of a mind to."

"And that is?"

Me, I taken some money from my pocket. "Buy a marker for the grave of Felix Yant," I said, "a man of taste who would not settle for enough."

"You'd buy a stone for a man you killed?"

"He did it for pa. I want to kill no man. As for him, he put in his bid but he couldn't meet the price. One thing I've learned, Mr. Burns, when you buy chips in the pistol game, you'd better have enough to raise the ante."

Burns got to his feet. "You will be leaving town then?"

"For a rising young man of business," I said, "it seems an awful lot of towns want me to move on. Yes, I'm going."

"We wouldn't want to bankrupt you," Burns said, "buying tombstones."

I walked to the door with him, and he held out his

hand to me. I took it and he smiled a little, then said, "We found the remains of Judge Blazer in your burned-out cabin. We had a warrant for him from Kansas for misappropriation of public funds."

"You talk to Wacker?"

"Left the country. We did talk to your Indians, and they verified your story."

When he walked away, I closed the door. Pistol had gone to bed and so had Mrs. McCrae.

Well, I just looked at Laurie and asked, "You mean it?"

"I mean it," she said.

And I believed her.

AUTHOR'S NOTES

The trails followed by Kearney McRaven in this story are all there. Some are now highways, some jeep trails, and others can be followed only by riding a good mountain-bred horse or by backpacking. It is high country, rough country, mountain country. It is also some of the most beautiful country on earth.

The cliff dwelling where Kearney took shelter is now known as Eagle's Nest. Those of us who know it feel it was something very special, and there is none other quite like it.

The Hotel de Paris is still there in Georgetown for all to see. It was as described.

The Denver and Rio Grande Narrow Gauge still carries passengers to Silverton from Durango, tourists now, instead of miners, gamblers, and prospectors. Many of them still eat at the Bent Elbow, formerly the Tremont.

Tom Speers was well known in Kansas City, as were the Livestock Exchange and the House of Lords.

Bill Tilghman, gentleman, frontier marshal, and buffalo hunter, was a friend of my brother's. He showed us one day, in the North Canadian River bottom, how it was done with a six-gun.

Walter, Baron von Richthofen, whom the conductor in Chapter XIX talks about, was an uncle of the famed World War I flier. He lived in Colorado for some years, became an American citizen, and wrote *Cattle-Raising on the Plains of North America*.

The ruined stage station in Chapter XX is now on the Wineglass Ranch.

Otto Mears, mentioned briefly here, built railroads and roads where others said it couldn't be done. He was a western man who had a simple way of making the impossible possible.

ABOUT THE AUTHOR

Louis L'Amour, born Louis Dearborn L'Amour, is of French-Irish descent. Although Mr. L'Amour claims his writing began as a "spur-of-the-moment thing," prompted by friends who relished his verbal tales of the West, he comes by his talent honestly. A frontiersman by heritage (his grandfather was scalped by the Sioux), and a universal man by experience, Louis L'Amour lives the life of his fictional heroes. Since leaving his native Jamestown, North Dakota, at the age of fifteen, he's been a longshoreman, lumberjack, elephant handler, hay shocker, flume builder, fruit picker, and an officer on tank destroyers during World War II. And he's written four hundred short stories and over fifty books (including a volume of poetry).

Mr. L'Amour has lectured widely, traveled the West thoroughly, studied archaeology, compiled biographies of over one thousand Western gunfighters, and read prodigiously (his library holds more than two thousand volumes). And he's watched thirty-one of his westerns as movies. He's circled the world on a freighter, mined in the West, sailed a dhow on the Red Sea, been shipwrecked in the West Indies, stranded in the Mojave Desert. He's won fifty-one of fifty-nine fights as a professional boxer and pinch hit for Dorothy Kilgallen when she was on vacation from her column. Since 1816, thirty-three members of his family have been writers. And, he says, "I could sit in the middle of Sunset Boulevard and write with my typewriter on my knees; temperamental I am not."

Mr. L'Amour is re-creating an 1865 Western town, christened Shalako, where the borders of Utah, Arizona, New Mexico, and Colorado meet. Historically authentic from whistle to well, it will be a live, operating town, as well as a movie location and tourist attraction.

Mr. L'Amour now lives in Los Angeles with his wife Kathy, who helps with the enormous amount of research he does for his books. Soon, Mr. L'Amour hopes, the children (Beau and Angelique) will be helping too.